Praise for the Shamus Award–Winning
Nathan Heller Novels
by Max Allan Collins
"THE MASTER OF TRUE-CRIME FICTION."
—*Publishers Weekly*

CHICAGO CONFIDENTIAL

"Mixes a compelling story with a handful of real-life characters. . . . Collins doesn't see the past through rose-colored glasses but rather the sight lines of a nine-millimeter automatic. Excellent hard-boiled fare."
—*Booklist*

"When it comes to noirish hard-boiled PI thrillers, few writers can compete with Collins. The sex is hot and the killings cold. What else could you ask for?" —*Library Journal*

ANGEL IN BLACK

"Who killed the Black Dahlia? Collins's may well be the ultimate answer. Believable . . . entertaining . . . amazing . . . seamlessly blends fact and fiction." —*Los Angeles Times*

"The glamorous and the gruesome come together in this fictionalized retelling of the famous 1947 Black Dahlia murder. . . . Max Allan Collins weaves a colorful tale."
—*New York Daily News*

"Collins's take on the Black Dahlia may be less brooding than James Ellroy's version, but it's also more entertaining and will appeal to a wider audience."
—*Booklist* (starred review)

"Max Allan Collins blows the glitter off Tinsel Town with some of the grittiest writing in his hard-boiled career. Perfect-pitch dialogue . . . and a sleight-of-hand knack for fusing true crime with heart-wrenching fiction. . . . Few writers of any genre can match Collins's skill."
—*The News-Press* (Fort Meyers, FL)

continued . . .

STOLEN AWAY

"Collins triumphs with the art form he invented—the hard-boiled historical novel—with the added bonus of a plausible solution to the crime of the century."   —Andrew Vachss

"The yardstick against which further work of true-crime fiction will be measured."   —Lawrence Block

"A thoroughly intriguing 'what-if' tale."   —Clive Cussler

MAJIC MAN

"Refreshingly gritty. . . . There's magic of a literary kind here: full-bore suspense coupled with an ingenious take on an overworked pop-historical touchstone."
    —*Publishers Weekly* (starred review)

"Four Stars. . . . Collins turns real-life events into a cogent fictionalized mystery plot and real people into full-fleshed fictional characters. . . . A remarkable series."
    —*Ellery Queen Mystery Magazine*

FLYING BLIND

"Buckle your seat belt and get ready for a journey into a world of intrigue, espionage, betrayal, and a rousing good time. Collins is at his best."   —*Mostly Murder*

"A brilliantly realized conclusion to one of history's most spellbinding puzzles."   —*Kansas City Independent*

"Highly entertaining . . . snappy dialogue and jet-paced action."   —*Los Angeles Times*

CHICAGO CONFIDENTIAL

A NATHAN HELLER NOVEL

Max Allan COLLINS

A SIGNET BOOK

SIGNET
Published by New American Library, a division of
Penguin Putnam Inc., 375 Hudson Street,
New York, New York 10014, U.S.A.
Penguin Books Ltd, 80 Strand,
London WC2R 0RL, England
Penguin Books Australia Ltd, 250 Camberwell Road,
Camberwell, Victoria 3124, Australia
Penguin Books Canada Ltd, 10 Alcorn Avenue,
Toronto, Ontario, Canada M4V 3B2
Penguin Books (N.Z.) Ltd, Cnr Rosedale and Airborne Roads,
Albany, Auckland 1310, New Zealand

Penguin Books Ltd, Registered Offices:
Harmondsworth, Middlesex, England

Published by Signet, an imprint of New American Library,
a division of Penguin Putnam Inc. Previously published
in a New American Library hardcover edition.

First Signet Printing, May 2003
10 9 8 7 6 5 4 3 2 1

 REGISTERED TRADEMARK—MARCA REGISTRADA

Printed in the United States of America

PUBLISHER'S NOTE
This is a work of fiction. Names, characters, places, and incidents either are the
product of the author's imagination or are used fictitiously, and any resemblance
to actual persons, living or dead, business establishments, events, or locales is
entirely coincidental.

For Gary Warren Niebuhr
and
Ted Hertel,
neither of whom is in this book.

Although the historical incidents in this novel are portrayed more or less accurately (as much as the passage of time, and contradictory source material, will allow), fact, speculation, and fiction are freely mixed here; historical personages exist side by side with composite characters and wholly fictional ones—all of whom act and speak at the author's whim.

"Chicago is the heaven and haven
of mobsters, gamblers, thieves, killers,
and salesmen of every human sin."

Jack Lait and Lee Mortimer

"The Mafia is no fairy tale. It is ominously real,
and it has scarred the face of America."

Senator Estes Kefauver

"Murder is the essence of Chicago,
just as blackmail is the essence of Hollywood."

Florabel Muir

1

In Chicago the price is up front, at least, if nonnegotiable. In Hollywood, you don't even know what you're buying—just that somewhere beneath the tinsel, down under the layers of phoniness, there's going to be a price tag.

Maybe that was why this girl Vera Palmer was so refreshing. She still had a wholesome, smalltown, peaches-and-cream glow, for one thing; and for another, she wasn't even a starlet, just a college girl, out at UCLA. The shimmering brunette pageboy, the heart-shaped face, the full dark red-rouged lips, the wide, wide-set hazel eyes, the impossible wasp waist, the startling flaring hips and the amazing full breasts riding her rib cage like twin torpedoes, had nothing to do with it.

"Mr. Heller, I'm afraid of Paul," she said. Her voice was breathy yet musical—something of Betty Boop, quite a bit of the young Shirley Temple. A hint of Southern accent was stirred in there, too, despite my best efforts.

She was sitting across from my desk in a cubicle of the A-1 Detective Agency in a suite of offices on the fifth floor of the Bradbury Building in Los Angeles, California. It was mid-September 1950—the air conditioners were shut off, and the breeze through the half-open windows was crisp as an icy Coke. The girls were wearing their skirts long, but the way this one's shapely legs were crossed under pleated light blue rayon, plenty of calf and even some knee was exposed. Her blouse was the same powder blue with navy trimmings: gaucho collar, edged short sleeves and slot pocket; her elaborately brassiered breasts punched at the light fabric like shells almost breaching a submarine's hull.

Before this mammarian rhapsody continues, I should point out a few facts. Though I was stuck back among the lowly operatives in this partitioned-off bullpen, I—Nathan Heller—was in fact the president of the A-1 agency. My partner Fred Rubinski—vice president of the A-1—had the spacious main office next door, here in our L.A. branch. My real office was back in Chicago, in the heart of the Loop (the Monadnock Building), and twice the size of Fred's. I had taken this humble space, in my back corner near a gurgling water cooler, because I was making a temporary home of Los Angeles.

I had recently divorced Peggy—on grounds of adultery, which considering most of my income came from working divorce cases is the first of numerous cheap ironies you'll encounter in these pages—but was staying close to her to be near my toddler son. My ex-wife and I had taken to spending Sunday afternoons in Echo Park together, enjoying our kid, thanks to the understanding nature of her movie director fiancé. Some of my friends suspected I was hoping to reconcile with that faithless bitch, and maybe I was.

In addition, I was laying low because Chicago had been crawling of late with investigators looking to enlist witnesses to sing in Senator Estes Kefauver's choir. The Tennessee senator had, starting back in May, launched a major congressional inquiry into organized crime—with Chicago a prime target—and I was not anxious to participate. While not a mob guy myself, I had done jobs for various Outfit types, and had certain underworld associations, and hence did know where a good share of the bodies were buried. Hell, I'd buried some of them.

So my associates in Chicago were instructed not to forward my calls, and—just to occupy myself—I was taking on occasional jobs for the agency, routine matters I handled only when my interest was piqued. And the bosomy, long-stemmed college girl named Vera Palmer had certainly piqued it.

She was only nineteen years old, whereas I was not a teenager. I could barely remember having been a teenager. I was a well-preserved forty-five years old—ruggedly handsome, I've been told, with reddish brown hair going gray at the temples, six feet carrying two hundred pounds, chiefly scar tissue and gristle—with precious few bad habits, although my major weakness was sitting across from me with its legs crossed and its breasts staring right at me.

"We broke up at the start of the summer," she said breathlessly, leaning forward; she smelled good—not perfume, but soap . . . I made it as Camay. "Paul went off to ROTC—he's in the reserves—and he kept writing me letters. I never answered them."

"This was in Dallas?"

Her hands were folded in her lap; lucky hands. "Yes. We were both at the university there. Freshmen. We'd dated in high school. Paul wanted to get married, but I wasn't ready. Anyway, a month or so after he went off for training, I headed out here."

The muffled voices of ops making phone calls—credit checks mostly—and others working typewriters—detailed reports made billing clients easier—provided an office-music backdrop for our conversation.

I asked, "You didn't tell your ex-boy friend where you were going?"

"No. I didn't tell him I was going *anywhere*. Heck, I wasn't even answering his silly letters. And I gave my mother strict orders not to tell Paul where I'd gone."

"But she must've spilled the beans, Miss Palmer. Or maybe a friend of yours told Paul where—"

She shook her head and the brown hair bounced. "No. He found out when he was home on leave, and saw my picture in the paper."

"Why was your picture in the paper?"

Her smile was a lush explosion; her whole face went sunny. "Why, don't you think I'm pretty enough to have my picture in the paper?"

Her shoulders were back, her chin up, the submarine hull threatened worse than ever.

"I think you're a lovely young woman . . . but papers need a reason, or anyway an excuse, to run a picture, even of a pretty girl like you—so why's a Los Angeles picture of Vera Palmer running in a Dallas paper?"

"I'm in a beauty contest. I'm one of the twenty finalists."

Seemed Miss Palmer had registered at the *Daily News* to enter the Miss California contest. Naive, she hadn't brought along an 8" by 10", and a news photographer, overhearing this, had volunteered to shoot her picture—he even fronted five bucks for her to go buy a bikini.

"He was so nice," she purred. "So generous."

"Yeah, sounds like a real philanthropist."

The *News* had run a story about the guileless girl who had wandered in to enter the Miss California contest, and how the *News* had helped her out by buying her a swimsuit and taking a photo . . . which the paper ran. And the wire service picked up.

She shrugged. "I don't know what's so special about a picture of me in a bikini."

Despite her wide eyes, I was starting to understand that she knew very well what was special about her, in or out of a bikini.

"Paul," I said, getting her back on track.

"Paul," she said, with a nod. "Last week Paul caught up with me. . . . He follows me around campus, shows up at the rehearsals for my play, calls my room."

"Are you in a dorm?"

"Yes, at the MAC."

"The MAC?"

"That's short for Masonic Affiliates Club or Clubhouse or something. It's a student activities center. They have several dorms there. It's also where we're rehearsing the play. I'm in a play. I'm a drama major."

I should've known—scratch a college girl out here, find a starlet. Still, she seemed so fresh, so sincere. . . .

"You can ask my two roommates," she was saying, "ask the girls if Paul hasn't been a pest."

"Has he gotten physical?"

She frowned. "I wouldn't have sex with him again for a million dollars."

"I mean, has he hit you?"

"He's grabbed me." She turned her palms up and I could see small bruises on her inner forearms.

"We can get a court order," I said.

"What?"

"A restraining order, where he can't come within a hundred feet of you."

"No! No, I don't want to involve the authorities. That's why I came to you, Mr. Heller."

"I understand you requested me, specifically?"

"Yes, I read about you in the newspapers."

I'd had coverage, locally, when I'd been involved on the fringes of the notorious Elizabeth Short murder, the so-called Black Dahlia slaying. Other cases of mine over the years had hit the national wire services, too; I was a minor celebrity myself, even if I didn't look good in a bikini.

"Well," I said, "you're lucky to find me. Usually I'm in the Chicago office."

"Will you take my case?"

"First you better tell me what it is you want me to do. Scare him, hurt him, what?"

She shook her head, eyes tightening in a frown. "I don't really want him hurt. I was . . . fond of him, once."

"Okay. What, then?"

"Just protect me. Talk to Paul. . . . He's pretty tough, though. He's a soldier."

I smiled. "That's okay. I used to be a Marine."

"Ooooo, really?" The "ooooo" had been a sort of squeal. "I love men in uniform."

"Except for Paul."

Her smile disappeared, and she nodded, like a schoolkid realizing she'd gotten a little too wild in the classroom. "Except for Paul. . . . What do you charge? I don't have a lot of money."

"We'll work something out," I said.

And all I meant by that was I'd take into consideration that she was just a college kid, a sweet girl from Texas trying to get an education. Really. Honest. No kidding.

"I'm sure we will," she said, her expression and tone mingled with lasciviousness in a unique way that somehow scared me a little. I felt like the Wolf discovering Little Red Riding Hood was packing heat.

I agreed to meet her in the assembly hall of the MAC at UCLA around seven; she was rehearsing *Death of a Salesman*, of all things.

"I'm afraid I play a sort of floozy," she said.

"I didn't think you were playing Willie Loman."

"You know the play?"

"Saw Lee J. Cobb in it in the Chicago run, early this year. Good show—won't make much of a musical."

She blinked. "Are they making a musical out of it?"

"That was just a joke."

Her smile looked like a wax kiss. "You're quite a kidder, aren't you, Mr. Heller?"

"I'm hilarious."

Now she was studying me. "Are you depressed?"

"Depressed? No. Hell no."

"Did . . . somebody die in your family?"

Just my marriage.

"No. But you're a funny kid yourself, Miss Palmer."

Now her smile shifted, dimpling one cheek. "You think I'm stupid, don't you? From that musical remark. Well, I have a high IQ, I'll have you know . . . and I'm going to make something of myself. That's why I'm enrolled in college . . . and that's why you have to make sure Paul doesn't spoil things."

"I'll see what I can do. You have a photo?"

"Now I do! I had scads taken, after that business at the *Daily News*—"

"No, I mean of Paul."

"Oh! Yes. Of course." She dug into her purse and handed me a photo of herself and Paul, dressed up for the prom, apparently; Vera was smiling at the camera—and why not, it loved her—and he was a dark-haired handsome kid with thick dark eyebrows, a weakish chin, and a glazed expression.

"Can I have the photo back when you're done?"

"Sure," I said, not getting why she wanted a keepsake of her and this harasser.

She beamed at me, stood, slung her purse strap over a shoulder, and reminded me where I was to meet her; we exchanged goodbyes and I watched her walk away. It was a hell of a thing, her walk, a twitchy affair that seemed to propel her as far to the sides as it did forward.

About two minutes later I was still contemplating that walk when my phone rang. It was my Chicago partner, Lou Sapperstein—bald, sixty, a lean hard op who looked like an accountant, thanks to the tortoise-shell glasses—and his Crosbyish baritone over the long-distance wire was edged with irritation.

"You gotta get your ass back here and do something about your pal," Sapperstein said.

"My pal? I got lots of pals, Lou. You're my pal."

"Screw you. You know who I'm talkin' about—Drury!"

I sighed. "What's he up to now?"

"Well, for one thing, he hasn't followed up on half a dozen assignments I've given him. And for another, he's spending his time playing footsie with Robinson."

George S. Robinson was Kefauver's stalking horse, the Senate Crime Investigating Committee's associate counsel, who'd been working in concert with the Chicago Crime Commission, a citizens' watchdog group dating back to Prohibition.

"Christ," I said. "He's going to get me shot."

"No, Nate—he's going to get *me* shot . . . you're on the lam in sunny southern Cal, remember?"

"Yeah, and Bugsy Siegel didn't get nailed out here in his goddamn living room, I suppose? Fuck—can't you handle him, Lou?"

"He's your friend."

"He's your friend, too!"

We all dated back to the Chicago P.D. pickpocket detail, in the early thirties, Sapperstein, Bill Drury, and me. After that, Lou and I and Bill's partner Tim O'Conner played poker together, for years.

"Bill promised he'd lay off," I said, "while he was on salary with us."

"Drury is a lunatic on a crusade. Nice guy, great guy, but he's supposed to be working for the A-1 and instead he's out gathering evidence for that hick senator in the coonskin cap."

Kefauver had worn a coonskin cap as a gimmick in his Tennessee campaign to win a Senate seat despite the best corrupt efforts of Boss Crump's Dixiecrat machine.

"I'll call Bill," I said into the phone. "I'll talk to him."

"You need to fire him."

"He's my friend, Lou—one of my best friends."

"Then come back and talk some sense into him."

"I'm in the middle of a job out here."

"Right—blonde or brunette?"

From the photo on my desk, Vera's boy friend Paul was looking up at me accusingly. "I won't dignify that with a response."

"Look, you can't duck this Kefauver thing. You need to get back here, meet with those sons of bitches, tell them you don't know anything, that they're wasting their damn subpoenas, and—"

"And go to jail for contempt, and smear our agency's good name."

Lou blew me a long-distance raspberry. "Our agency's 'good' name is built on your unsavory reputation, Nate. Don't kid a kidder."

"Lou—I'll talk to Drury."

"Are you coming back? Should I put a light in the window?"

"I'll talk to Bill, Lou. Goodbye."

And I hung up.

I got myself a Dixie cup of water and sat and sipped and thought about Bill Drury and what a schmuck I'd been to hire him onto the A-1. I shook my head. This was one of the rare times when I'd fucked myself over by being too nice a guy. . . .

My friend Bill Drury, former lieutenant on the Chicago P.D.—who'd been unadvisedly taking on the Chicago mobsters since he first came on the job, back when Capone was still in power—had been railroaded off the force (not for the first time) two years ago. He had been fighting for reinstatement in the courts, while writing antimob columns for the *Chicago Herald-American* and the *Miami Daily News*. Last year, when the Illinois Supreme Court refused to hear his case, Drury found his services as a crime reporter were no longer in demand, and he came to me, looking for a job as a private investigator. I had given it to him, on the condition he lay off the mob busting.

I knew I had to talk to him, but I didn't feel ready to head back to Chicago. I enjoyed the Sunday afternoons with my sweet lovely son and my sweet lovely goddamn faithless bitch of an ex-wife. I'd gotten attached to the sunshine and the work was easy, and Kefauver's people—some of whom were investigating out here, also, but looking for California crooks, not Chicago ones—hadn't bothered me.

Both Bill Drury and his poor common sense were no longer in my thoughts as I parked on Le Conte Avenue, not far from the front gate of UCLA. I wandered through Westwood Village—a collection of attractive boutiques and intimate restaurants in handsome Mediterranean-style buildings—enjoying the cool evening under a clear sky flung with more stars than Hollywood. The night was almost cold, a breeze biting through the slacks of my blue glen plaid tropical worsted, as I approached the building called the MAC.

An example of Southern California architecture at its best, the MAC was a mission-style castle with stone-tile masonry walls, a square tower, and a red clay tile roof. I strolled through a charming stone-and-landscape courtyard, across glazed ornamental tile, into a sprawling building rife with hardwood interiors, wooden beams, and decorative ironwork.

I soon found myself in a lounge, where pretty coeds and lucky college boys were laughing and talking, sipping Cokes, having smokes, a few gathered around a wood burning fireplace with a crackling fire going; some card playing and Ping-Pong was going on, too, and a couple couples were doing the hokey pokey to some music on the radio. I asked a coed for directions, then headed past a library, various conference rooms, a dining room, and the kitchen, into the large assembly hall where, on stage, the rehearsal was under way.

I sat with my hat in my lap, amid a scattering of students involved in the production. Vera did indeed play a floozy, and she did a bang-up job of it; but her part was small, and after about an hour, during which her scene was run through half a dozen times, she'd been dismissed, and joined me in the sparse audience.

"Any sign of Paul?" she asked. She was in the same fetching powder blue outfit she'd worn to my office, plus spike heels that may have been part of her *Salesman* characterization.

"Nope," I said.

She craned around to look. "I'm surprised. He's been haunting rehearsal all week."

"How long do you have to stay?"

"I'm done, now. Would you walk me to my dorm? The entrance is around back of the building. . . ."

We headed out through the courtyard, where we paused to admire a colorful tiled fountain in the shape of an eight-pointed star; lighting within the fountain painted the dancing spray with a rainbow effect. Her arm was in mine, and she was leaning against me; the smell of Camay soap in the fresh crisp air was bewitching. She was a young, shapely, pretty girl and I was a lonely divorcé in his forties, and I was distracted.

Which is why he was on us before I even knew it.

The guy grabbed Vera by the arm linked with mine, and yanked her away.

"Paul!" she squealed.

Paul was tall, knife-blade thin, wearing his army uniform, which was rumpled and wouldn't pass inspection. Despite his weak chin, he was handsome enough, or would have been if his eyes hadn't been so wild, and his nostrils flaring.

"What are you doing with this old fart?" he demanded of her. His fists were clenched. He looked like he might hit her at any moment.

But the real reason I sucker punched him was the "old fart" remark. I caught him in the side of the face with a hard left hand and he collapsed like a card table.

Vera stepped back and covered her mouth; college-kid faces began popping up in the arched windows along the ersatz stone facade of the building edging the courtyard. Smiles and wide eyes and pointing fingers. . . .

"Don't hurt him," she said, but it wasn't clear who she meant.

"Leave her alone," I told him.

He was a pile of long limbs in khaki down there on the ornamental tile. His eyes were crazed, his lower lip trembling.

"She doesn't want you bothering her," I said, patting the air with my palms. "Just keep your distance—"

But something was coming up from deep within him, a scream of agony that took the form of words: *"Bothering her!"*

And suddenly he was reassembling himself, like a played-backward newsreel of a building demolition, and he was on his feet and hurling himself at me before I could say another word.

I did have time to throw a punch, which caught his jaw and should have sent him down again, but he was fueled by rage, and shook it off and came windmilling at me, fists flailing, one catching my chin and stinging. I backed away, but had forgotten the fountain, and tripped over a star point and tumbled back into the water in a spattering spray. Then I was the one who was flailing, floundering on my back in the shallow water, lucky not to have cracked my skull or broken a damn rib or something.

He was laughing at me, pointing, hysterical, out of control, he had never seen anything so fucking funny, and he was still laughing when I rose like a human wave and leapt out of the fountain at him, dripping wet, hopping mad, doubling him over with a right to the belly, straightening him with a left under the chin, putting him down with a right to the side of his face.

Then he was on one knee, as if proposing. He was not about to get up, not soon, not now. I was dripping water, but he was dripping blood, one side of his mouth a pulpy mess.

Vera stood with a hand to her dark red lips, looking at him with pity, but making no move to go to him.

I just stood there, drenched, waiting to see if a reconciliation was going to take place. Wouldn't be the first time an old boy friend got beat up by a girl's new savior, only to renew her sympathy and interest in the old beau.

Not this time. Vera took my wet arm and said, "We need to get out of here, before the campus police come."

I nodded, and we left him there, on his hands and knees, his breath heaving, mouth dripping; maybe he was crying.

I was a little out of it, from the scuffle, and I don't remember exactly how we wound up at my car—a '50 Packard, a dark green number that belonged to the A-1. But we were sitting in it—me behind the wheel, getting the upholstery wet—and Vera in the rider's seat, looking at me with concern.

"I don't want to go back," she said.

"Back where?" I was still a little groggy.

"To the MAC . . . to the dorm. Paul's still back there. He might cause more trouble."

"You want to bunk on my couch?"

She nodded. "You want me to drive?"

"No. I'm okay."

"Is it far to your place? You need to get out of those wet things."

"No, it's close. Hop, skip, and a jump."

When I pulled in at the Beverly Hills Hotel, Vera's hazel eyes grew huge. "You *live* here?"

"Sort of. I have use of a bungalow. We handle their security. Management likes having me around. . . . They have a clientele that needs discreet assistance, sometimes."

"But those bungalows are expensive!"

"Well, I'm in one of the Howard Hughes bungalows. He rents four of 'em, at all times, but only shows up occasionally. And one is for security, so even when he's around, I can stay put."

"Howard Hughes? You know Howard Hughes? What is he like?"

"Nuttier than a fruitcake. But he'd go for you."

"You think so?"

"Oh yeah. . . ." He would take one look at this doll and start designing a cantilevered bra.

Soon I was walking Vera down a sidewalk bordered by

palms and flowering shrubs, and she was commenting on how Clark Gable and Carole Lombard had supposedly started their romance in one of these bungalows. I had no reply—I was busy shivering in my wet worsted on this cool night.

Then I ushered Vera inside and she ooohed and aaahed at the marble fireplace, the French doors leading to the private patio, the French provincial furnishings, and the pale pink decor with the pale green touches. The console television, which was neither pink nor green, amazed her; she stared at it like a savage contemplating a crashed airplane. I told her the sofa—a comfy overstuffed pink-and-green floral number—was all hers.

I wasn't planning anything. I was sore from the punch I'd caught and the fall I'd taken; maybe I was an old fart at that, because the lovely coed in the other room interested me less than a hot shower.

After which, soothed, and sleepy—though it was only around nine-thirty—I went to the bathroom closet and put on one of two Beverly Hills Hotel white terrycloth bathrobes hanging there, and draped the other over my sleeve, like a waiter serving a meal.

When I returned to the living room, the lights were off and the fireplace was on. Still in that powder blue ensemble, she was sitting in front of the flames, legs tucked under her, the spike heels off, staring at the dancing orange and blue, which reflected on her pretty features.

"Would you like to sleep in this?" I asked, holding out the robe.

She rose, took the robe, and asked, "Do you mind if I take a shower, too?"

"No. Go right ahead."

I sat in my bathrobe on the sofa with nothing on but the robe. Still not planning anything, listening to the muffled dance of water needles seep through the bathroom door, I wondered if maybe Vera had something in mind.

She did.

Her brunette hair damp, bangs turned into gypsy curls, she returned smelling like Lifebuoy (no Camay in my soap dish, unfortunately) with all the makeup washed away, looking fresh and innocent. Or anyway she looked fresh and innocent until she dropped the terrycloth robe to her feet, a puddle of white she stepped out of, letting the flickering flames dance all over her.

But even in the glow of firelight, her skin was creamy, and her figure was astonishing—tiny waist, wide hips, perfectly shaped, pink-tipped breasts displayed like awards on a wide rib cage.

She slipped her arms around me and said, "Thank you for saving me," and presented her pretty face for a kiss.

Who was I to argue? The full lips were warm and moist and her tongue flicked at mine; then she was tugging that bathrobe off me, and we fell onto the couch and necked in the nude like we were both teenagers. A few minutes later her damp hair was tickling my thighs as she suckled me, making giggling, gurgling sounds, like she couldn't have been having a better time with a lollipop; and when she crawled around on top of me, so she could continue her oral indulgence while I returned the favor, nose deep in curls, I realized this Texas teen was not as wholesome as first I had thought. We took a quick time out for me to find a Trojan, and I sat on the couch and she sat on me, and rode me like a kid on a carousel, making delicious little sounds, squeals and coos, my hands on her rounded bottom as I nuzzled first one ripe breast, then another, inducing further girlish glee. She was so fun-lovingly feminine, she was almost a cartoon—but a cartoon in *Esquire*.

Later she came back from the bathroom wrapped in the robe, saying, "That was a ball!"

Sitting on the couch in my own robe, I managed a nod. I felt like a truck had hit me—a 115-pound, well-stacked one.

"What do you want to do now?" she asked, plopping next to me, cuddling against me.

"Sleep?"

"No! It's early. What about that place you own part of?"

"I don't own part of anything."

"Didn't I read you own some restaurant on the Strip?"

"Sherry's? No, the papers got that wrong. . . . It's my partner, Fred Rubinski's place. You want to go there?"

She wanted to go there.

*   *   *

Sherry's was a study in glass and chrome, ornate in a modern manner, and often was jumping, even on a Thursday night like this. Tonight was no exception at the Sunset Strip café, customer chatter colliding with clanking plates and the tinkle of Cole Porter on the piano, though the brightly illuminated restaurant seemed short on famous faces. Of course my gangster acquaintance Mickey Cohen had stopped hanging around here, after he and his entourage got shot up out on the sidewalk, last year.

Though it was open for dinner, Sherry's was known as an after-hours joint, the likes of which had been suffering due to a postwar decline of nightclubs and theater; Ciro's and the Mocambo were still doing good business, but many other clubs had shuttered, and big-name nitery talent had migrated to Las Vegas where top dollar awaited. Also, the Big Bands weren't drawing like they used to—dancehalls had tumbleweed blowing through them, now that the kids were listening to Frankie Laine and Patti Page. Hadn't been the same in this town since '48, when Earl Carroll's closed down after the boss died in a plane crash.

We were shown to seats by a waitress I didn't make eye contact with (we had history); nonetheless, I was the owner's partner, and got treated right by way of a cozy booth. Even in a starlet-laden burg like Hollywood, Vera's striking figure caught many an eye; her simple powder blue college-girl attire was at odds with the after-theater finery around us. But a body like Vera's in a town like this made up for a lot of sins. So to speak.

We ordered coffee and pastry—I had a Napoleon and Vera a cream puff, which we were in the middle of when Fred Rubinski came over to say hello (and to be introduced to the gorgeous brunette).

"Sit down, Fred," I said, and Fred slid in next to Vera. "This is a client of ours—Vera Palmer. She has an ex-boy friend who hasn't come to terms with the 'ex' part. Vera, this is my partner at the A-1, Fred Rubinski."

"I've read about you, Mr. Rubinski," she said with a grin, then shook hands with him as she licked custard from one corner of her mouth.

This action froze Fred for a moment, but he managed to smile and say something or other. Fred—a compact, balding character who resembled a somewhat better-looking Edward G. Robinson—was as usual nattily attired. He had opened a one-man P.I. agency in the Bradbury Building before the war, gradually garnering an enviable movie industry clientele; my national reputation had been growing at the same time, and in 1946, we had thrown in together, in what was now the L.A. branch of the A-1.

"You must want to be an actress," Fred said.

Vera said, "That's what I'm studying at UCLA."

"She's a finalist in the Miss California contest," I said.

Fred was patting Vera's hand. "Well, when you're ready to talk to the studios, don't forget us."

"Oh, I won't!" And she giggled and cooed—sounds I'd last heard when she was on my lap.

Then Fred turned his sharp, dark eyes my way; his rumpled face tightened, as much as it could, anyway. "Sapperstein called me today."

"Yeah. Me too. He thinks I'm needed in Chicago."

"I agree with him. You gotta get back there and deal with your friend Drury."

"Not you, too, Fred! I'll call him. . . ."

Fred waggled a scolding finger. "Nate, this is bad for business. Neither one of us—in either of our towns—can afford to have the kind of enemies Drury is making for us."

"I'll handle it."

Fred shrugged, but his eyes were unrelenting. Then he asked Vera if she minded if he smoked, and she said no, she was finished with her dessert and was going to have a smoke, herself.

So Fred lit up a Havana and Vera had a Chesterfield. I just had my coffee. I was not a smoker—I had only smoked during the war, when I was overseas, on Guadalcanal. The only times I craved a cigarette now were certain kinds of stress reminiscent of combat.

"Listen, Nate," Fred said, "Frank's here."

"Which Frank? I know a lot of Franks."

"Frankie."

"Oh," I said. "That Frank."

Vera was trying to follow this. "You don't mean Frank Sinatra?"

I nodded and her eyes glittered.

"He's been wanting to talk to you for a couple weeks," Fred told me. "Remember, I said he called? . . . Why don't you go back and say hello, get this out of the way. He's with Ava."

Vera's hazel eyes popped. "Ava Gardner?"

I shook my head. "Poor kid's on the way down."

Fred shrugged. "He just had a hit record."

"Yeah, well his tank's on empty and he's running on fumes. He's had his run, Fred."

"Boy's got talent."

"The public's gonna have his ass, leaving Nancy."

"Maybe. Say hello to him. Maybe you can see what this job he has for us is all about—he won't tell me."

I nodded again, and got out of the booth. Vera looked at me like a greedy child who wanted a pony.

"Come along," I sighed.

Frank and Ava were at a booth near the kitchen—not really such a good seat, but out of the way. I didn't know Ava very well—only that, beautiful as she was, she was a hard-nosed broad with a vicious streak.

"Nate!" Frank said, bolting to his feet; he stuck out his hand, which I took.

He looked skinnier than ever, sporting a Clark Gable mustache that was wrong for him. He swam in a tan gabardine sportcoat and a yellow shirt with an open collar; he wasn't wearing a rug and his thinning hair made him look old for his thirty-five years. Next to him, in a foul mood that rose from her like heat off asphalt, sat Ava; she was smoking a cigarette and her makeup seemed heavy to me, though she was unquestionably lovely, her attire simple but striking: an orange blouse with a mandarin collar.

I said, "Hiya, Frank. Ava."

The actress looked away.

Frank said, "Have you been ducking me, Melvin?"

He was calling everybody Melvin that year.

"No. Uh, this is Vera Palmer. She's a client."

Frank beamed at the girl and extended his hand. "Pleasure, Miss Palmer."

Ava stamped out her cigarette on the tablecloth and said in her husky alto, "I suppose you're sleeping with this broad!"

Frank looked at her, aghast. "What? I just met her! Are you crazy?"

"I must be," Ava said, and scooted out of the booth, grabbing her wrap, and then stormed out through the restaurant, brushing Vera roughly aside.

"Excuse me," Frank said, and followed her.

Vera looked at me as though she'd been poleaxed.

I shrugged. "That's pretty much par for the course with those two. Let's go back to our booth."

Which we did, and we were on our second cup of coffee (Fred was off schmoozing with other customers) when Frank—looking like a whipped puppy—came back in, spotted us, and joined us, sitting next to me.

"Jesus," he said. "All I have to do is look at a pretty girl, and bam, Ava and me, we're off to the races."

I didn't say anything. I was irritated with him; we'd known each other a long time, and I knew he was a tomcat, but I didn't think he'd ever leave Nancy and the kids. And after what I'd been through myself, I wasn't too keen on cheaters.

"I can't stay," Frank said, "but I'll be in Chicago next week, at the Chez Paree. Are you heading back, by any chance?"

"I don't know," I said. "Maybe."

"Well, either way, we need to talk. Listen, Melvin, I'm in a world of shit. This guy Miller at Columbia has me making novelty records, trying to compete with Frankie the fuck Laine, for Christ's sake. Then I managed to piss Mayer off and lost my movie contract. I do have a TV series coming up—CBS. That's a good thing."

"That's a very good thing, Frank. TV's the hot deal, these days."

"Yeah, and those lousy Senate hearings are all over it!

That's what's really got me in a vise. The feds . . . these fucking feds. . . . Excuse me, Miss Palmer."

Vera was gaping at him like she was a tourist and he was the Grand Canyon. "That's all right, Mr. Sinatra."

"Fucking feds," he continued, "they're squeezing me like a goddamn pimple."

"How so?"

"That hick from Tennessee wants me to talk about Charley and Joey and the boys."

The "boys" he referred to were mobsters, mostly from Chicago—like Charley, Joey, and Rocco Fischetti, Capone cousins who were high in the Outfit.

"I've been ducking that bastard Kefauver myself," I admitted.

Frank was lighting up a cigarette. "Yeah, but at least you don't have that cheese-eating Red-baiter on your butt."

"What, McCarthy?"

He smirked. "Yeah, I'm not just a gangster, you know—I'm a Red!"

"McCarthy thinks all Democrats are communists."

Sinatra's fabled blue eyes locked onto me. "You *know* him, don't you?"

"Some. I did a job for Drew Pearson involving McCarthy, and got to know the guy."

Pearson was a nationally known muckraking syndicated columnist I'd handled occasional investigations for over the years: Senator McCarthy had been a source of his I'd checked.

Sinatra's eyebrows climbed his forehead. "So you're friendly with McCarthy?"

"Friendly enough to drink with."

"Great! Perfect, Melvin." And the skinny singer stood, patting me on the arm, flashing me his charismatic if shopworn smile. "We'll talk soon. . . . I gotta try to catch up with that crazy broad."

And he was gone.

"He seemed nice," Vera said.

"He can be. You ready?"

"It's too late for me to go back to the dorm. Can I stay at your place?"

"Sure."

We went out the glass doors and walked arm in arm under the Sherry's canopy, with Vera leaning against my shoulder.

"You know a lot of famous people, don't you?" she asked. Her spike heels clicked on the sidewalk.

"That's part of my business, Vera. You want to be famous?"

"Oh, yes. My parents brought me to Hollywood on vacation, when I was a little girl—about ten. I stood on the corner of Hollywood and Vine and I just knew this town would belong to me someday."

We walked around and up the incline into the parking lot.

"And here I thought you were just a college girl," I said.

"I'm a college girl studying to be a movie star."

"Careful what you wish for, Vera. . . ."

We were approaching the Packard when he stepped out from between two cars: Paul, his army uniform looking stained and rumpled. His fists were clenched, but he did not charge at us or anything—just stood with his weak chin high. The wild look was out of his eyes: despair had taken its place.

"Keep your distance, mister," he said to me.

Poor bastard had been following us all night—first saw me take his girl to the hotel, then to Sherry's. . . .

I said, "Paul, that's good advice—keep *your* distance, or I'm turning you over to the cops for harassing this girl."

His voice quavered, but there was strength in it, even some bruised dignity. "I just want to talk to my wife."

I glanced sharply at Vera. *"Wife?"*

She swallowed and avoided my eyes, though still hugging my arm.

To the solider, who was maybe ten feet away, I said, "You're her husband, Paul?"

Traffic sounds from the Strip provided dissonant background music for this second sad confrontation.

"That's right," he said. "And Jaynie's afraid I'll tell the Miss California people she's married, and a mom, and they'll toss her out on her sweet behind."

I winced at Vera. "Jaynie?"

Paul answered for her: "Her name is Vera Jayne, mister. And Palmer's just her maiden name. Our little baby girl, just a few months old, is home with Jayne's mother."

Mildly pissed and vaguely ashamed of myself, I turned to the coed. "This boy is your husband? And you have a baby back in Texas?"

She still wasn't looking at me; but she nodded.

"Go talk to him," I said, suddenly exhausted. "I'll wait— I'll still drive you back to your dorm, if you want. But first talk to him."

I leaned against the Packard while they talked. I didn't eavesdrop, and anyway they kept their voices down. Finally they hugged. Kissed, tentatively.

Vera came over and said, "Paul's been called up to active duty—he's going to Korea. He wants me to be with our little girl, back home in Dallas, and be with him as much as possible. . . . When his hitch is up, he says he'll bring me back out here, and let me take my shot at stardom. That's two years. You think I'll still be pretty enough, in two years, to try again?"

"Sure, Vera."

Her eyes shimmered with desperation. "Can I call you, then? For a reference to the studios?"

"Sure—me or Fred, either one of us will help you, Vera."

"Really, it's Jayne. And my married name's Mansfield."

She kissed my cheek and trotted over to rejoin her soldier-boy husband. That motion in her caboose—side-to-side as she moved forward—was worth watching.

They were still standing there talking when I pulled the Packard out of Sherry's parking lot, heading for the Beverly Hills Hotel.

But let's face it: I was on my way to Chicago. Far as Hollywood was concerned, my roll in the hay with Vera Jayne Mansfield had been the last straw.

2

Lake Shore Drive's majestic mile—once an endless array of magnificent mansions—was now a row of high-rise tombstones; grand residences survived here and there, as a privileged few stubbornly clung to the city. Starting at the crossroads of the Gold Coast, where Lake Shore Drive and Michigan Avenue met, posh hotels and plush shops lined the avenue, serving their wealthy, discriminating and oh so exclusive clientele.

Minutes away, on Clark and Rush Streets, proprietors weren't so fussy—anyone with five hundred bucks could deflower a virgin, and you don't want to know what kind of wilted rose three bucks would buy. Guns (from a snubby to a burp), dope (from reefer to horse), and booze (from untaxed bubbly to rotgut whiskey) were available at prices even the middle class could afford.

It was good to be home.

The beautiful parks fringing the lake were still greener than money, no sign of the leaves turning yet; these land-scaped acres and the broad lakefront boulevards of Chicago's Northside were a reminder of how the city's planners had intended things, before commerce and human nature took over. Lake Shore Drive—up which I was tooling my dark blue 1950 Olds 88—had once been strewn with the elaborate domiciles of the wealthy; most of those structures remaining had been converted into schools and other institutions—the U.S. Court of Appeals, for one.

The remaining members of the old wealthy class—those who had not yet had the decency to die, or move to the suburbs or Florida—lived in the towering modern apartment buildings here and on the other lake-facing avenues, Lincoln Parkway and Sheridan Road, and their cross streets. These über-flats also put roofs over the heads of the Windy City's new nobility: high-rolling gamblers, mistresses, tavern owners, and, top of the heap, mobsters.

One block south of Belmont Avenue, where the shore-line curved around glimmering lagoonlike Belmont Harbor, I located something even the most skillful Chicago detectives didn't often find—a parking place—right across from the nondescript brown-brick building at the corner of Barry and Sheridan. The late Al Capone's cousins, the Fischetti brothers, nested in the top three penthouse floors, which were set back a ways, sitting on the fifteen stories below like a brimless, too-small top hat.

The doorman of Barry Apartments, a paunchy fiftyish guy with a drink-splotched face that went well with his red uniform, did not seem to be a Fischetti bodyguard in liveried drag. At least it didn't look like he was packing, anyway.

"Visiting someone here, sir?" he asked, hands locked behind him, rocking on his heels.

"Yeah. I'm sure my name's on your list."

"I don't have a list, sir."

"Sure you do. Name's Lincoln." And I gave him my identification.

He looked at the fin, nodded, said, "Yeah this is you, all right," and slipped the bill in his pocket. "But the top three floors is off-limits, unless the elevator man is expecting you."

So the elevator man *was* a Fischetti watchdog.

"I don't know anybody in the penthouse," I said. "I just want to talk to the building manager."

"We don't have one on site. We do have a janitorial supervisor. He's got a staff of three, and an office around back."

I nodded. "Any building inspectors, or fire marshals come around lately?"

"Matter of fact, yeah. Building inspector last week."

"Well-dressed for a building inspector, was he?"

"Funny you should say that. He was a real dapper dan. Nice fella. I sent him around back to see the janitor, too."

"Thanks." I turned to go, then glanced back at him. "This conversation is confidential, by the way."

He shot me a yellow grin in the midst of the red-splotchy puss, and touched the brim of his cap. "Mum's the word, Mr. Lincoln."

I walked around back; the paved alley was a single narrow lane, widening into the recess of the building's modest loading dock, next to which was a door, unlocked. It opened onto an unfinished vestibule with double PUSH doors to the left, the wooden slats of a service elevator straight ahead, and a corner turned into a sort of office at right, with a desk and a couple battered file cabinets in the middle of stacked boxes and bucket-size barrels, all squatting on the cement floor. The air wafted with the bouquet of disinfectant.

The janitor was skinny, but he had a round piggy face; a balding guy in his forties in wireframe glasses and bib overalls, he had his workshoe-shod feet up on the scarred desktop as he sat reading the *Police Gazette* with Jane Russell on the cover. A cup of pencils (perhaps abandoned by a blind beggar), several empty pop bottles, and wadded-up balls of grease-spotted brown sandwich paper were the extent of the work spread out on the desk.

At first I didn't think he'd heard me come in, but then he chimed out, in a whiny tenor, "Didn't you see the sign? No soliciting."

"I'm here about the guy in your basement," I said.

The magazine dropped to his lap. His pig's nose twitched and so did his buck-toothed mouth; his eyes—a rather attractive china blue, in the midst of all that homeliness—

were as round and hard as marbles. But there was fear in them.

"Nobody in the basement," he said.

"Sure there is," I said, and tossed a fin on the desk.

He just looked at it; after a while, he blinked a few times.

"I'm not from the cops," I said, "and I'm not a Fischetti boy. The guy in the basement? I'm his boss."

And I tossed an A-1 Detective Agency business card his way. He took his feet off the desk and sat forward and studied the card, which he held in two hands, like a Treasury agent examining a counterfeit bill.

Then I plucked the card back—it was nothing I wanted to leave lying around the Fischetti homestead—and said, "Just point me, and there's another fivespot in it for you, on my way out."

"I could really get in trouble, you know."

"How much is my op paying you?"

"Don't you know? You're his boss."

"I'm the boss, but he's kind of his own man. What's he paying you?"

The janitor shrugged. "Ten bucks a day. Plus the original C note."

"And you do know who lives on the top floor of this joint?"

His lips farted. "Sure I know."

I shook my head. Some people didn't put much of a premium on their own skins. "Yeah, you could really get in trouble. . . . Point me."

There, amid the labyrinth of pipes and ductwork and the typical junk accumulated in any basement, under the open beams of the low ceiling, in a pool of light provided by a bare hanging bulb, at an old battered table, wearing a dark blue vested suit with gray pinstripes (jacket draped over his chair), his back to the wall, sat former police lieutenant William Drury, like a man preparing to eat a meal. With the exception of a thermos of coffee, the array of items spread out on the table before him, however, wasn't my idea of nourishment: a .38 revolver; a sawed-off shotgun; a notebook; assorted pencils; his gray homburg; and two suitcase-style Revere tape recorders trailing wires that disappeared into the ductwork. The reels of one of the sleek white machines in the hard-shell brown carrying cases were turning, the other two spools staring up at me like big plastic eyeglasses, the machine not recording, at the moment.

He had headphones on, but arranged to leave an ear uncovered; so he'd heard me approach—his right hand hovered over the .38—then smiled in chagrined relief when he saw it was me. And the hand moved away from the gun.

For a guy five foot nine, broad-shouldered Bill Drury had incredible physical presence. But the dark blue eyes, which had always danced with intelligence and good humor, were pouchy now, and the dimpled jutting chin sat on a second, softer one. His complexion had a grayish cast, and his dark thinning hair—combed over ineffectively—was touched with gray; and that ready smile seemed strained.

"I guess if somebody's gotta nail me," Drury said, sheepish, "I'd rather it was you."

"Christ, Bill," I said, shaking my head. I felt woozy, like all the blood had drained out of me; my stomach was turning flip flops. "You're going to get yourself killed, this time. Worse, you're going to get *me* killed."

He waved that off, made a dismissive face. "The Outfit doesn't kill cops."

"Fuck me! We're not cops. I haven't been a cop since 1932! And you, Bill—you're not a cop, either. Not anymore."

His eyes tightened. "I will be again. I will be, Nate."

"How, by illegal wiretap?" I was still shaking my head. I gestured to the machines on the table. "Why two recorders, Bill?"

"I've got the phone line tied into this one," he said, nodding toward the Revere at his left, "and this other one I can switch between various rooms in the three apartments."

I noticed a small black metal box with several knobs, and said, "The recorders I recognize—they're the A-1's. When Lou said you'd checked them out, I figured you were up to something like this. But who made you the gizmo? Somebody on Kefauver's staff?"

"I'm not working for the Kefauver Committee, Nate. This is strictly my own show."

"No, Bill. This is the A-1's show—you're my operative, and those are my machines. You get busted by the cops, or the Fischettis, I get to take the ride with you . . . whether it's to the station house or a ditch."

He was shaking his head. "Nate, I'd never let that happen."

I threw up my hands. "You are letting it happen! Where's your goddamn judgment gone? Sapperstein warned me about hiring you."

"Nate. . . ."

"You've always had a hard-on for these Outfit guys, but breaking into their homes and bugging them? Setting up a listening post in their fucking basement? It's insanity."

Jaw muscles pulsing, he stood; he pointed a finger— Uncle Bill Wanted Me. "Sitting back and watching these bastards get away with murder, *that's* insanity! Looking the other way while the city we love falls under gangster control—that *is* insanity!"

I found a crate to sit on and sat and sighed, leaning an elbow on my knee; I held a hand to my face. I said nothing. Finally Bill, perhaps a little embarrassed, sat back down, himself.

His voice was almost a whisper when he added: "Somebody has to stand up against these barbarians."

"Bill," I said, softly, looking up at him. "When exactly wasn't this city under gangster control? Name a time."

He swallowed, shook his head. "That doesn't make it right."

Unlike almost every other cop in Chicago history, Bill Drury hadn't pulled political strings to land his badge; no graft had been involved, and there was no Outfit connected ward committeeman or alderman or judge in the woodpile. Instead, he had studied hard and scored record high marks on the P.D. entrance exams, and passed the physical requirements with grace and ease, former Golden Gloves champ that he was. The closest thing he'd had to an "in" was that his brother John was a well-known reporter on the *Daily News*; the department didn't mind getting a little good publicity now and then, and having a reporter's kid brother on the job couldn't hurt.

That had been the late twenties, when gangster rule in Chicago was at its most blatant and violent—from the train-tunnel slaying of newsman Jake Lingle to the blood spattered warehouse of the St. Valentine's Day Massacre. A bright young idealistic go-getter—a natural athlete, a scholar—could get ideas about playing Wyatt Earp, and cleaning up this dirty town, like a modern Tombstone or Dodge City. My friend Eliot Ness certainly grew such notions; and so did Bill Drury.

Moving from patrolman to detective in under a year—another Chicago P.D. record—Drury had decided a police officer ought to do something about Al Capone and his boys, and had targeted the Outfit for special attention. Whenever he would spot a known Capone associate, Drury slammed the guy against the nearest wall and made him stand for a frisk.

And Drury didn't care where this took place—a restaurant, the racetrack, a men's room, a street corner—and he would gladly embarrass these hoods when they were out with their wives and kiddies.

"Let these families know," he'd say, "what kind of coward is the head of their household."

Soon the papers had dubbed Bill the "Watchdog of the Loop"—his sports background, his brother being a reporter, and his own gregarious nature led to friendships with countless newspapermen, who constantly gave him glowing mentions in the press—and the Syndicate boys were scratching their heads wondering why they were paying good dough to Drury's superiors, when they were getting ballbreaking treatment like this. Before long, Bill was taken off the street and assigned station house duty; then he was transferred to the pickpocket detail, where I first met him. In neither case did these assignments prevent the Watchdog of the Loop from pursuing his mission in life.

Drury spent his off-duty hours sauntering along Rush Street and Division and other Loop thoroughfares, prowling for hoodlums. When he spotted a millionaire thug like Tony Accardo or Murray Humphries, he demanded their identification and leaned them against the nearest building, legs spread, arms and hands and fingers outstretched, patting them down for concealed weapons.

Such vicious killers as Spike O'Donnell, "Machine Gun" Jack McGurn, and Frank McErlane were among those he fearlessly badgered. He arrested Louie "Little New York" Campagna on State Street, catching the Capone crony packing a .45. In a North LaSalle office, he nabbed ten mobsters, catching Charley Fischetti carrying heat; and he arrested Jake "Greasy Thumb" Guzik, the notorious Outfit accountant, outside Marshall Field's, to the delight of jeering onlookers.

"You son of a bitch," the pudgy, iguana-like Guzik had sputtered. "I'm no vagrant! I got more money in my pocket right now than you earn in a fucking year!"

"Two more words, Jake," Drury said, "and I'll snap the cuffs on you. Two more sentences, I'll get you fitted for a straitjacket."

This kind of showy bravado had made Bill a favorite of the reform crowd. A socially concerned segment of the social register—with names like Palmer and McCormick—singled him out as their police mascot; he was hired to stand guard in black tie, tails, and top hat at fancy weddings and various fashionable doings (and made the papers doing so). When the swells had jewels, furs, or works of art to be guarded, off-duty Drury would moonlight for them; the Opera House became his second beat. Much as he despised graft, he accepted generous fees from his wealthy patrons, and he always drove a nice car and was widely known as the best-dressed honest cop on the force.

We had a long and tangled history, Bill Drury and me. He had saved my life, back in pickpocket detail days, in a shootout at Lincoln and Addison with a car thief named Thomas Downey, who'd been eluding the cops for weeks. For that Bill had won the Lambert Tree commendation— the department's "Medal of Honor" for bravery in the line of duty; he also won my undying friendship.

In 1943, when an old girl friend of mine, Estelle Carey, was murdered viciously—tortured and torched—Drury doggedly pursued the Syndicate angles of the slaying. He turned up the heat on various hoods, subjecting them to polygraphs, and this led to trumped-up charges that Drury—then acting captain at Town Hall station—had looked the other way where gambling in his district was concerned. Bill and his friend Tim O'Conner—another rare Chicago cop with an honest reputation—were suspended, though both fought through the courts and were eventually reinstated.

I had also been involved in the case that had finally brought him down: the shooting of James Ragen, who had been rubbed out when he refused to turn his racing news wire service over to the Outfit. Ragen had been my client— I'd been his bodyguard driving down State Street in the heart of Bronzeville when the shotgun assassins opened up on us from a truck otherwise filled with orange crates. The bullets didn't kill Jim, not immediately; but he died in the hospital, with the help of a mobbed-up doctor who introduced infectious staphylococci into the wounds.

Jim Ragen's niece, by the way, was Peggy Hogan; and Peggy had been my girl friend at the time (right now she was my ex-wife).

So I had helped Bill track down a trio of colored eyewitnesses to the shotgunning—a Pullman porter, a steel worker, and a drugstore clerk—and three West Side gunmen were indicted for the Ragen killing. But one of the witnesses was bumped off, and the other two recanted . . . and both claimed Drury had offered to share the reward money with them in exchange for their testimony. Bill and his partner Tim O'Conner were called before a grand jury demanding details on their dealings with the two witnesses; when they refused to testify unless granted immunity, the Civil Service Board dismissed both from the force.

Now, as his court battles continued, and his chance of returning to the Chicago P.D. grew ever more remote, Bill Drury was staging a last ditch effort to bring down the Outfit guys who had derailed his career.

"I trusted you, Bill," I said, still seated on the crate, sighing, shaking my head. "And you've put me on the spot."

Sitting before his feast of tape recorders and guns, he

didn't look at all contrite. He smiled like Father O'Malley and held out his open hands. "Nate . . . join me."

"What? Go to hell."

Now, ridiculously, he looked around as if to make sure no one was eavesdropping; and very quietly he said, "I'm not just investigating, and helping out the committee. . . . I'm testifying."

"You're going on TV?"

He ducked that. "You know about my files, my notebooks, my journals."

I nodded. Over the years he'd made a hobby of it, following day-by-day movements of Outfit leaders, compiling names, dates, places, which had been useful when he'd turned to writing those newspaper columns. Few people understood the inner workings of the Chicago mob better than Drury; and no one else had chronicled them in this fashion.

"Well," he said, basking in self-satisfaction, "next Tuesday I'm meeting with Kefauver's staff. I'm turning over all my notebooks, records, card files, tape recordings, everything."

I couldn't stop shaking my head. "Why not just limit it to that, behind closed doors—why advertise it by testifying?"

He sneered. "I'm not afraid of these dago bastards. I don't operate in the backroom—I'm taking this out in the open!"

Which was why he was sitting in a basement, I supposed, making illegal wiretap tapes.

"Don't go pious on me, you dumb mick," I said. "You figure if you can't wangle your way back on the department, at least you'll be famous. Maybe write a book—maybe open your own detective agency."

He had the expression of a lovesick fool proposing to his girl. "I'd rather stay on at the A-1 with you, Nate. We could make that place something special."

"Yeah—a parking lot."

"Nate. You have to do this."

"Do what?"

"Join me. Come with me, Tuesday. Meet with Kefauver's people. Agree to testify."

I stood and almost bumped my head on the rafters. "Testify! What, are you smoking the evidence?"

He placed his hands on the table; the recorder continued to whir. "Nate. Look—you're the only guy in this city *not* mobbed-up who knows the mob like I do. . . . Fact, you know things I don't. You worked for them. You were practically Frank Nitti's goddamn protégé."

That was overstating it: I had done jobs for Nitti, and he had done me favors, like not having me whacked. We had come to respect each other—maybe we'd even grown to like each other. I'd even been sorry to see him die.

But all I said was, "Nitti was the best man in his world— that's all that can be asked of anybody."

His eyes widened and rolled. "Bullshit, Heller! He was a killer and a thug and a goddamned extortionist and . . . hell, you know that, you know damn well you should join me and help cleanse this city."

Now my eyes widened. "Did you say that? Did you really say that? 'Cleanse this city?' Can Bill Drury be that naive? That stupid?"

He folded his arms. "I'm not stupid and I'm not naive. And while I don't share your admiration for Frank Nitti, I do admit he was a damn sight better than the boys upstairs."

And he jerked a thumb at the ceiling, where fifteen floors above, the Fischettis' three-story penthouse began.

I wasn't really following this, and said so: "What makes the Fischettis so special, all of a sudden?"

Leaning forward, he shared his secrets, like a swami who had traded his crystal ball in on firearms and tape recorders. "The power is shifting. Guzik's way down the ladder, now . . . last of the old guard. Accardo wants to retire, and there'll be a successor named, soon. And right now, first in line, is Capone's sweet cousin, Charley—the worst of a sick lot."

I shrugged. "The worst I ever heard about Charley, and his brother Rocco for that matter, is they're woman-beaters."

"That's an indication of their savagery, sure. Nate, since the war, Charley's moved the Outfit full-scale into narcotics . . . which was something Frank Nitti would never have done."

That was true about Nitti, and I knew narcotics use in town was up, but I said, "I thought Fischetti's agenda was encouraging the boys to invest in legit enterprises. All I hear from Outfit sources, these days, is Wall Street and Texas oil."

He smirked. "Oh, yeah, they're investing in stocks and bonds and petroleum, all right. But they're also investing in human misery." He began counting on his fingers, though the numbers he began tossing around didn't correlate. "There are fifty thousand drug addicts in this city, Nate—about half of them colored, on the South Side. You know what a habit like that takes to maintain? You got to steal over a hundred bucks worth of goods a day. You add it up."

"Save the speeches for Kefauver."

But he was rolling. "Did you ever see a schoolkid hooked on heroin? I have. Think about your baby son, Nate . . . think about him."

"Maybe you should think about your own family, Bill."

"You know I don't have any kids."

"No—but you got a wife, a beautiful one who loves your foolish ass. And your mother lives with you, right? And your sister? And her husband? And their kid? It's not just your life, and mine, you're risking, you know."

That chin jutted even more than usual. "Annabel knows what we're up against. She's been at my side for a long time, Nate, through all my wars. . . . You know that."

My turn for a speech. "Here's what I know, Bill—you can talk about justice, and wave the flag, and play the violin about schoolkid junkies all you want. . . . But you know and I know that this isn't about justice. It's about getting even."

He started to respond, then stopped.

I went on: "You picked out these Outfit guys for a target, when you were a bright-eyed, rosy-cheeked punk kid, looking to make a reputation. Well, you made that rep, and along the way, also made the worst kind of enemies. They didn't shoot you, oh no—they killed your career instead, because the way this city . . . hell, this country . . . works is, the public wants what the Outfit is selling, and so the politicians and the civil servants, like the whores they are, do their part by climbing in bed with the mob guys. You can't do anything about that, Bill—people like money, and they like sex, and they like all kinds of things that are bad for them, like gambling and booze and dope. This isn't about any of that, though, is it, Bill? This is about you getting even with the bastards who took your career away from you . . . and if you deny it, I'm going to stick that illegal sawed-off shotgun up your ass."

He avoided my gaze, studying the tape recorder whose reels were whirling, gathering more tainted evidence. Finally he said, "They can subpoena you. I'll tell them that you know plenty."

"Then I'll lie through my teeth, and save my ass."

He gave me a long, withering look. "You did that once before."

That was a low blow. I knew exactly what he was referring to. When I was a young uniformed cop, I had lied on the witness stand as part of a Capone mob cover-up. My father was an old union guy with a leftist bookstore on the West Side, and I knew if he didn't get an influx of money, and soon, he'd go under. So I lied on the stand, and got the money, and was promoted to detective, and Pop shot himself through the head with my nine millimeter Browning automatic at his kitchen table in the living quarters back of the bookshop. It was still the gun I carried, when I carried a gun, which I wasn't right now. That gun was the only conscience I had.

"When it's safe," I said, calmly, gesturing to the Revere machines on the scarred table, "haul this stuff out of here. Take the recorders, and any other A-1 property you've checked out, back to the office."

He shrugged, nodded. "All right."

"And Bill? You're fired."

Of course, he knew that already; he said nothing else as I found my way out. I paid the janitor his second fin, and walked around the front of the building. I was going to lay a twenty on the doorman, to make sure he forgot my visit.

I was in the process of giving him the bill when Joey Fischetti came out through the lobby and recognized me.

3

Grinning, Joey Fischetti—having just exited the elevator—trotted across the narrow, modern lobby of Barry Apartments, with its ferns, mirrors, and luxurious furnishings; his footsteps echoed like gunshots off the marble black-and-white tile floor, the first few making me flinch. About five eight, slender, darkly tanned and immaculately groomed, Joey wore the kind of "casual" outfit it took half an hour to select from a well-stocked closet: a brown-with-white patterned sports jacket, a blue-on-white tattersall vest, gray slacks, a red-and-blue patterned tie, and a sporty charcoal hat with a fuzzy red feather that looked like a fisherman's fly.

At forty, Joey was the baby of the Fischetti triumvirate, the only one not actively involved in criminal capitalism, with a blank arrest record to prove it; he was generally considered the best-looking of the brothers (though Charley might have taken issue), and the dumbest (no likely challengers on that point).

The latter quality was what I was counting on.

"Nate Heller!" he said, joining the doorman and myself in the crisp fall afternoon air. He was an animated guy drenched with show biz sincerity. His voice had a husky, high-pitched enthusiasm, and his eyes were as bright as he wasn't. "Goddamn. Do you believe it? What a coincidence!"

"Isn't it, though? Good to see you, Joey. Frank sends his best."

Sinatra and Joey Fischetti were bosom buddies.

He grinned—big glistening white teeth that were either caps or choppers—and shook his head. "You believe that? That's the second coincidence!"

I still didn't know what the first coincidence was.

Now his eyes narrowed, in an approximation of thought. "What are you doin' around these shabby digs, Nate?"

The Barry Apartments were anything but shabby: this was as fashionable as Chicago neighborhoods got, and the Fischetti clan's luxurious triplex penthouse had once been occupied by Mayor Thompson and Mayor Cermak . . . one at a time, of course.

I gave him half a smile and said, "I was just bribing your doorman to see if I could come up and see you, without an appointment."

The doorman's eyes widened with alarm.

But Joey waved off my remark. "Ah, you don't need to waste your money on that! Don't take his money, George."

George swallowed and said, "No, sir," and handed the twenty back.

As I was returning the bill to my pocket, Joey slipped his arm around my shoulder and walked me a few steps down the sidewalk, for a little privacy; the baby Fischetti smelled like a Vitalis and Old Spice cocktail. "My brother's been wanting to talk to you."

"Rocky or Charley?"

"Charley. Rock'll probably be in on it, though. See, I was supposed to call you, but I got busy making arrangements for Frank. That's where I was headed, right now—paving the way for the Voice with Dave Halper, at the Chez Paree."

Dave Halper was one of the new owners of the club, which Mike Fritzel and Joe Jacobsen—the longtime hosts of a venue that had provided first breaks to the likes of Danny Kaye, Betty Hutton, and Danny Thomas—had sold to him last year. The Fischettis had an interest in this, the city's biggest, biggest-time nitery: they owned the Gold Key Club, the Chez Paree's backroom casino.

"See, I kind of had to talk Dave into booking Frank," Joey said.

"Yeah, the kid's career's in a tailspin."

"Naw, Nate, it's just a bump in the road."

I wasn't going to argue the point. "Well, don't let me keep you, Joey. I'll be on my way, and you call my office, and we'll—"

But, oh fuck, now he was walking me back toward the apartment house. "Don't be silly," he was saying, squeezing my shoulder. "Seeing Halper can wait. Frank don't open till Friday. Let's go up and see Charley."

George got the door for us—I didn't tip him—and Joey and I clip-clopped across the lavish lobby.

"Would you do me a favor, Nate?"

"Name it, Joey."

We stepped into the elevator, which was attended by a blue-uniformed guy with blue five o'clock shadow, a nose with minimal cartilage, cauliflower ears, and a bulge under his arm that wasn't a tumor.

Joey said to him, "I'm making a stop at Rocky's floor."

"Yes, Mr. Fischetti," the elevator man marble-mouthed.

To me Joey whispered, "Don't mention to Charley I just run into you by accident. I wanna tell him I called your office and you come around on purpose."

"Fine by me, Joey."

"Sometimes Charley thinks I'm a fuck-up, and it's nice to show him I got organizational abilities. I'm doing more and more in the entertainment field, you know."

"Are you managing Frank?"

He grinned, shrugged. "Not exclusive. Several people I know got a piece of Frank."

This did not surprise me. Since the decline of his career, Sinatra had been working mostly in mob rooms—Skinny D'Amato's 500 Club in Atlantic City; Moe Dalitz's Desert Inn in Vegas; Ben Madden's Riviera in New Jersey; and of course the Chez Paree here in Chicago.

At the seventeenth floor, the uniformed thug deposited us in an entryway about the size of my first apartment. The plaster walls were light gray and the penthouse door—and

another around to the left labeled FIRE STAIRS—a deep
charcoal. A few furnishings—a table with cut flowers in a
white vase under a mirror, a golden Egyptian settee with
a scarlet cushion—hugged the walls, and a sunburst clock
opposite the penthouse door matched the sunburst doorbell, which Joey didn't press—he used a key.

"Hey, Rocky," Joey called, cracking the unlocked door.
"It's me—Joey! Are you decent?"

Now there was a question.

The only response was a muted railroad whistle—*woo!*
woo!

Joey grinned at my confused expression. He said, like I'd understand, "Sounds like Rocky's in his own little world again."

I followed Joey inside. The spacious living room had the
same light gray walls and a charcoal slate floor, warmed up
by pastel furnishings, including two peach sofas facing each
other over a coffee table on a white carpet near a fireplace
over which hung a big gilt-framed painting of peasants pic-
nicking in what I'd wager was a Sicilian countryside setting.
Past a grand piano, through sheer drapes, I could make out—
through the wall of glass doors—the terrace-style balcony with
its white wrought iron furniture and millionaire's lake view.

"Not bad, huh?" Joey said, as I took the place in. Occasional little railroad whistles—"Woo! Woo! Woo! Woo!"—
punctuated this nickel tour.

"Nice," I said, thinking it didn't look like anybody lived
here; an adjacent formal dining room looked similarly showroom perfect. Of course I knew the Fischettis only stayed in
Chicago about half the year—must have been about time for
them to head down to Florida, where they wintered (and
supervised their criminal activities in that state).

The ostentation didn't surprise me, though—one of
Rocco's nicknames was Money Bags, because he liked to
flash his dough around.

Joey led me down a hallway off of which were a spotless
white modern kitchen and a bathroom. Finally, he knocked
on a door, edged it open, stuck his head in, and said, "Hey,
Super Chief! We got company."

"Yeah, yeah," a gruff voice said.

I followed Joey in—possibly designed to be a master bedroom, the large room's only furnishings (other than a few scattered movie-set type canvas-and-wood chairs) were tables of various sizes and various heights, the central one a good four feet by six, to accommodate the towns and villages, the valleys and mountains, the tunnels, bridges, loading platforms and stations, of an enormous, sprawling, demented model railroad.

Miniature freight elevators unloaded grain, water tanks filled the steam engines of locomotives, and a coal mine provided chips of real coal. Tiny conductors, engineers, railroad workers, and passengers inhabited this landscape, as did billboards, farmhouses (with livestock), and much else. On shelves were model trains of every conceivable sort: steam, electric, freight, military, passenger, one of which was on the tracks now, taking the incredibly elaborate journey through the world Rocco Fischetti had created.

The Almighty God of this mini-universe was a homely, pale, pockmarked, shovel-headed hood with a wide yet sharp chin, a long knobby nose, and dark close-set eyes under slashes of black eyebrow; his hair was black with skunk streaks of white. Five-ten, sturdy-looking, he sat mesmerized before a control panel of switches—watching his train take its circuitous, even dangerous, route—wearing a maroon silk house robe and slippers—and a railroad engineer's cap.

He wasn't alone: seated across from him, bored senseless, was a cute shapely twentyish blonde (I thought I recognized her from the *Chez Paree* chorus line) in a silver silk robe and her own engineer's cap. Also, a black eye.

"Sorry to bother you, Rock," Joey said.

The train said, "Woo woo! Woo woo!"

Rocco's back was partly to me—he had not seen me yet, or anyway not acknowledged in any way that he had. "I'm busy," he said. "Don't I look busy?"

"You look busy, but I got Nate Heller here with me."

After a tough day beating up his girl friends, or a hard night torturing an informer, a guy needed to let his hair down. And Rocco had found a way to unwind while expressing his creativity, fashioning this intricate model railroad complex.

He threw a few switches and his train slowed to a halt, its last "woo woo" sounding a little weak, even sad.

He looked at me, and said, "So how's the dick?"

"Swell," I said. "And you mean that in a good way, right, Rocky?"

He smirked; we knew each other a little—though I now knew him better, having glimpsed Model Train Land—and we always spoke, even kidded some. He was the kind of guy who expected respect but liked being treated like a regular joe.

"We been wanting to talk to you," Rocco said, "Charley and me." Rather resignedly, he plucked the railroad cap from his head and tossed it on the control panel. To his brother, he said, "Go on up and see Charley . . . I'll get dressed and join you."

The girl said, "Should I get dressed, too, Rock? Are we going out for dinner?"

He glared at her. "Did I ask you anything?"

"No."

The flatness of their voices in the room was almost a surprise: yelling across the mountainous landscape between them, you'd expect an echo.

"Did I fucking ask you anything?"

"No."

"That's right. Go on and get dressed. Put something on that eye—it's ugly."

"Yes, Rock."

"And call Augustino's and get us the regular table."

"Yes, Rock."

But she hadn't moved from her perch. She was waiting, respectfully, for us to leave. I guessed.

Rocco ushered me out of the railroad yard, putting a hand on my arm, giving it a gentle, friendly squeeze. He too smelled of Vitalis and Old Spice, though less potently than Joey, who trailed down the hallway behind us.

"You gotta be tough on these dames," Rocco said. "Gotta know how to handle 'em."

"You've certainly got a touch."

He knew I was kidding him, and he liked it. "You're a card, Heller."

"Yeah, a joker!" Joey chimed in, grinning, pleased with his wit.

Rocco gave me a look that admitted his baby brother's

idiocy, but fondness was in there, too. And before we left, he patted Joey's cheek and said, "Ask Charley to wait for me, before you talk business."

So we were going to talk business. Wasn't that a delightful notion.

We summoned the elevator and its cauliflower-eared guardian, who delivered us to the eighteenth floor. The entryway was identical to the floor below's, only this time Joey pressed the sunburst doorbell.

"I don't ever just bust in on Charley," Joey said. "He don't like it."

"Maybe we shouldn't bother him," I said. "We can do this some other time. . . ."

But Joey rang the bell again, and before long, Charley—presumably after checking the peephole—revealed himself in the doorway.

Broad-shouldered, kind of stocky, Charles Fischetti was around fifty, an almost-handsome guy with an oval face, bumpy nose, knife-scarred jaw and small mouth that could flash in a surprisingly mischievous smile. Under black slashes of eyebrow that reminded you he was Rocco's brother, Charley's hazel eyes beamed an icy, unblinking intelligence. Charley dyed his gray hair platinum and combed it back in traditional George Raft gangster style; he seemed taller than his brothers, but that was the elevator shoes.

"Sorry to drop in on you, Charley," Joey said.

No dressing robe for Charley Fischetti: his pin-striped single-breasted Botany 500 was so dark a gray, it looked black; his shirt was a light blue and his tie a slip stitched gray with dots of red, like precision splashes of blood.

"Joey," Charley said, in a mellow, mildly scolding baritone, "I told you bring Heller around, but I didn't say just pop by with him."

Joey had a panicky look, so I jumped in with, "It's my fault, Mr. Fischetti." I didn't know Charley very well, and couldn't take the same liberties as with Rocco. "I got the date wrong, but Joey said I might as well come on up, anyway."

Charley smiled at his forty-year-old baby brother, and patted his cheek, much as middle-brother Rocco had. "You're a good boy, Joey. I shouldn'ta doubted you."

I said, "If you have another appointment . . ."

"I do have somebody coming around . . ." He checked his watch. ". . . but that's not for almost an hour."

Joey explained that Rocco would be joining us.

"Well that's fine," he said to his brother. Then, as he gestured for me to step inside, he said, "And let's make it 'Charley' and 'Nate.' "

"Thank you, Charley."

"Hey—any friend of Frank Nitti's is a friend of mine."

We had stepped into the living room when I replied: "Frank was a fine man. He was almost a father to me."

That was overstating it, but I wanted to be welcome in these circles, and of course Nitti had been the successor to their beloved cousin Capone.

"Do you like modernist?" Charley asked. "I like modernist."

Charley liked modernist, all right. The penthouse had the same layout as Rocco's, with the same light gray walls and charcoal slate floor, but offset by the turquoise of a biomorphic-shaped sofa, the forest green of a sculpted ply-wood lounge chair's webbed upholstery, and the salmon pink throw rug (with black geometric squiggles) on which this stuff sat in front of the out-of-place traditional fire-place, over which a huge metal-framed Picasso lithograph squinted with its various eyes.

"Oh yeah," I said, amazed and appalled by the array of atomic age nonsense: kidney-shaped glass on a claw hand of sculptured walnut serving as a coffee table, green Fiber-glas chairs with black wire legs, black metal floor lamp that looked like a praying mantis.

"Most of this," he said, gesturing expansively, "I buy overseas. The Scandinavians get all the credit, but the best modern design is Italian. Carlo Mollino, Gio Ponti, Gian-franco Frattini. . . ."

"No kidding."

"Take a look at this," Charley said, waving me over to several framed paintings on the wall (Joey had taken a three-legged Fiberglas chair, proving it could be sat in). The canvases were abstractions, doodlings in color and geometry.

At his side, I regarded these masterpieces, wondering if Drury's microphone was snugged behind one of them.

"You know, the great artists, they all had patrons," Charley said. "In the Renaissance. Guys like Da Vinci, Michelangelo. It was an Italian thing."

"So I heard."

"See, I have a lot of fine pieces in my collection. I have three Dalís. That's a Picasso over the fire. I got a Miró, and a Klee. Worth a goddamn fortune. But these, these mean more to me."

"I take it these are new painters."

The tiny mouth curved in a slice of a smile. "You know, Nate, you impress me, your sensitivity. Your insight."

"Thanks."

"You're absolutely right. I'm tight with Ric Riccardo. He's my artistic advisor."

An accomplished artist himself, Riccardo ran a popular, artsy café on Rush Street out of a converted warehouse, where he had single-handedly started the local craze of restaurants and merchants exhibiting artists and sculptors.

Charley was saying, "Ric only recommends the best of the new young talent."

What, as compared to the old young talent?

"You see, Nate, I'm not just a collector—I'm a patron."

Like the Borgias, I thought.

"Take this one here," he said, pointing to a canvas that appeared randomly splattered with green, brown, and black. "Ric says this fella is going to be the next Jackson Pollock."

I didn't burst Charley's bubble and point out there already was a Jackson Pollock; I merely nodded and murmured appreciatively if nonverbally.

He slipped his arm around me. He smelled like Vitalis, too, but the cologne was something more expensive than Old Spice—something more expensive than I could recognize.

"Nate," he said, "I feel comfortable with you. I really do. I am so used to uncouth company."

"Yeah, I hate that."

"I hope you feel comfortable with me. A lot of people get the wrong idea about me, you know."

"I know what you mean."

"People like us—you're from the West Side, right?"

"Right."

"Maxwell Street?"

I nodded.

Stepping away, he shrugged elaborately. "You know about coming up from the streets. Rough beginnings." He leaned near again and put a hand on my shoulder and whispered: "That's the trouble with Joey. We pampered him. He come to be a man when we already had our family position, our fortune."

"That can be hard on a kid." Even a forty-year-old one.

"What I mean is, coming up, we all make youthful indiscretions. Now, I'm a respectable businessman—and a connoisseur of the finer things."

"Obviously."

"I'm not gonna kid you, Nate—you swim in the same Chicago sewers I do. . . ."

From connoisseurs to Chicago sewers, in one leap.

". . . and you know I have to keep my hand in certain areas of . . . we'll call it entertainment. Servicing public needs. You were Frank Nitti's friend, and you know that it was his dream to be entirely legitimate."

"Problem is," I said, "these days, legitimate business isn't entirely legitimate."

He patted my shoulder, twice. "Excellent point. Excellent point. And politics . . . which is an area of expertise of mine . . . it's no better. The reality of business is compromise. Only in the arts can a person be truly uncompromising."

He continued showing me around his sky nest—spent a good fifteen minutes showing off his collection, about a third of which was valuable stuff by name artists, the rest junk by "up and coming" new "talents." Charley spoke well for a mob guy, but he wasn't fooling me.

For all his posturing and pretension, and his man-of-the-world airs, this was still the same Charley Fischetti who'd been his uncle Al Capone's bodyguard/chauffeur, and nick-named Trigger Happy.

This was the same Charley Fischetti who started as an alky cooker and rose to be Capone's top lieutenant, who had been implicated in several murders though arrested only once—by Bill Drury—with a conviction for carrying a concealed weapon (reversed in the higher courts).

And this was the same Charley Fischetti who was the Outfit's top political fixer, funneling endless money into local and national campaigns, whose criminal business interests extended to St. Louis, Kansas City, Las Vegas, and Miami.

Gambling. Prostitution. Narcotics. Extortion. Usury. Bribery. Murder. Those were the arts Charley Fischetti was a patron of.

"Hey, I don't want you thinking I'm a goddamn snob," Charley said. "Let me show you my TV room—we'll talk there. . . . Joey, wait out here and bring Rocky in, when he shows."

My host took me by the elbow—he had a barely perceptible limp, from a long-ago gun battle—and soon we were in a more casual room, with cork-paneled walls and windows with closed venetian blinds and geometric-design drapes. A pair of boxy pink foam-cushion couches hugged two walls to form a V, with a couple chairs of the same ilk, only light blue, forward of the couches at left and right, all squatting on fuzzy white wall-to-wall carpet, sharing space with light-blond oak tables. The seating faced a blond console—as wide as the couches—with a TV in the middle with a huge screen . . . twenty-one inch, easy . . . and built-in radio and record player and album storage bins, with a cloth-covered speaker as big as the picture tube.

"Yeah, I'm a TV fan," Charley said, man of the people that he was, slipping behind the blond oak bar along the side wall. "Care for something?"

"Rum and Coke, ice."

"I got martinis made."

"That's fine."

He poured from a pitcher. "I'm addicted to that damn

tube . . . Ed Sullivan, Sid Caesar, and this *Studio One*—
now that's serious drama."

"So is watching Jake La Motta catch Dauthille with a right."

He came around, a martini with olive in either hand.
"No frog is gonna send one of my people to the canvas."

By "my people," I wasn't sure whether Charley meant
an Italian or a mob-owned boxer—La Motta fit either cate-
gory, after all.

We sat on the pink sofa opposite the massive TV console
and he gestured toward it, with his martini. "What I'm afraid
of is this Kefauver clown will be the next Uncle Miltie."

"They've been televising some of these hearings."

"Yeah, and 'cause of the response, *all* the New York hearings, after first of the year, are going nationwide!" He shook his
head. "That's why I can't testify. . . . Not that I have anything
to hide, but the bad publicity. . . . That I can't abide."

He set his martini on the coffee table and reached in a
sportcoat pocket for a small round silver box, the lid of
which he popped off; he selected two small pink pills and
took them with a drink of martini.

"This bum ticker of mine," he said, shaking his head.
"Goddamn business pressures."

Joey and his brother Rocco came in—Rocco had traded
in his maroon robe and railroad cap for a dark brown
sportcoat, lighter brown slacks, and a yellow shirt.

I nodded to Rocco, and he nodded back; he went behind
the bar and came back with a bottle of beer. He and Joey
sat on the adjacent sofa.

"What took you?" Charley asked Rocco, a faint edge of
crossness in his voice.

Rocco's ugly face got uglier. "That cunt—she got mouthy
again. She's fuckin' worthless. I told her to pack her fuckin'
bags. She's got half an hour and then I throw her down the
fuckin' stairs."

Shaking his head, Joey said, "She used to be such a
nice kid."

Rocco sneered, shook his head once, and had a gulp
of Blatz.

Charley sipped his martini, shrugged, and said, "Sooner
or later they all wear out their welcome. . . . Rock, we

were just getting started, here. I explained to Nate how we don't like this bad publicity."

Rocco nodded, belched. "This traveling dog-and-pony show, it's really just a sham, y'know. Kefauver don't know his dick from a doughnut."

"A sham?" I said.

"Don't misunderstand my brother," Charley said. "The senator is a sincere, honest man—but he's a man, with weaknesses, or anyway . . . traits."

"What kind of traits?"

"Well, he's impulsive for one. Look at him, bull in the china shop, with this investigation. Not thinking about the political ramifications for his own party."

"What I heard," I said, "was he's not coming to Chicago till after the election."

Which was only a month and a few weeks away. This was an off-year national election, after all, and Kefauver's fellow Democrat Senator Scott Lucas—a powerful man in Washington, the Senate majority leader—was up for re-election. And the Demos locally were running Captain Dan "Tubbo" Gilbert, chief investigator of the State's Attorney's office, for Cook County sheriff.

Both Lucas and Gilbert were bedfellows of local political boss Jake Arvey—which meant they were also bedfellows of the blond-haired art connoisseur sitting next to me.

"Also," Charley was saying, "Kefauver's ambitious. He wants to be the next president."

"So you think this gangbuster stuff is just publicity-seeking."

Rocco said, "Goddamn right."

"Whatever the case, the more stable minds around Kefauver," Charley said, "were either able to maneuver him, or talk reason to him. Anyway, even though he's got staff poking around here, he postponed the Chicago hearings, yes, till after the election; he's in Kansas City, now."

"Truman must love that," I said, thinking about the President's own ties to convicted felon, Boss Tom Pendergast.

Chariev was beaming at me; he hadn't noticed I hadn't touched my martini—I hate the things. "Now, Nate, I won't insult you—I guess we know where you stand, if you get called to testify."

I shrugged. "Nobody's talked to me yet."

"They'll get around to you."

I didn't question how he knew this, I just said, "They'll be wasting their time."

Rocco sat forward and said, "You heard about this fifth amendment thing, ain't you? Charley, tell him about this fifth amendment thing."

Charley's small mouth formed a smile large with condescension. "I believe our friend Mr. Heller knows his constitutional rights, Rock."

Rocco said to me, "Even if they get us on contempt, for not answerin'? A few months and you're on the street again."

"Rocky," Charley said, "Nate can decide for himself how to handle this unpleasantness."

So that's what this was about: getting my assurance that the Outfit had nothing to worry from me, if I testified.

Or so I thought, till Charley went on to say: "What we really want to talk to you about is this guy Drury, who works for you."

"He doesn't work for me anymore."

"You let him go? Fired him?"

"That's right."

"When?"

"Recently."

Charley thought about that, then sighed and said, "I understand you're friends—you were on the department, together. He saved your life. That has to carry weight."

"Bill is still my friend. But he's his own man."

"You need to talk to him. He's making trouble. Settle him down."

I gestured with an open hand. "I don't carry *that* kind of weight with him. Nobody does."

Charley's eyes narrowed under the dark slashes of brow. "You could offer him his job back—at an increased salary, if he concentrates on his work for you. I could arrange to pay you the difference, every month."

"That's generous, Charley. But I don't understand—if you're not really worried about the Kefauver Committee—"

"I told you: it's the bad publicity. This lunatic Drury,

he'll testify, he'll bring up all kinds of ancient history, he'll spin his yarns, and we'll look like a bunch of gangsters."

Can you imagine that?

"He's a hard-headed Irishman," I said. "Proud as hell and twice as stubborn—you can't buy him, and you can't scare him. And if you . . . do anything else, you'll really have bad publicity."

Rocco glared at me. And this time I didn't feel like kidding him.

Charley looked unhappy, too, as he got up and poured himself another martini. Still over at the bar, he said, "What you're implying is out of line, Nate. That's the old school. This is not 1929."

Joey said to Charley, as he was sitting back down, "Ask him about Frank."

Charley sipped his fresh martini and said, "You ask him. Frank's your friend."

Joey swallowed and sat forward. "Nate, you must've seen Frank out in Hollywood."

"Just the other night, actually. Why?"

Joey's handsome face contorted as he said to me, "I can ask him, but what's he gonna say? I mean, to me? Being who I am. What do *you* think?"

I said, "What the hell are you talking about?"

Joey held out open palms. "Where does Frank stand?"

"Oh. Well—he's scared right now. The feds are squeezing him—you want bad publicity, try being a show business guy labeled a Red."

"Never mind that," Charley said. "What's your opinion of Sinatra's integrity?"

"I can't see him selling you guys out," I said.

Rocco asked, "Too scared?"

"No. He likes you guys. Respects you. You know how some people feel about movie stars? That's how he feels about you."

Charley thought about that, nodded, set his martini glass on the coffee table. "Appreciate your frankness, Nate. Your insights." He checked his watch, then patted my shoulder. "Gotta chase you out, now—before my next appointment."

When Charley stood, so did I, and his brothers. I shook hands with Charley and Rocco, and Joey walked me to the elevator.

"Thanks for standing up for Frank," Joey said, in the entryway. "I'll get you a ringside table, opening night."

"Make it a booth," I said.

Afternoon was turning to dusk, as I reached my car, parked across from the apartment house. I sat for a while, wondering if Drury had gotten his ass out of there yet. But I was also waiting to see who the next appointment was.

A heavy-set man in an expensive topcoat with a fur collar walked up the sidewalk to where George the doorman held the door open for him, like he was a regular. Maybe he was: the guy was Captain "Tubbo" Gilbert, candidate for Cook County sheriff.

I was chewing that over when the blonde showgirl with the black eye came out, wearing a pink long-sleeve sweater and pink slacks and carrying two big pink suitcases with a gray garment bag over her arm. I had a hunch her railroad cap wasn't in either suitcase.

She was stumbling; she'd been crying. George looked like he might want to help her, but didn't.

She must not have had a car of her own, because she hauled the suitcases to the corner and sat on them, like she was waiting for a bus. A cab might come by, eventually—maybe she'd called one. I knew I should mind my own business.

Instead, I called out, "Hey!"

She looked up and squinted across the street at me.

"You need a lift?" I asked.

She swallowed and nodded.

So I got out and went over and helped with her bags, and loaded them—and her—into my Olds.

As I headed back to the Loop—it was on the tail end of rush hour on the Outer Drive—she looked over at me, timidly, using big brown eyes that were beautiful even if they were bloodshot. "You . . . you're not one of *them*, are you?"

I figured she meant, was I a mob guy?

"No," I said, and hoped to hell I was right.

4

At the time of its construction before the turn of the century, the sixteen-story Monadnock Building in the south Loop had been the world's biggest office building, as well as the last—and largest—of the old-style masonry structures, with walls fifteen feet thick at the base. The dark brown brick monolith nonetheless had a modern, streamlined look— thanks to its flaring base, dramatic bay windows, and the outward swell at the top, in lieu of a cornice. A classy building, a classic building—and home of the A-1 Detective Agency.

The A-1 had begun back in December '32 as a single office over a blind pig in an undistinguished building on nearby Van Buren, sharing a street with hockshops, taverns, and flophouses, with fellow tenants numbering abortionists, shylocks, and a palm reader or two. It was always an awful place, but my friend Barney Ross, the boxer, owned it, so that's where I got my start.

By '43 I'd expanded to a suite of two offices and had taken on two operatives (including Lou Sapperstein, who was now a partner) and a knockout secretary named Gladys, who was unfortunately all business; we eventually took over most of the fourth floor. After the war we were briefly in the Rookery, but the space was limited and the rent wasn't.

So we now had the corner office on the seventh floor of the

venerable Monadnock, with a view over Jackson Boulevard of the Federal Building. I had four full-time operatives and two part-time, who shared a big open bullpen of desks; Lou had a small office and I had a big one (Gladys had a reception cubbyhole). We were close to the courts and the banks, and yet still within spitting distance of the Sin Strip of State Street. It was everything a private eye in Chicago could want.

I even looked like one, in the military-style London Fog raincoat and my green Stetson fedora, as—on the cool, overcast September morning after my meeting with the Fischetti boys—I strolled in the Monadnock's main entrance at 53 West Jackson. Plenty of natural light filtered through the store windows on either side of the corridor—the building was narrow and these were the back-end show-window entries of stores facing Dearborn and the glorified alley that was Federal. The Monadnock had open winding stairwells all the way up, beautiful things, but I took the elevator to seven.

I took a left as I got off on my floor and strode down to the frosted-glass-and-wood wall behind which was our reception nook—or was it a cranny? In bold black, the door said:

A-1 DETECTIVE AGENCY
Criminal and Civil Investigations
Nathan S. Heller
President

and in smaller lettering,

Louis K. Sapperstein
Senior Operative

I went in and Gladys Fortunato looked up from her work. A busty brown-eyed brunette with a sulky mouth, primly professional in a white blouse and dark-framed glasses, Gladys was sitting behind her starkly modern plywood and aluminum desk with its phone, typewriter, and intercom.

"Good morning, Mr. Heller."

"Morning." I had my hat off; Gladys had long since taught me respect.

Behind her was another wood-and-frosted-glass wall. On the walls to either side hung framed vintage Century of Progress posters, under which resided boxy lime-color wall-snugged couches, a low-slung plywood and aluminum coffee table in front of each, well stocked with various *True Detective* magazines that featured stories about me.

Gladys and I had never been an item, but after her husband (an operative of mine) had died at Guadalcanal, she and I had finally become friendly. Her smile was genuine as she handed me a pile of mail and magazines.

"Glad to see you drag in," she said.

"I didn't have any appointments. Nobody knows I'm back in town."

"Somebody does. You have an appointment in half an hour with Captain Gilbert."

"Hell! Why did you take that?"

"I didn't—he did. His secretary asked if you had a ten o'clock appointment, and I said no, and she said to put Captain Gilbert down and that was that."

"Damn."

"And Mr. Sapperstein wants to talk to you."

I sighed. "Send him over."

"I can get you some coffee, if that'll help."

"No thanks."

I went through another frosted-glass door out into the bullpen—Lou's office was straight ahead, door closed. The area was fairly open—I don't like butting desks up against each other—and (while I was no modernist in Charley Fischetti's league) the office furniture I'd chosen was the latest stuff: plywood, Fiberglas, perforated aluminum, and wire, sleek and efficient. We were in an ancient building, with foam green plaster walls and dark molding, and I wanted to send a contemporary message.

About half the desks were filled—my ops spent a good share of their time in the field, and of course Drury's desk was vacant—and I nodded a couple hellos as I headed around to the right, stopped to get a Dixie cup of water from the cooler, then went through the door marked PRIVATE.

I hung up my hat and coat in the closet. My office was a spacious affair with a comfortable couch, padded leather client

chairs, wooden file cabinets, and—positioned against the opposite wall to take advantage of the big double bay windows—the
mammoth old scarred desk I'd had since the beginning. I wasn't
going to subject myself to any of that atomic age nonsense.

My office walls were decorated with framed, mostly signed
photos of celebrities, sometimes with me, sometimes not. A
few magazine covers were framed as well—a *Real Detective*
that covered my handling of the Sir Harry Oakes "locked
room" murder, a *Daring Detective* showcasing my cracking
of the Peacock homicide, a couple others—an egotistical
array, but it impressed clients.

I leaned back in my swivel chair and sipped my water,
wondering if Captain Dan "Tubbo" Gilbert—who I'd seen
yesterday afternoon, going in for the next appointment with
Charley Fischetti—had spotted me, as well.

Two raps on the door announced Sapperstein, who did not
wait for a response, just ambled in, shutting the door behind
him, and pulled up a chair. He had his suitcoat off, exposing
dark suspenders and the rolled-up sleeves of his white shirt;
despite this casualness, his royal blue tie wasn't loosened.

My bald, bespectacled partner—who at sixty could still
kick the hell out of most men half his age, belying his librar-
ian looks—said, "Did Gladys mention you'd had a number
of phone calls already this morning?"

"She said Tubbo's secretary called for an appointment."

He frowned. "Yeah, so I heard—what's that about?"

"What do you think? Drury. Tubbo's on his short list, right
next to Fischetti."

"Where *is* Bill this morning? Not that he's ever around.
Did you ever track him down yesterday? Not to mention our
tape recorders."

"I tracked him down, and he's not going to be around,
other than I hope to bring back those Reveres. I fired him."

Briefly, I told Lou how I'd caught our operative in the
basement of the Barry Apartments.

"Crazy bastard," Lou said, shaking his head. "He'll get us
all killed before he's through."

"No he won't. He's not part of the A-1, anymore. We
have nothing to do with him and his little war on crime."

"Let's see if you can convince Tubbo of that."

I raised an eyebrow. "I think I convinced Fischetti—or anyway, I thought I had. With Tubbo turning up on my doorstep this morning, who the hell knows?"

That astounded him. "You saw Fischetti yesterday? What, Charley?"

"Charley *and* Rocco. And Joey, for that matter."

I gave him the lowdown, quickly—I left out the part about me giving Rocco's discarded, battered showgirl a lift into the Loop . . . or that she was still in my residential suite at the St. Clair Hotel. (You'll get the lowdown on that, in due time. Patience.)

As I wound up my story, Lou lifted a pack of Camels from his breast pocket and lighted up. I could tell he was thinking about how to approach me, on something. Finally he waved out his match and said, "Those other calls I mentioned? They're all from Robinson—Kefauver's man."

"I know who he is."

Lou's eyebrows rose. "Oh, you've met him?"

"No. But I know who he is."

"Robinson wants to meet with you. No subpoena—just informal. Over at the Stevens Hotel."

"I heard they were camped out at the Crime Commission, with Virgil Peterson."

Lou nodded. "Officially, yes. But they're using the Stevens for talking to potential witnesses and, uh . . ."

"Informants?"

He shrugged. "Better a live informant than a dead witness. Anyway, you better get it out of the way. Go over there—see if you can convince them you don't know jack shit. Head this fucking thing off."

"You've talked to Robinson?"

Lou's eyes rolled. "Oh, only six or twelve times, about this. You want me to call, and set it up?"

I sighed. Nodded.

"For when?"

"Soon as the hell possible," I said. "This morning, even—just allow me time to deal with Tubbo."

Lou nodded, breathed dragon smoke, and rose. Heading for the door, he said, "I'll take care of it," and went out.

I was halfway through my mail when Gladys buzzed, and

informed me my "ten o'clock" was here. I told her to usher
him in, which she did.

"Quite a step up from Van Buren Street," Captain Dan
"Tubbo" Gilbert said jovially, after we'd shook hands and
he'd settled into a leather chair across from me.

If Bill Drury was the best-dressed honest cop in town, Dan
Gilbert was the best-dressed bent one . . . which was a bigger
distinction, after all.

Pushing sixty, a fleshy six-footer in a three-piece three-
hundred-buck double-breasted gray pinstripe suit with a
blood-drop ruby stickpin in his gray-and-blue tie and several
diamond-and-gold rings on various pudgy fingers, Tubbo sat
with an ankle on a knee and his pearl gray homburg in his
lap. His keg of a head sat on an ample double chin, and his
dark eyes in their pouches were sharp with cunning if not
quite intelligence. His nose was flat and pointed, like Jack
Frost's icicle snout starting to melt; his chin cleft, a Kirk
Douglas dimple; his hair neatly combed salt-and-pepper,
nicely barbered; his eyebrows thick dark slashes that might
have been borrowed from Rocco or Charley Fischetti.

"I guess you haven't been over to our new offices before,
Tub," I said, leaning back in the swivel chair, arms folded,
giving him a faint meaningless smile.

"You should come over to my suite at the Sherman," he
said. "Very nice. Nothing like an office with room service."

Tubbo was on leave of absence from the State's Attorney's
office, for the duration of his campaign for sheriff—not that
he'd ever spent much time at the office out of which he
supposedly supervised one hundred detectives.

"How's the campaign going?" I asked.

"Swell. Public's really responding to our message."

"What message is that? I've been out of town."

"Oh. Well. I'm going to drive all the gambling out of Cook
County—just give me your vote, and six months."

I had to grin. "Does that include that handbook of yours,
over on West Washington?"

Tubbo didn't take offense; he just flashed me a yellow grin,
and reached inside his suitcoat pocket. I knew he wasn't going
for a weapon—well, not a weapon that used bullets.

The envelope he flopped onto my desk would have green ammunition in it, no doubt.

"Take a look," he said. "Two grand in fifties."

During his thirty-three years as a police officer, Tubbo Gilbert had been a busy boy. He'd been a labor organizer prior to his first assignment on the P.D.—patrolman—and in less than nine years, he made captain. And it didn't interfere with his continued union organizing, at all. After he became chief investigator for the State's Attorney's office, few Chicago-area labor crimes were solved; and in his eighteen years with the State's Attorney, gambling flourished in suburban Cook County, while not one major Capone hoodlum went to jail—although Tubbo did find time to frame a few of the Outfit's competitors, notably bootlegger Roger Touhy.

These minor lapses didn't keep Tubbo from achieving distinction as a law enforcement officer in Chicago. He was considered the city's top cop—above the commissioner and the chief of police—and was undoubtedly the most important law enforcement officer in the county. His real claim to fame, however—cemented by various newspaper articles—was as "the world's richest cop."

An underpaid public servant could get wealthy, he explained to reporters, by investing wisely on the Chicago Commodity Market.

"It's two grand, all right," I said, thumbing through the greenbacks; then I tossed the envelope back on the desk—nearer to myself than Tubbo.

"Would you like to know what that's for, Nate?"

"I figure you'll get around to it."

"We've not had many dealings, you and I."

I'd seen to that: steered Tubbo a wide path.

He went on: "But we've had mutual friends, over the years. Frank Nitti said I was his favorite golfing partner."

"No kidding."

"None. We used to go down to the Arlington Hotel in Hot Springs, together—great golf course. Owney Madden used to join us. You know, I still use the clubs Frank gave me. Gold-plated. Frank was a generous man."

"The clubs he gave me were solid gold."

Tubbo frowned—the pouchy eyes seemed hurt, for an instant; then he grinned. "You're pulling my leg, aren't you?"

"A little. But I agree with you. Frank Nitti was a hell of a guy."

"He put the word out, you know—no one was to screw with Nate Heller. He liked you. You had his protection."

"But he's dead, now. Dead for what—seven years?"

Tubbo raised a plump, jeweled hand as if in benediction. "It still goes—you still benefit from his goodwill. His respect for you."

"Good to know." I didn't mention that Tubbo was referring to the same Outfit guys who had cornered Nitti into suicide.

Captain Gilbert folded his hands on his ample belly. "I don't see your associate, Mr. Drury, in the office today—or does he have a private office?"

Didn't Fischetti fill him in? "Bill doesn't work here anymore, Tub. . . . Still want to give me the two grand?"

"That's a token of thanks from certain individuals in return for your cooperation in this laughable 'crime' inquiry."

"Nothing more?"

"It could be considered a down payment. Have you had a falling out with Drury? Was it on bad terms, his parting from your employ?"

"Bill saved my life, once. We'll always be friends. I just don't want to have anything to do with his crusade."

Tubbo twitched a sneer. "Vendetta, you mean."

"You think he's singled you out, Tub?"

"Not me, really. Charles Fischetti. Drury's had a chip on his shoulder, for Charley, ever since Charley beat that gun rap, years ago. Silly damn grudge. Childish. As for me, I've always gotten along with Bill. I just ran into him in the Sherman Hotel drugstore, the other day—he plays handball in the gym, there."

"Really."

"Yes, and when you see him, tell him I was serious about my offer. It still stands."

I grinned again—trying to bribe Bill Drury? Who was Tubbo trying to kid—himself? "What offer was that, Tub?"

"After the election, I'll have an investigator's slot waiting for him, on the sheriff's department. He'd like to be a cop again, I hear. Well, I'll make him one."

"I'll pass that along. For what good it'll do."

He raised a fat finger. "You might advise him to watch the company he's keeping."

"What company is that?"

"These reporters. Did you see the *Collier's* piece, by Lester Velie?"

"I skimmed it."

His eyes tightened. "Your friend—your former employee—was the prime source. And of course he's still feeding Lait and Mortimer wild stories and exaggerations."

Jack Lait, a seasoned reporter and veteran of several Chicago papers, was now the editor of the *New York Mirror*; and Lee Mortimer was a syndicated columnist for that same paper. Starting with New York, they'd collaborated on several best-selling books on major cities—half smutty tour guide, half muckraking journalism. The latest one—*Chicago Confidential*, published early this year—had exposed to a national audience many Outfit secrets, including Tubbo's role as the "elder statesman of political corruption."

"I don't know anything about that," I said. "Bill was working for the *Herald-American* before he came to work with me. And his brother was a reporter. So he runs in those circles."

The pouchy eyes narrowed; for the first time, a faint edge of menace crept into Tubbo's voice. "You didn't know he was feeding these yellow journalists his tripe at the same time he was on your payroll?"

"I did not."

Tubbo shifted in the chair; the leather made a farting sound, as he crossed his other leg. "Have you ever seen these fabled notebooks of his?"

"The records, the files he keeps? I know about them. He's mentioned them. He certainly didn't keep them here."

The dimpled chin lifted and he gazed down the pudgy expanse of his excess-ridden face. "If you could find them, they would be . . . of interest."

"To you or to Charley Fischetti?"

An elaborate shrug. "Does that matter? Find them, secure them, deliver them—and there's fifty thousand in it."

"Jesus! Fifty thousand. . . ."

His smile seemed almost puckish. "I thought that might get your attention."

I picked up the envelope, riffled through the bills. This was the moment, in the pulps, in the movies, where the private eye threw that damn money in the crooked cop's face.

"Thanks," I said, and tossed the envelope in my top desk drawer. "I'll see what I can do. . . . But those notebooks are a long shot. I'm not promising anything."

Tubbo nodded, pleased. He got up—it took a while. He gestured for me not to show him to the door—I wasn't planning to, anyway. He was halfway there when he paused and asked, "Do you know this attorney—what is it, Bas? Marvin Bas?"

I shrugged. "Not well. He's a Republican, pretty active in his ward. Represents some nightclubs, strip joints, on the Near Northside."

Now his tone got casual—a little too casual. "Did you know Bas and Drury are thick, these days?"

"News to me, Tub."

"It's really too bad . . . distressing. You see, Bas is working for Babb."

That was a lot of *b*s, but what it meant was, Drury was tight with a high-ranking campaign worker of Tubbo's opponent in the sheriff's race. Drury might be digging up dirt on Tubbo—a job that wouldn't take much of a shovel—for that candidate.

"It's a pity," Tubbo said, and shook his head. "Beating Coughlan woulda been a damn cakewalk."

J. Malachy Coughlan, Tubbo's original opponent in the sheriff's race, had died in August; young, handsome, personable John E. Babb—an attorney and a World War Two hero—had been chosen to fill the slate.

"You're a Democrat, Tub," I said. "You got to try real hard to lose, in this town."

Tubbo nodded that I was right, waved a jeweled hand, and slipped out—and he was barely gone before Sapperstein slipped in. He trotted over and took Tubbo's well-broken-in chair.

"Robinson will see you at eleven-thirty at the Stevens," Lou said. "Suite 1014. Any objections?"

"No. Thank you for setting it up." I returned to my mail and then looked up and Lou, bright-eyed behind the tortoise-shells, was staring at me.

"Are you still here?" I asked.

"So?"

"So what?"

"So what's up with Tubbo—spill!"

I filled him in, and showed him the envelope of money.

"You're keeping that?" Lou asked, mildly surprised.

"Hell yes. I wasn't going to testify, anyway."

His eyes were wide, his brow tense. "Well, Christ—thanks for making me party to a bribe."

I shrugged. "In that case, this never happened, and this two grand goes into my pocket, and not the A-1 account, out of which you get a share."

Sapperstein smirked. "You're funnier than Kukla, Fran, and Ollie."

"All of them? Anyway, I was waiting for the other shoe to drop, and now it has."

"What other shoe?"

I leaned back, rocking in the chair. "It was too easy, yesterday, with Fischetti."

"How so?"

"Charley just asked me not to testify, and I said don't worry about it, and that was it. *Some* money had to change hands, or I'd be worried."

He frowned—and with that bald head, the frown went way back and never seemed to stop. "You're not going to sell Drury out, are you?"

I almost threw a paperweight at him. "What the fuck kind of thing is that to say? I got lines I don't cross, for Chrissake!"

He got up, patting the air with both palms. "I know, Nate, I know, I'm sorry. . . . It's just—after all these years, I still have trouble keeping track of what they are, exactly."

And he went out.

5

The Stevens Hotel was hardly an out-of-the-way hole-in-the-wall where an investigator might discreetly interview informants. On Michigan Avenue between Balbo and Eighth, overlooking Grant Park and Lake Michigan, the massive, rococo hotel was the world's largest, with its three thousand rooms, twenty-five stories and four finger-like skyscraper towers.

Still, it made some sense, Kefauver's team camping out, here. Uncle Sam had a relationship with the Stevens, which had been used by the military during the war, for offices, training, and even billeting. And with all these rooms, all this activity—who knew how many conventions and conferences were going on in the hotel right now?—anybody could get lost in the crowd, or at least have an excuse for being here.

Though the Stevens was only a four-block walk from the Monadnock, a light rain encouraged me to hop a cab, which dropped me at the Michigan Avenue entry. A corridor of storefront windows opened into a two-story, ornate lobby bordered by yawningly wide staircases, leading to ballrooms and, no kidding, an ice-skating rink. Shaking the drizzle from my fedora, I strolled on into the vast white chamber, a world of marble pilasters, luxurious Louis XVI furnishings, and fluffy clouds drifting on a high, carved-plaster, gold-trimmed ceiling's painted sky—what better setting for Chicago gangsters?

The elevators were to the left of the check-in counter, near an elegant sitting area of round button-tufted couches and overstuffed chairs. I spotted a small man in a brown suit and green snapbrim, seated in a chair between a couple of potted ferns, legs crossed exposing diamond-pattern socks over brown tasseled loafers. Though his identity was hidden by the *Herald-American* sports section, which he was holding high and close, something about the guy seemed familiar.

When I turned my back to this possible sentry—or spy—I continued to watch him in the polished bronze elevator door, to see if he peeked out over or around that sports section. He did not. Maybe I was just being paranoid—but that was okay, because I was, after all, a professional paranoid.

When I got off on the tenth floor, a short, burly-looking little guy—snappy, in a well-cut blue suit with blue-and-red-striped tie and gray feathered hat—was waiting to get on. His hair was black and his eyes were like black buttons in a rumpled oval face made round by five o'clock-shadowed jowls.

I knew him and he knew me—and we both froze there, long enough for him to miss the elevator. We understood at once why we both were on the tenth floor of the Stevens.

"Well, hello, Jake," I said, and offered my hand.

Jake Rubinstein's grip was firm, but his smile wasn't. "Been a long time, Nate. Since before the war, right?"

"Right. I thought you were in Dallas."

"Yeah, yeah I still am." He hitched his shoulders, Cagney-style, only without the confidence. "I had, uh . . . business back here."

We both knew what kind of business—the Kefauver variety—but that went unstated.

Jake punched the DOWN button, and said, "So is Barney in town?"

"No, he and Cathy are in L.A. They got remarried."

"Ah, that's great. I heard he shook that monkey off his back. That's great, too. Gutsy little bastard."

This strained exchange referred to our mutual pal, Barney Ross, who had come back from the war with a morphine habit that he managed to kick, going public with his problem.

All three of us had grown up in the Lawndale district, near Maxwell Street, and we'd all been little street hustlers as kids, only Barney went on to be a world's champ prizefighter, I became a cop, and Jake a strong-arm goon and bagman for local unions. A few years ago Jake had moved to Dallas, where (among other things) he managed the Silver Spur, a nightclub.

The elevator made a return stop, and Jake and I bid our goodbyes, and he went on his way, and I on mine.

Once you got away from the area around the elevators, the halls of the posh hotel got as tight as a train car. I took a right down to the door of the corner suite where I'd been told to come. I knocked on a gold-edged ivory door.

After peephole inspection, the door swung open and revealed Drury's fellow exile, ex-police captain Tim O'Conner, a lanky, blue-eyed, sandy-blond Irishman whose narrow, handsomely sharp-featured face was mildly ravaged by pockmarks (cheeks) and drink (nose).

"Doorman, now, Tim?" I asked, as he ushered me in. "That the only job available to an ex-copper these days?"

"I'm lucky anybody'll have me." Like Drury, O'Conner was well dressed for a cop, his off-the-rack brown suit livened up by a pale yellow shirt and dark yellow tie. "Actually, these gentlemen thought you might warm up to a familiar face."

I stopped him in the hall-like entryway of the suite, off of which were closets and a bathroom. "Are you working for the committee?"

He took my raincoat and hung it up; I kept my hat, but took it off.

"In a roundabout way," O'Conner said. "This local lawyer working with the committee, Kurnitz, I hired on as his investigator. He's here, you'll meet him, Kurnitz, I mean."

"I've met him before."

Kurnitz was an eccentric, full-of-himself lawyer in the Loop who did a lot of criminal work, both for white-collar criminals, like embezzlers, and blue-collar crooks, like heist men. He didn't mouthpiece for the mob, though, which explained the committee using him—a guy with connections in the underworld who wasn't connected.

O'Conner was saying, "The committee didn't want to hire either Bill or me, because we're controversial figures. We were fired off the police force, after all."

"I'd think getting fired off the crookedest goddamn force in the country would be a glowing recommendation."

"Doesn't matter. We're getting the job done."

O'Conner escorted me into the living room area of the nicely appointed suite, where my hosts were waiting. A sofa along the window overlooked Grant Park and the lake—a breathtaking view made irrelevant by the gray afternoon— with several easy chairs pulled up close, a coffee table between . . . a nice, cozy setting for an inquisition.

As we approached, the three men who'd been seated together on that couch rose as one. All three had dark-rimmed glasses and dark hair and receding hairlines—they might have been brothers.

Or maybe the Three Stooges—only all of them were Moes, albeit balding ones.

The one nearest me extended a hand—he was tall, lean, but sturdy-looking with an oblong face that had slits for eyes and a slightly wider slit for a mouth, which right now were combining to form a stern expression. Fiftyish, he wore a brown suit and a darker brown tie. "George Robinson, Mr. Heller, associate counsel. Thank you for joining us."

It was a firm handshake, and his words were cordial enough; but his manner made me think of a high school principal regarding a problem student.

"Rudolph Halley, Mr. Heller," said the man next to Robinson—a head shorter, a good ten years younger—in a high-pitched voice laced with a lisp. "Chief Counsel." A compact character in a blue suit with a blue-and-red bow tie, Halley had a moon face, its roundness offset by a cleft chin and hard dark eyes.

"Mr. Halley," I said, accepting his aggressive handshake. Then I turned to the remaining man, and said, "Mr. Kurnitz," nodding to the lawyer, who was at right, standing slightly apart from the other two.

"Mr. Heller," he said, nodding back, in a well-modulated courtroom baritone. He wore a gray suit, nicely cut, and a blue-and-gray tie, and would have been handsome if his intense brown eyes hadn't been too large for his face even before his eyeglasses magnified them.

They returned to the couch and I took a comfortable armchair opposite them, with the coffee table—piled with various files and notebooks—between us. Water glasses and a coffee cup also rested on the glass top. The grayness of the afternoon filled the windows behind them like a bleak expressionist painting.

O'Conner, standing near the other easy chair but not taking it, asked, "Anybody want anything?" To me he explained, "There's coffee and ice water and soft drinks."

"No pretzels?" I asked.

Nobody but me found that funny.

Robinson and Halley asked for refills of their water glasses, and Kurnitz requested another coffee, black. I asked for a Coke. O'Conner hustled over to the wet bar and filled everybody's orders. Glad to see the ex-cop had a significant job here on the Crime Committee.

"Mr. Heller, you've had an interesting and varied career," Robinson said. He managed to make that sound like an insult.

Sitting forward, Halley said, "You can understand why we would like to have your cooperation."

"I'm here," I said with a shrug.

O'Conner was in the process of serving everybody.

"You left the police force, locally," Robinson said, referring to a spiral notebook, "in December 1932, not long after an incident involving Frank Nitti."

"Two crooked cops tried to kill him," I said. "They expected me to lie for them. I didn't."

"You testified to that fact in April 1933," Halley said. Unlike Robinson, he didn't refer to any notes, and I guess I was supposed to be impressed.

O'Conner—after serving me last, handing me a water glass with ice cubes and Coke—settled into the easy chair at my right. He flashed me a nervous smile; he hadn't gotten himself anything to drink.

"I don't have anything to add, where that incident is concerned," I said. "It's all part of the public record—my testimony speaks for itself. Besides, that's ancient history, isn't it? Frank Nitti is dead."

"Killed himself," Robinson said, in a "crime does not pay" fashion.

I shifted in my seat. "Why do you need to ask me things you already know the answers to? If you have the FBI file on me—"

"We don't have your file, Mr. Heller," Halley said. That nasal voice of his was weirdly hypnotic. "J. Edgar Hoover has gone on record with his opinion that the Mafia is a myth—we are receiving no cooperation whatsoever from the FBI, which is why we have to work so hard investigating, on our own steam."

I kept a poker face, but relief was flooding through me. I knew for a fact—because just last year, I'd been confronted with it in an interrogation in Washington, D.C.—that the FBI had a file on me as thick as the Chicago phone book. Once, a long time ago, I had told J. Edgar to go fuck himself (that's not a paraphrase, by the way) and he had ever since taken a personal interest in my welfare. I had been expecting Kefauver's advance team, here, to have that handy little reference tool to guide them.

"We do have the cooperation of the IRS," Robinson said. "And Frank J. Wilson gives you high marks."

Wilson had been one of the IRS agents who had nailed Capone; until recently, he'd been head of the Secret Service, another Treasury Department operation.

"That's nice to hear," I said.

"Eliot Ness also regards you highly," Robinson said, referring to the former T-man who had been key in the Capone case. "He indicates you helped him, and effectively, on several matters in Cleveland, during his years as Public Safety Director."

I said nothing.

He went on: "You are aware, certainly, that we're concentrating on illegal gambling, in general, and the racing wire racket, in particular."

"I am." I grinned at him, which seemed to unsettle him. "And just why is that, Mr. Robinson?"

Robinson frowned in genuine confusion. "What do you mean?"

"Why gambling? Why aren't you dealing with narcotics, or loan sharking, or prostitution? Or perhaps the relationship between machine politics and the mob? Or maybe the criminal infiltration of labor unions?"

Robinson looked at a page of his spiral notebook. "We have to begin somewhere, Mr. Heller. Gambling is our focus."

"Gambling is a safe target, you mean—you don't step on as many toes, in an election year. You can play Joe Friday, and look good, and still not get yourselves or your political parties in any trouble."

Halley had been sipping his coffee; he set the cup down in its saucer, clatteringly. His nasal lisp notched up, in volume and indignation. "Mr. Heller, if that's going to be your attitude, we won't do you the courtesy of meeting with you in private. We'll send you a subpoena and put you on public display with the rest of the hooligans."

I saluted him with my Coke glass. "Oh, this is a courtesy? Five'll get you ten—hypothetically speaking—there's a mob watchdog in the lobby keeping track of every informant coming up the elevator to see you. Charley Fischetti and Jake Guzik and Paul Ricca and Tony Accardo and assorted 'hooligans' will all know Nate Heller was meeting with the Kefauver quiz kids, this afternoon. And I'll have some explaining to do."

"You have some explaining to do, right now," Robinson said. The slit of his mouth curled in contempt. "You were James Ragen's bodyguard the day he was shotgunned in the Chicago streets, were you not? In June 1946?"

"Yeah. I was Mayor Cermak's bodyguard, too, and Huey Long's." I took a swig of Coke, and swallowed obnoxiously. "How's that for a track record?"

"I'm afraid your point eludes me," Robinson said.

"My point is, I do that sort of thing for a living . . . not always very well, obviously. It doesn't mean I'm a mobster or that I have any particular insights into the breed. Look, I testified at the Ragen inquest; it's all in the public record."

"Ragen was your wife's uncle, I understand."

"She was my girl friend, at the time. She's my ex-wife, now."

O'Conner said to me, "Bill Drury thinks the way to bring the racing wire mobsters down is to crack Ragen's murder. After all, Ragen was murdered so the Capone crowd could take over his racing wire business."

I didn't respond; I mean, it wasn't a question.

Frustrated, O'Conner pressed on: "Back in '46, you and Bill Drury searched out the eyewitnesses, Nate. You helped Bill!"

"We did find the eyeball witnesses," I admitted, "and they ID'd the shooters—a trio of West Side bookies."

Robinson read from his notebook: "David Finkel, Joseph Leonard, and William Yaras. Yaras is still a Chicago resident, and Mr. Drury would very much like to see him brought to justice. The whereabouts of Finkel and Leonard are unknown, though I'm sure Mr. Drury would like to see them brought to justice, as well."

It was too late for Bill Drury or this committee or anybody short of God Almighty to bring Davey Finkel and Blinkey Leonard to justice, because I already had. I'd shot them both on a lonely moon-washed beach on Pacific Coast Highway, the night they blew Ben Siegel away.

But I decided not to share that tidbit with the Crime Committee's representatives.

"The witnesses recanted," I said. "Except for the one that was murdered."

Robinson blinked. "Doesn't that make you . . . angry?"

"It makes me . . . cautious."

"Mr. Heller, do you really want us to call you as a witness?" Halley lisped. "Wouldn't you prefer to help us, behind the scenes?"

"Gentlemen, call me to testify if you like. My answers will fall into two categories: taking the fifth amendment, against self-incrimination; and invoking attorney-client privilege."

Halley reacted like I'd thrown a drink in his face. "You're not an attorney!"

"Individuals you might assume are clients of mine are, in most instances, actually the clients of attorneys I represent. . . . The attorney-client privilege pertains."

All three of them were lawyers; none of them disagreed with me.

Kurnitz, though—who had stayed silent, thus far—seemed vaguely amused; his arms were folded—he was leaning back. "Where *do* you stand, Mr. Heller, where these gangsters are concerned?"

"You do criminal law around these parts, Mr. Kurnitz. I would imagine you just do your best to serve your clients' interests and keep your head above these murky Chicago waters."

Kurnitz smiled, arching an eyebrow.

"We can seriously embarrass you, Mr. Heller," Robinson said, "if you force us to."

"Mr. Robinson," I said, "let me explain a couple things. First, the more sleazy and connected to gangsters you make me sound, the more desirable and glamourous I'll seem to potential clients. Second, I'm a decorated veteran of the recent war, a Bronze Star winner. Maybe *you* boys would like to be embarrassed."

"You were mustered out on a Section Eight," Halley said.

I sat forward. "I was honorably discharged, after fighting on Guadalcanal—what's your war record, Four-Eyes?"

Halley huffed, "I served my country," but he didn't say how.

"But thanks for reminding me," I said. "I had amnesia, induced by battle fatigue, what they used to call shell shock. How's that for a reason not to be able to recall this and that?"

"You're a very unpleasant man, Mr. Heller," Halley said.

"You're not exactly Norman Vincent Peale yourself," I said, and got up. "Thanks for the Coke. . . . By the way, that fella out in the hall, getting on the elevator when I arrived?"

They all frowned, but they knew who I was talking about.

"Jake Rubinstein?" I reminded them. "Is he the kind of informant you're counting on?"

"I don't think that's any of your concern," Robinson said.

"Just be careful, is all. Whoever advised you to fly that guy in from Dallas, take a close look at."

Halley sneered. "And why is that, Mr. Heller?"

That sneer deserved a smirk in return. "Here's one free tidbit I will give you. My understanding is Jake is the liaison between the local mob and the Dallas boys. I've known Rubinstein for years . . . or, what is it he's calling himself these days?"

"Jack Ruby," Kurnitz offered.

The other two lawyers glared at him.

"A rose by any other name," I said. "Never take a guy like that at face value. Any 'informing' Jake's doing is likely a cover for what he can find out about what you fellas are up to."

"That's the chance we take when we deal with these kind of people," Robinson said stiffly. "By necessity, informers come from the ranks of the gangsters themselves."

Pompous ass.

"Swell," I said, "but Jake, or Jack, is an old union goon, with strong ties to Captain Dan Gilbert—you know . . . Tubbo? Do you really want somebody from Tubbo's camp pretending to be your buddy?"

Robinson and Halley exchanged glances.

Kurnitz said, "You must be aware, then, that your friend Mr. Drury is investigating Gilbert."

"Sure, hoping to expose him before the election—but *my* knowing that isn't important. The key thing is, Tubbo knows." I made a sweeping gesture with my fedora, then put it on, saying, "Good afternoon, gentlemen. Lots of luck in your fine effort to wipe out gambling."

O'Conner didn't walk me out. I had a feeling he'd probably given me a pretty good build-up—friend of Drury's, ex-cop who'd stood up against mobsters—and I'd made him look like an idiot.

When I got off the elevator in the lobby, the guy in the green snapbrim was still reading the *Herald-American* sports section, but he had moved to one of the round couches. I settled in beside him.

"I thought that was you," I told the guy.

Sam Giancana looked over at me from behind the paper, lowered it to his lap, and under the brim of the green hat, his gray-complected oval face, with its lumpy beak and close-set mournful eyes, gave me no clue to how he was reacting.

They called the little hoodlum Mooney because of his

crazy unpredictability. The former chauffeur/bodyguard of Tony Accardo, and Paul Ricca's likely heir as Chicago mob boss, Giancana was a quietly self-confident psychopath.

He smiled. "That's what I like about you, Heller."

"What is, Sam?"

"That you're not afraid of me."

"Maybe I'm just not afraid of you in the lobby of the Stevens at lunchtime."

He laughed; it was a raspy, death rattle of a laugh. "That's the other thing I like: you're a funny guy. Natural fuckin' wit."

What he really liked about me was my discretion. I had done a job for him a couple of years ago, getting an embarrassing photograph back. He had paid well, and hadn't forgotten I'd done right by him.

Also, he was probably comfortable with me because we were both Westside boys, though he wasn't a Maxwell Street kid like Barney and me (and Jack Ruby); he was a product of the Near Northside's infamous Patch, and a veteran of the vicious street gang, the 42s. His legend was based upon having endured an abusive father until he finally grew up, beat the shit out of the old man, and took over the household.

I said, "I hope you don't mind my sitting down to say hello."

"Not at all." He folded the paper and put it next to him on the tufted couch. "You weren't upstairs long. Having a quick one? What's her name?"

"Kefauver."

He twitched a sick smile. "I didn't think 'she' was in town."

"No, but her sisters are."

"Good-looking girls?"

Now I twitched a smile. "Sam, don't ask me to tell you who I talked to up there."

"Did I ask? I don't remember asking."

"You see, the way this works, Sam, is I don't inform on anybody, on either side. I'm not playing—I'm not even in this game."

One shoulder shrugged. "If you don't want to tell me you talked to Robinson and Halley and Kurnitz and Drury's pal

O'Conner, that's fine. But I would like to know what you told them."

I shrugged both mine. "I told them if they're dumb enough to call me as a witness, my amnesia will recur. Or I'll plead the fifth, or attorney-client privilege."

The cold eyes were studying me. "That's all you told them?"

"That's all. . . . Well—you saw Rubinstein, I take it?"

"Am I gonna not notice another Westsider? I saw the prick."

"Well, I told them Jake went way back with Tubbo, and if he told 'em anything, they should consider the source. And that's all the help I gave them."

"That's all?"

"That's the boat."

He nodded slowly. "I appreciate this. Your frankness."

"Can I ask a favor?"

"Ask."

"I told Charley Fischetti I wasn't going to cooperate with these clowns; I think he knows I can be trusted. Sam, would you make sure Guzik knows? And Accardo, and Ricca?"

"I can do that."

"I don't need anybody thinking I'm a problem."

"Like your friend Drury is a problem?"

"Like that."

"What *about* your friend Drury?"

"He's still my friend, Sam. But you probably heard, I fired him."

"I did hear. That's for real?"

"That's for real."

"Okay. Appreciate it."

I knew this friendly, even charming little man could turn on a dime, but I had to risk it. . . .

"Sam—these guys, these Crime Committee guys, you know they're not worth killing anybody over."

He had his shark eyes fixed on me. "What are you trying to say, Heller?"

"Bill Drury—and Tim O'Conner, for that matter—are just a couple of cops trying to get their badges back. Bill's still flogging the Ragen shooting. Two of the shooters are long since missing, and the other one, well . . . that's your world, not mine."

"Seems like yesterday's news to me."

"I'm just saying, these committee guys—they got no power of arrest. The FBI wants no part of them. All Kefauver can do is turn what they find over to local law enforcement. So suppose they come up with some stuff, and then what? Turn the evidence over to Tubbo Gilbert?"

Giancana laughed, once. "You make a good point. But these things sometimes got a way of getting out of hand."

"Well, Frank Nitti used to say, 'Don't stir up the heat.' That's good advice, Sam. 'Cause if this turns bloody, all bets are off."

Kefauver wouldn't even have been in the crime-busting business if somebody—probably Charley Fischetti—hadn't ordered the slaying of slimy politico Charley Binaggio in Kansas City, last April. Binaggio had failed to deliver a post-'48-election wide-open K.C. to his out-of-town mob investors. The classic gangland hit—Binaggio and his top goon were found with two bullets in the head each, in the straight-row "two deuces" formation that signified a mob welsher's ultimate payoff—made embarrassing national headlines . . . in part because the bodies were found in the local Democratic headquarters under Harry Truman's picture.

"Are you saying if Drury has an accident," Sam asked, "your attitude toward testifying might change?"

"Draw your own conclusions, Sam."

Giancana reached out and gripped me by the arm. He was smiling and his voice hadn't changed tone . . . he was still his charming self . . . letting his words convey the menace.

"You want to be careful, Heller, about threatening me. I like you, you're a smart guy, and I like that smart mouth; it's cute. But you don't want to fuckin' threaten me."

I don't know where he came from; I don't know if he was staking out the lobby himself, or was on his way up to join his friend O'Conner with the Kefauver advance team.

But suddenly Bill Drury was yanking Sam Giancana to

his feet, Giancana's hat flying off, his grip on my arm popping open, just like the gangster's eyes were popping when he saw the brawny Drury—in topcoat and homburg—right on top of him, all but screaming in his face.

"Are you getting rough with my friend?" Drury asked Giancana, gripping him by a bicep, looming over him.

I got up, saying, "Jesus, Bill—back off!"

Drury's flushed Irish puss made a stark contrast with Giancana's grayish Sicilian pallor. "You don't want to get rough with my friends, Mooney."

Giancana's teeth were bared, like a growling dog. "You're not a cop anymore, you dumb mick!"

Drury clutched Giancana's other bicep, holding it as if to shake him. "I'm a licensed private investigator, Mooney. I'm an officer of the court. Are you packing? Care to stand for a frisk?"

I grabbed onto Drury and pulled him away from Giancana, whose eyes were wide and wild. I said, "Don't do me any goddamn favors, Bill!"

People in the lobby, guests getting off the elevator, were noticing this, some frozen, others moving quickly on, but all of them wide-eyed and murmuring.

I turned to Giancana. "Sam, I apologize."

His suit rumpled from Drury's hands, Giancana was breathing hard, trembling with rage. He wasn't looking at me: his crazed glazed gaze was strictly on the grinning Drury.

Giancana's voice was soft—a terrible kind of softness: "You ain't at fault, Heller. It's your friend who has the problem."

With me standing between them, my arms out like a ref who broke up a basketball court scuffle, Drury shouted at Giancana. "You're goddamn right! I'm your problem, and all of you Sicilian sons of bitches better pack your bags, 'cause you're either going to jail or back home to the motherland!"

Giancana picked up his hat, dusted it off.

I reached a hand out and said, "Sam. . . ."

Snugging the snapbrim down over his bald pate, Giancana said, "Heller—you're not to blame. You're not to blame."

And then the little gangster made a beeline through the white marble lobby, toward the Michigan Avenue exit, leaving his sports section behind.

Drury looked at me with concern. "Are you okay, Nate?"

"Am I okay? Are you drunk? Are you fucking crazy? That's the looniest homicidal son of a bitch in the city! If you want to die, that's your business—leave me the hell out of it!"

A hotel employee approached, a youngish man in a blue Stevens blazer. "Gentlemen—I'm afraid we can't have a scene. . . . You'll have to leave."

Scowling, Drury got out his badge—his P.I. badge—and flashed it and said, "I'm a cop. This is police business. You just get back to your desk."

"Yessir," the hotel guy said, and scurried.

I sat back down on the round couch, and flopped back, stunned.

Drury plopped down next to me, grinning, pleased with himself. "They're all cowards at heart. . . . Are you all right, Nate?"

"No, I'm not all right! What the hell was the idea?"

"That bastard was getting tough with you."

"Do I look like I need you to defend me? If I want saved, I'll go to a goddamn revival meeting. Jesus! Stay away from me, Bill—just stay away. I don't want to be in your line of fire."

Drury was spreading his hands. "What? What did I do?"

"You're not a cop, anymore, Bill. They can shoot at you now—get it?"

He patted beneath his arm, where his shoulder-holstered .38 lived. "Let 'em try."

"Oh, they will," I said. "They will."

He waved me off. "Don't be an old woman."

"The point is," I said, getting up, "to be an old man."

And I left him there to ponder that—though I doubted he would.

6

The black-eyed blonde's name was Jackie Payne—Jacqueline, really, but nobody called her that except her parents, who she hadn't seen in some time.

She was born and grew up in Kankakee, in the shadow of the state insane asylum, and as omens go, that was a hell of a one. Her parents were "real religious"—a polite way to say goddamn zealots—who had been ashamed of her wild behavior in high school, which is to say she'd been a cheerleader and in drama club.

A talent scout at the county fair—where she tap-danced and won five dollars—had encouraged her to look him up in Chicago; so, three and a half years ago, shortly after graduating Kankakee High, she had hopped the Twentieth Century east and, with the talent scout's backing, took up residence in the Croyden, a Near Northside hotel catering to showgirls.

Let me interrupt this soap opera to mention that the Croyden was one of several such hotels on the Near Northside. A nicer example, the St. Clair—just off Michigan Avenue's magnificent mile, at the corner of Ohio and St. Clair—catered to both typical travelers and longer-term residents; but showgirls and strippers loved the St. Clair, and many lived there, whether a few nights or a few years were involved.

The St. Clair was a classy but unostentatious hotel, twenty-some red-brick stories with a set-back penthouse. After my divorce, and the sale of our Lincolnwood bunga-low, I had established my Chicago home address at the St. Clair, taking a fifteenth-floor suite; before my marriage I'd lived in a similar but smaller apartment at the Morrison Hotel, which was closer to my office; but living north of the Chicago River expanded my world to the upper levels of Windy City society.

At the St. Clair, I was just a few blocks south of the Gold Coast; from my corner suite, I could see the lake from my bedroom window, and from my living room win-dow (looking south) I could wave to Colonel McCormick in his Tribune Tower aerie. My neighbors included the Wrigley Building and the Water Tower, as well as enough exclusive shops to send a kleptomaniac into a seizure. But the neon sleaze of Rush Street, with its cocktail lounges, pizzerias, taverns, and nightclubs, was just on the other side of Michigan Avenue, with the Chez Paree only two blocks away.

My old friend—sometime girl friend—Sally Rand had recommended the St. Clair, and Beth Short, another old flame (since sadly extinguished), had lived there briefly as well. Photographer Maurice Seymour had his studio among the businesses on St. Clair's upper floors—conveniently next to a beauty parlor—and he had contracts with damn near every burlesque house and nightclub in town, shooting portraits of entertainers and models and, in particular, showgirls and strippers.

Nothing unusual, at the St. Clair, about seeing Gypsy Rose Lee or Ann Corio or Georgia Southern traipsing through the small, nondescript lobby, carrying suitcases jammed with their seductive wardrobes, from sheer stock-ings to pasties to G-strings; or Rosita Royce swaying her hips as she carried cages of doves, or Sally with her (feath-ered) fans—not to mention Zorita tugging along her airhole-punched trunk on wheels with the python in it.

Though the lobby had practically no sitting room, a cof-fee shop was off to one side, and the Tap Room—with its famous Circle Bar—was off to the other. Grabbing a cup of morning java or a noon sandwich, you were surrounded by beautiful girls; catching a cocktail after work or in the evening, ditto. Those girls were sometimes in pin curls and little or no makeup, of course, though a man with my deductive skills knew evidence of pulchritude when he saw it.

I loved the St. Clair.

Another nice thing about the hotel was the no-questions-asked attitude of the management. When the evening before, after my confab with the Fischettis, I had escorted Jackie Payne through the St. Clair's front revolving door—carrying her two suitcases for her, while she lugged a train case—past a newsstand on one side and a bank of pay phones on the other, across the small dark-oak lobby to the elevators and up to my suite, the guy at the desk didn't blink. Of course, this was hardly the first time he'd spotted me with a showgirl in his lobby, if the first time for one sporting a shiner.

When Rocco unexpectedly tossed Jackie out on her sweet behind, she was flat busted (in one sense, anyway), and I'd mentioned she could camp out on my sofa, for a night or two; she had girl friends at both the Croyden and the St. Clair she could contact, and maybe move in with one, until she got a job and a little money.

"But I'd kind of like to wait until this heals up," she said in her small sweet voice, embarrassed, pointing to the black eye. She was sitting on the plump-cushioned sage green mohair couch, legs curled up under her; I was next to her, but not right next to her. She had slipped her shoes off and her toenails were painted red; her long-sleeved pink sweater and slacks showed off her trim shapely figure, and her shortish honey blonde hair was a tousled nest of curls.

Room service had brought us up a couple of burgers with french fries, and I'd plucked cold Pabsts from my refrigerator. A coffee table by the couch was the repository for our plates and beers and my stockinged feet. We only had one light on, a lamp on the end table near me, creating a forty-watt pool of glowing light. The mood was one of casual intimacy—for complete strangers, we were surprisingly comfortable with each other.

My apartment, by the way, was functionally furnished, a

page torn from a Sears and Roebuck catalog—living room, bedroom, small spare room I used as a home office, and modest kitchen. I'd dressed the living room up with a television and a radio phonograph console—the radio on, at the moment, Nat King Cole softly singing "Mona Lisa" accompanied by traffic sounds from Michigan Avenue below—but I wouldn't kid you: the apartment was really just a hotel room got slightly out of hand.

"Haven't your girl friends ever seen a black eye before?" I asked her.

"It's just—Ginny, the one I'll probably call, she warned me about Rocco, way back when, and I didn't listen."

"Yeah, nobody likes 'I told you so.' "

She shrugged. "I'd rather not have to answer questions. Anyway, I heal really fast. I'll be out of your hair before you know it."

"You can stay as long as you like—don't worry about it. Listen, I could even stake you to a room here at the scenic St. Clair, for a few nights, if you'd rather."

In the dim light her heart-shaped face with the pretty features took on an angelic radiance. "Why are you so sweet to me?"

"I'm just one of those Good Samaritans you hear so much about. Why, if you weighed two-sixty and had warts all over your face and two double chins, I'd probably do the same thing. . . . Probably."

She laughed at that, and we'd talked. She told me the story of her Bible-thumping parents and the talent agent, who (unbelievably) had done good things for her, though she mentioned offhandedly she'd lived with him for a while. Smalltown or not, she seemed to understand the big-city rules.

"Do I look familiar to you?" she asked, rather coyly. This was on the second beer, the burger and fries a memory.

"Sure," I said, sipping my own second Pabst. "I saw you at the Chez Paree—you were one of the Chez Adorables."

Which was what the chorus line there was called.

"Till six or eight months back I was, but that wasn't what I meant. About two years ago, I was Miss Chicago."

"No kidding!"

"Yeah, in the Miss Illinois pageant. I was in all the papers."

"Well, sure, I remember now. How could I forget that face?" Of course, I didn't remember her. Cheesecake photos were a dime a dozen in the Chicago press, and cute as this little doll was, she was just another showgirl . . . albeit one with a black eye.

"Of course, I didn't win the state title," she said, "and go on to Atlantic City or anything . . . and I didn't have any use for the scholarship money. . . . College was never in the cards for me."

"And so your friend the talent agent got you an audition for the Chez Paree."

She nodded. "I was always a good dancer. I worked at a grocery store, in high school, to pay for ballet lessons that my parents didn't know I was taking."

"Which is where you met Rocco. . . . The Chez Paree, I mean, not the grocery store."

She laughed and nodded again. "I know you won't believe this, but he was really sweet, at first. Rocco, I mean. He's no matinee idol, I admit . . ."

"Maybe if the matinee is a horror triple feature."

She smiled at that, a little. "He took a big interest in me. I didn't want to just be in the chorus—I wanted to be featured, to be a headliner someday, to sing and dance, like Judy Garland or Betty Hutton. He said he'd get me lessons."

Rocco had encouraged her to quit the Chez Paree chorus line—she was too good for that, he'd said—and she had moved in with him, in the penthouse on Sheridan. After all, Rocco and his brothers, particularly Joey, had all sorts of show business connections.

But the lessons never happened—Rocco claimed he couldn't find teachers worthy of Jackie's talent—and before long, she was shoveling coal on the Fischetti model railroad.

"He was sweet for the longest time," she said. "Then one day I asked about my lessons—I wasn't snippy or sarcastic or anything, that's not my way—and I'd asked lots of times before, about the lessons, plenty of times . . . but this time he slapped me."

I felt my eyes tighten. "Why didn't you leave?"

She was staring at her hands in her lap. "I don't know. . . . For quite a while, the beatings were real occasional—'cause he was drunk or in a bad mood or I said the wrong thing. Somehow I convinced myself each time was a fluke. He'd apologize. Give me flowers. Be sweet again."

That was the pattern of these woman-beating bastards.

She was saying, "Anyway, I knew I couldn't get my job back at the Chez Paree, 'cause he and his brothers were in business with the owners. And nobody in town would hire me if Rocco said don't hire me, right?"

"Right."

"It's a beautiful penthouse—I was alone a lot. You didn't see some of the rooms, with the Italian Renaissance antiques—Charley picked them out; that was his passion, antiques, before he started in on that modern stuff; he gave those pieces to Rocco."

Hadn't she realized she was in a well-appointed prison?

She went on. "I'd use the piano—I can play a little—and practice my singing. Sometimes Rocky was gone for weeks at a time. There are servants, I was waited on hand and foot, fed like a queen, treated like I was still Miss Chicago or maybe Miss America, after all . . . except by Rocco, when he got mad."

I was sitting closer to her now; I took her hand and held it, squeezed it gently. "I can't imagine you doing anything that would ever make me mad."

Jackie wasn't looking at me; her voice was soft and small—barely audible above Vic Damone singing "You're Breaking My Heart" on the radio.

"The last few weeks," she said, "Rocky would just yell and slap me and hit me without me even saying anything. I think . . . I think he had just got tired of me. I see that all the time with his trains."

"His trains?"

"Yeah. He would send away for expensive model trains and when the delivery man brought them, he would tear into the packages like Christmas. And for a week, maybe two, he'd sit and play with that new train in that room of his—hour after hour, with this dumb little smile on his face. Then he'd get bored and put them on the shelf . . . and buy something new."

After that we talked about me, for a while. About my marriage, and how my wife had cheated on me and ruined everything, and about my son, who was going to be three years old in a few days, and how I wouldn't be there to see it. That made her sad, and she came closer, very close, and put her arms around me, and kissed me, very soft, very tender. . . .

I was twice her age, and then some, but I didn't give it a thought: she'd been living with Rocco Fischetti, who was older than me and a homely fuck to boot.

So I had no pangs of conscience about accepting affection from this girl, who badly needed some affection herself, right now. Most strippers, most showgirls, were much younger than me, and damaged goods; this was nothing new. But she had this special sweetness, like she'd wandered off the set of an Andy Hardy picture into *Little Caesar*.

She asked me to switch off the light and I did, and then in the dimness of unreal blue-tinged city light coming in from Michigan Avenue, she tugged off the pink sweater by its long sleeves, revealing a white lacy bra, which I undid for her. Miss Chicago was not as voluptuous as the would-be Miss California I'd been with not so long ago, but she was stunning nonetheless, with uptilting breasts that made perfect handfuls and a dramatic rib cage and a tiny waist.

That she was a dancer became obvious when she stood before me, arms outstretched, naked to the waist, with the formfitting slacks still on. There was something fabulously sexy, wonderfully dirty, about her standing there in just the slacks, with her hands on her hips and the cupcake breasts thrust forward for my viewing pleasure; the experience tickled her lips into a smile, even as my mouth gaped open like an idiot staring at Mount Rushmore.

That baby doll face took on a brazen confidence as she watched me drink in her bare loveliness; then she turned her back to me and unzipped her slacks at the side and shimmied out of them, swaying to Patti Page singing "The Tennessee Waltz," leaving only a second skin of sheer white panties over a rounded tight behind, the sweep of her back dimpling above the cheeks.

She looked over her shoulder at me, and giggled at the sight of my reaction, and came over and sat on my lap, a child asking Santa for toys, her arms around my neck, and we kissed and kissed, and nuzzled each other's throats and ears, and she moaned as I kissed her breasts, the tips hardening under my lips. . . .

Finally she stood before me again, with her back to me, and slid the panties down, dropping them in a puddle, then turned and held her arms out again—tah *dah!*—showing all of herself to me, the slightly muscular dancer's legs, the tufted pubic triangle as brown as her eyes, her faint smile inviting me to her.

I stood and she began undressing me; drunk from her beauty—and three beers—I allowed her to do all the work, and finally we were both naked, standing there, the small shapely thing plastered to me, her sweet face turned upward, wanting kisses, aching for affection, hooded eyes yearning for love.

Then she was on the couch, lips open, arms open, legs open. I said I would get something, meaning a rubber, and she said, no, it's a safe time, don't use anything, I want to feel you inside me, and the warmth of her swallowed me, and her eyes rolled back in her lovely face as her hips churned with a desperation that made me drunker still and the intensity was dizzying, like a fever dream, and when she came, she cried, and maybe I did, too.

She kept crying, my little black-eyed blonde, and I held her and comforted her, for all the shit she'd been through, soothing her, kissing her, loving her, consoling her, assuring her I'd be there, and finally I took her hand and led her to my bedroom, where she slept with me that night.

On my back in bed, naked as the day I was born but with considerably more scars, staring at the ceiling like a man in a trance, I felt physically and emotionally drained. Making love with Vera Jayne had been a joyful carnival ride; making love with Jackie had been a different kind of ride entirely.

Jackie—who had crawled in bed in just the sheer panties—was asleep and the lights of the night were filtering in off the lake, bathing her in blue-tinged ivory. She looked lovely, childlike, her face puffy from crying, but also from youth; her mouth had a swollen bruised look that had nothing to do with Rocco's abuse. When she turned toward me, the covers pulled down off her mostly naked form, I reached over to pull them back up, and tuck her in, like daddy's little girl.

That was when I noticed the needle tracks.

This morning, in the cold light of day, we had talked about it, at my kitchen table, over the breakfast I'd prepared.

"I've been on it for six months," she said.

"Why? Doesn't make any sense, Jackie—a smart, talented kid like you, with ambition enough to buck her parents and pay for your own dance lessons. . . ."

She wasn't looking at me; she was staring down into the eyes of her sunny-side up eggs. "I got depressed. Rocky, when he was acting nice, said he could help me. Get me medicine. So I wouldn't be blue."

Wrapped up in the silver robe I'd first seen her in at Fischetti's, she didn't look at all bad—she certainly didn't look like a junkie, and her young, pretty features, sans makeup, served her well.

"He got you medicine, all right," I said.

She was shaking her head, stealing a look at me, now and then. "I was so damn depressed, I would have tried anything . . . including razor blades. Now . . . what am I going to do, Nate? I don't even have a supplier—Rocky gave me the stuff, himself."

"That fucking asshole."

She heard the rage in my voice, and it startled her, scared her. Her eyes were wild, a hand held like a claw at the side of her face as she said, "You're going to kick me out, too, aren't you?" She looked down into her coffee cup; she hadn't eaten a bite of her toast and eggs. "You're going to throw me out on the street. Just like Rocco!"

"Shut up."

The wild eyes dared me. "You want to slap me? Go ahead! Slap me!"

I almost did. But instead I just said, "When's it going to get bad for you?"

She sighed, swallowed—air, not food. "Sometime this morning it'll start."

"Jesus."

"I . . . I might be able to call a girl I used to know at the Chez Paree. I think she's still at the Croyden. She smoked reefers all the time . . . she's got a connection, maybe I could—"

"But you don't have any money, Jackie. It costs thirty bucks a day, at least, to support a habit like yours."

The eyes stayed wild but the voice turned timid. "Maybe . . . maybe you could loan me some. If I can have my medicine, I can get myself put together and go out and get a job—maybe now that Rocco doesn't want me anymore, I can get a job singing or dancing somewhere."

I shrugged, stirring sugar into my coffee. "You could always strip. You did a hell of one for me last night."

I'd meant that as a dig, but instead it had only got her going.

"I think I could do that. . . . I think I could stand to do that. It's dancing, right? It's a kind of dancing."

I looked at this girl, this sweet smalltown girl, and knew how close she was to the abyss.

"You'll get a job, all right," I said. "You'll be over at the Mayfair Hotel with the other hookers."

Horror filled the brown eyes, including the black-and-blue one. "No. . . . No I would never do that. How can you say that? Last night you were so kind. . . . How can you. . . ." And she put her right hand over her face and began to cry.

She was trembling a little too, but I was afraid it had more to do with the stuff she was starting to crave than any sorrow or shame she might be feeling.

I sat forward. "Now listen to me—a friend of mine got

hooked on morphine. He was on it for years, and he kicked it. You've only been riding the horse for a few months. Do you want to get off it?"

Shuddering, she said, "Oh yes . . . oh yes."

"I can help arrange that. I'll have to make a few calls, but I can arrange it."

Her eyes searched my face. "How can I pay for that . . . for treatment?"

"I'll float you a loan." I had a sip of coffee. "And until we can get you into the right clinic, I'm going to make a few other calls."

Her eyes narrowed. "What do you mean?"

"Somebody'll be around this afternoon with what you need."

"Do I . . . understand you right?"

"You do. For the next few days, I'll support your habit. The guy who comes around, he'll be colored. You can trust him, far as it goes. You've got the works?"

"The what?"

Christ, she was a junkie and she didn't even know the lingo. Can you beat that? A sheltered drug addict. Fucking Rocco Fischetti.

Patiently, I asked, "You have your own needle and so on?"

"In my suitcase, yes."

"Do you have something nice to wear?"

"What? Why?"

"Because once you've had your medicine, and've had a chance to relax, I want you to make yourself presentable. We're going out tonight."

She was shaking her head, as if trying to clear her ears. "You're taking me out?"

"That's what I said."

So when I came back to the St. Clair—after my meeting with the Kefauver crowd, and my encounter with Sam Giancana and Bill Drury, at the Stevens—she was herself again . . . a lovely, doll-faced innocent in a dazzling black cocktail dress, black crepe off-the-shoulder V-neck top and ruffled tiers of black net over a taffeta skirt. The sleeves of the black top, however, came down midforearm, covering sins. Pearls at her throat, cherry lipstick, white gloves. . . .

"Do you approve?" she asked, bright as a penny, again outstretching her arms in *tah dah* fashion.

Her medicine had done wonders.

"You're a knockout."

She took my arm; she smelled wonderful—Chanel No. 5. "Where are we going tonight, my love?"

I grinned at her. "My pal Frankie is opening, tonight."

"Frankie? Sinatra? Isn't he . . . isn't that . . . the Chez Paree?"

"That's right."

She looked horror-struck. "But Rocco and his brothers are bound to be there. . . ."

"I know."

"Oh, Nate . . . Rocco could start something."

"One can always hope," I said.

7

Like most of us in Chicago, the Chez Paree—that garish, glitter-and-glamour nightclub at Fairbanks Court and Ontario—had humble roots: the Near Northside's fabled bistro had once been just another warehouse, before Ben Hecht's artist pal Pierre Nuytens turned it into a fortress of festivity in the late twenties. A few years later, tired of paying off cops and fending off gangsters, Nuytens sold his Chez Pierre to Mike Fritzel, an old hand in the nightclub game, who, with Joe Jacobsen, immediately redubbed the gaudy barn the Chez Paree, inviting "the Last of the Red Hot Mamas," Sophie Tucker, to crack a bottle of bubbly over the building's name plate. Twenty years later, Sophie was still returning annually to celebrate that christening with maudlin tunes and filthy jokes.

The bright, immense showroom seated five hundred, and presented entertainment of the first magnitude, including such $10,000-a-week stars as Jimmy Durante, Henny Youngman, and Martin & Lewis, with orchestras like Ted Lewis, Paul Whiteman, and Vincent Lopez, all augmented by the prettiest chorus line in America. Add fine dining (not your typical nightclub's third-rate food at cutthroat prices), and the joint almost didn't need its backroom gambling casino, the Gold Key Club, to make it the top after-dark spot in town.

Almost.

Not that the celebrated showroom didn't have draw-backs: its very size and noonday-sun brightness seemed at odds with the postwar trend for intimate clubs. Then there were the massive square pillars, causing patrons viewing problems; an art moderne pastel wall mural of the planets that dated the joint; and all those linen-covered tables mashed together treating high-class customers like passengers in steerage. Plenty of good seats to be had, though, arranged as they were around the dance floor onto which the Chez Paree showgirls frequently spilled down from the stage/bandstand to do their elaborate production numbers.

Tonight, on the occasion of Frank Sinatra's opening, the showroom seemed especially packed, and I suspected extra tables had been crammed in. Normally such a great crowd would have spelled good news for Sinatra, who wasn't drawing mobs like he used to, except for the Fischetti variety.

Unfortunately, the size of tonight's Chez Paree audience probably had more to do with morbid curiosity than any new wave of Swoonatra frenzy. Frank had been scheduled to appear at the Chez a few months ago, but had to cancel, after he'd lost his voice and coughed up blood on stage during a Copa engagement in New York. The doctors called it a vocal cord hemorrhage and sentenced him to silence for several weeks.

In fact, the Chez was so jammed tonight, I didn't think the fiver I slipped headwaiter Mickey Levin would do the trick, particularly since we'd skipped dinner. But the five-spot—which Mickey pocketed, of course—turned out to be unnecessary, as Joey Fischetti had kept his word and saved me a booth along the wall.

The booths weren't the best seats in the house by a long shot, in terms of seeing the show, but they were comfort-able and somewhat private. As we settled in, the floor show had already started. The Chez Paree Adorables—ten dolls in Hollywood's idea of Dodge City dancehall-girl costumes, with red garters and mesh stockings—were parading around singing that annoying Teresa Brewer tune, "Music! Music! Music!," accompanied peppily by the Lou Breese orchestra.

I sipped a rum and Coke, and Jackie—looking like a movie star in the black cocktail dress—had not touched her Tom Collins. She was rubbing her hands together.

"Take it easy," I said.

"Don't you see him?" she said, alarm dancing in her lovely brown eyes. The black eye had mostly gone now—she really was a fast healer—and makeup hid what remained.

"I see him," I said.

On our side of the room, but still separated from us by a sea of people, Rocco and Charley, with two beautiful young girls in low-cut gowns, sat ringside, craning around at the moment to watch the Adorables out on the dance floor. Charley was married, by the way, but his wife lived in Florida when he was in Chicago, and in Chicago when he was in Florida.

"Why did you bring me here?" she asked, not angry, more confused.

"I thought you could use a night out."

"You could have taken me anywhere but here."

"Jackie—I'm making a statement: I'm letting the Fischettis know that you're under my protection."

". . . protection?"

"This is a very tense time for them. You're aware of this investigation, this Kefauver thing?"

"Vaguely."

"Well, you lived in their penthouse for over a year. You saw people come and go. And you were rather rudely thrown out."

"I'm not sure I understand . . ."

Or maybe she just didn't want to.

I said, "You're a potential witness, if those Crime Committee boys get wind of you."

"Are you saying . . . I'm in danger?"

I nodded toward Rocco and Charley, who didn't seem to have noticed us yet. "Not when these sons of bitches see that you're with me. That you're my girl."

"Am I? Your girl?"

"If you want to be—position's open."

She clutched my hand. "Oh, I do, I do . . . and Nate—I'll go wherever you want, to get well, to a clinic or hospital or whatever—"

I gave her a sharp but not unkind look. "We're not talking about that, here. We left that behind, for tonight."

". . . okay."

"I really do want you to have a good time."

"I'll try."

"I'll introduce you to Frank."

"Oh, I met him when I was still in the chorus, here. He may not like seeing me very much."

"Why?"

"I think I'm the only girl, except for a couple of married ones, who wouldn't sleep with him."

When the Chez Adorables had finished their number, the expected timpani roll and offstage intro of the headliner did not occur; instead, Lou Breese and his boys played "Begin the Beguine." Murmurs of discontent and curiosity rumbled across the room—why wasn't Sinatra coming on?

Suddenly Jackie jerked back in the booth—like maybe she'd seen a ghost, or a Fischetti—and her sharp intake of air made me jump.

I almost went for the shoulder holstered nine millimeter Browning, which my dark suit (tailored for me on Maxwell Street) was cut not to reveal. Normally I wouldn't pack heat on a night out on the town . . . normally.

It wasn't a ghost, just a Fischetti—the harmless one, the good-looking not-as-smart one, Joey, looking like a mâitre d' in his black tie and tux.

"Thanks for the booth, Joey," I said.

"You gotta help me, Nate," Joey said from the aisle, leaning against the linen tablecloth. He hadn't noticed yet that the pretty blonde sitting next to me was his brother Rocco's ex-punching bag.

"Slide in—join us."

He did. His eyes were darting, his expression twitchy with panic. "Frank won't go on."

"Why not?"

"That fucker Lee Mortimer's in the audience. I could kill Halper for not catching that reservation, and squelching it."

I shrugged. "Just ask Mortimer to leave—refund whatever money he's spent—"

"Nate, you know that bastard. He'll make a scene. It won't just be in his column, it'll be in every paper in the country."

"What do you want me to do about it?"

He clutched at my arm. "Go back and talk Frank into going on."

"Jesus, Joey, he's your friend, too. You guys are bosom buddies."

"Yeah, but he don't respect me like he does you, Nate. Please. You gotta go talk to him—look at the size of the audience. He stiffs this crowd, his career really is over."

Joey seemed so pitifully desperate, I gave in, asking, "Where's Mortimer sitting?"

"Three booths down."

"I'll talk to *him*, first. Mortimer, I mean. I know him, a little. Maybe he'll listen to reason."

Joey was shaking his head; strangely, there was no rattle. "Anything, Nate. . . . Oh—hiya, Jackie. What are you doing here?"

"I'm with him," she said, nodding to me.

Joey looked from her to me and back again, a couple times.

"Joey," I said. "One problem at a time?"

"Right," he said, nodding, as if acknowledging there was only so much room inside there. "Right."

"But you have to do me a favor."

"Anything, if you just talk to Frank."

I was already out in the aisle. "You sit here with Jackie. If your brother notices her, and comes over, you have to protect her for me."

"What? But Rocky's—"

"You just tell him you're warming my seat up while I'm doing you this favor—you can do that, Joey. You're up to the job."

He sighed and nodded and said, "Yeah. Yeah. Go! Do it!"

To the tune of the orchestra playing "Enjoy Yourself (It's Later Than You Think)," I made my way down a few booths, and found Sinatra's nemesis.

Small, well-groomed, in his early fifties, Lee Mortimer had gray hair, a gray complexion and a gray suit; his tie was gray, too . . . but also red, striped. His eyes were tiny and hard-looking and his nose was large and soft-looking; his chin was pointed and his lips full and sensual. Seated in the booth beside him was a good-looking green-eyed brunette in a green satin low-cut gown; she was twenty-five and I recognized her from local TV commercials and print ads, a busty, raving beauty. Sinatra had spread the word that Mortimer was a "fag" and the reporter was overcompensating.

Mortimer was smoking—using a cigarette holder (maybe he wasn't compensating enough)—and his hooded eyes opened slightly as he smiled in recognition.

"Nate Heller," he said. "The man who doesn't return my calls."

"Can I join you, Lee?"

"Please. Please. . . . Linda, this is Nate Heller."

She offered her white-gloved hand. "I recognize him. . . . Mr. Heller, you make the papers now and then."

"So do you—Miss Robbins, isn't it?"

She was pleased I knew her name, and she seemed genuinely impressed with a local celebrity like me. Shallow girl. I filed her away for future reference.

Mortimer was born and raised in Chicago, but he left in the twenties for New York, where he'd become a gossip columnist at the *Mirror*. I had ducked him when he was in town researching his *Chicago Confidential* book, and I'd been ducking him lately, too.

"What can I do for you, Nate? Not that I owe you any favors, rude as you've been."

"You want me to be one of your sources, Lee . . . but I have a relationship with another columnist, and besides, you have Bill Drury in your pocket."

The mention of "another columnist" perked him up. "Are you and Drew Pearson friendly again? I heard you were on the outs."

"We patched it up. He paid his back bills, gave me a new retainer, and I forgave him his sins."

"Chicago-style penance."

A waitress brought Mortimer and the brunette a martini and Manhattan, respectively; I'd brought my rum and Coke along for the trip.

"You know, Lee, I just might give you an interview, at that."

His hooded eyes seemed languid, but they didn't miss a thing. "Really? Including information that I can't get from your associate?"

"If by my 'associate,' you mean Bill Drury, he doesn't work for me anymore."

He plucked the martini's toothpick from the drink and ate the olive. "I heard you met with Halley and Robinson today."

"Am I supposed to be surprised you know that, Lee? It's not 'confidential' that you and Kefauver are thick as thieves."

He sipped the martini. "We aren't anymore."

"Why not?"

A sneer twisted the sensual mouth. "That son of a bitch Halley has come between us."

"How so?"

"Chief Counsel Halley advised Kefauver against hiring me as an official investigator for the committee—me, whose book, whose original research, only inspired the goddamn inquiry!"

Mortimer's desire to work for the committee in an official capacity was, of course, laughable: Kefauver could hardly hire a member of the press.

But I humored him. "What a crock. . . . I understand Halley didn't want Drury or O'Conner hired, either—not officially, anyway."

"Right! And those two know more firsthand about the Chicago underworld than almost anyone alive—and Halley says they're not viable because they were 'fired' from the force—fired! Rooked off the crookedest department in the country, because they were honest, fearless—"

"You're right. Doesn't make sense."

He blew a smoke ring and sent me a sly look. "It does if you realize Rudolph Halley is as dirty as Tubbo Gilbert."

I grunted a laugh. "That's a tough one to buy."

"Listen—Halley's law firm represents a railroad that the New York Syndicate boys hold scads of stock in. And I spotted the bastard at the El Morocco, cozying up to movie company executives—who are his firm's clients, now. You don't see Kefauver going after the *Hollywood* connection, do you?"

"No. Of course you know, I'm close to Frank."

His upper lip curled in contempt. "Frankie boy? I know you are. You should have better taste."

I swirled my drink, idly. "I've gotten friendly with Joey Fischetti, too. Maybe I can find out something about Halley and his Hollywood connivings for you."

His eyes and brow tightened. "You'd do that?"

"Sure. We can talk about it later. Only, right now you have to do *me* a favor."

"What's that?"

"Leave."

"What?"

"Lee, you and I both know you're here just to rankle Sinatra, to get under that thin Italian skin of his."

Mortimer's sneer turned into a sort of smile as he puffed on the cigarette-in-holder. "I paid the cover charge. My pretty friend and I have a right to be entertained."

"You leave, and maybe we'll do business. Otherwise forget it."

Mortimer thought about it. "All right. We'll talk tomorrow."

"Fine. Call me at my office. . . . Pleasure, Miss Robbins."

The brunette smiled and said, "Pleasure, Mr. Heller."

I slipped out of the booth as Mortimer was paging a waiter to get his check. Then, nodding to Joey (sitting in the booth quietly with Jackie, who appeared calm), I headed backstage, where a couple of thugs who were Sinatra's current retinue recognized me and showed me into the great man's spacious dressing room. In addition to the usual makeup mirror, there was a couch and several comfy-looking chairs, as well as a liquor cart and a console radio.

Frank—still wearing that silly Gable mustache—was seated at the makeup mirror in his tux pants and a T-shirt; he looked lean and fairly muscular, not quite as skinny as many thought him to be. He sat hunched over the counter, smoking a cigarette, with a glass of whiskey nearby. His face had a ravaged look—hard to believe that, not long ago, he'd been the idol of countless girls and women.

"I'm not going out there, Nate—I'm not doing it. Not as long as that fucking fag cocksucker is in the house. No way, man. No fucking way."

Lee Mortimer had blasted Sinatra countless times in his columns. Frank claimed it was because the reporter had once tried, unsuccessfully, to sell the singer a song ("a piece of shit!"). Mortimer had had a heyday running the story about Sinatra accompanying Rocco and Joey Fischetti to Havana for the big confab with Lucky Luciano in '47, attended by a rogues' gallery of mobsters. As a celebrity who could travel unhindered, Frank had reportedly carried a bag filled with tribute, the greenback variety. Though Frank attended none of the business meetings, he hobnobbed with Luciano in the casino of the Hotel Nacional, and even had his picture taken with the deported ganglord.

A while back Sinatra had spotted Mortimer in Ciro's, and attacked the reporter, who won an out-of-court settlement from Frank, when Louis B. Mayer forced him.

I pulled up a chair. "I got rid of Mortimer, Frank. He's gone."

Sinatra looked up, the famous blue eyes taking on a startled-deer aspect. "No shit?"

"No shit."

"How did you manage it?"

"I had to promise you'd blow him. I hope you don't mind."

He looked at me blankly, and then he burst out laughing. He laughed until he cried, and I laughed some, too.

Smiling, standing, he said, "You're not kidding—he is gone?"

"I'm not kidding . . ."

Sinatra looked relieved.

". . . you do have to blow him."

Sinatra grinned, shook his head. "You fucker. . . . He's gone?"

"Out at home plate. A ghost. A distant bad memory."

As he got into his shirt and tie, Sinatra said, "You're just the guy I wanna see, anyway."

"Yeah?"

"What I said out in Hollywood, at Sherry's—it still goes. I want to hire you. I can have a thousand-buck retainer for you at your office in the morning."

"For what?"

"I want you to fly out to D.C. and talk to this son of a bitch."

"Kefauver?"

"No! Fuck Kefauver. It's McCarthy I'm sweating, man. If they label me a pinko, I really am washed up. You said you know the guy—through Pearson, right?"

"I know McCarthy. He's a good joe to drink with."

"Well, find out what it'll take to get him off my ass. See if he wants money, or if he wants me to sing at a fund-raiser or what the hell. But I got to put a stop to this shit. Mortimer's starting to spread that pinko crap around, already. People thinking I maybe have some gangsters as friends is one thing—they think I'm a Commie, man, I'm dead. Capeesh?"

"Capeesh," I said.

"How's the tie look?"

"It looked better when Nancy was making 'em."

"Don't start with me. What are you, my Jewish mother?"

"No, I'm your Irish rose. Get out there and try not to cough up blood."

He smirked at me. "Sweet, Melvin—you're a real sweetheart."

Sinatra was great. The crowd loved him. His voice did seem to have a rasp tonight, a kind of burr in it, but it was attractive, somehow, more mature. His ballads were heartbreaking—during "I'm a Fool to Want You" Jackie began to cry—and he seemed to have a new energy in the up-tempo stuff, like a peppy version of "All of Me" and the swinging "Saturday Night (Is the Loneliest Night of the

Week).'' Maybe he did have some career left out in front of him.

By the time Frank got on stage, however, Rocco had noticed us—and he would, from time to time, shoot daggers toward Jackie and me. Charley seemed to be trying to settle him down, touching his brother's hand, even sliding an arm around Rocco's shoulder, whispering.

In the middle of "The Hucklebuck"—a terrible song, typical of what Columbia was sticking Sinatra with these days—I told Jackie I needed to step out to take a leak. She was aware, of course, that Rocco had been shooting us death rays, and claimed to have to go herself.

While she was in the ladies' room, I was—and I'm sure this will come as no surprise—in the men's room. This wouldn't be worth noting, if—just after I zipped up—Rocco hadn't come striding in.

The men's room at the Chez Paree—this one, anyway (there were several)—was good-size; we had it to ourselves, Rocco and I, the show being in progress and all.

"Hi, Rocky," I said, voice echoing in this cathedral of porcelain altars and Crane confessionals, and went over to the sink and began washing up.

His voice, like his footsteps, echoed, too: "What's the idea, Nate?"

I let the water run, soaping my hands. "Oh, I always wash my hands after I piss or shit—you ought to try it, Rocky. Latest thing."

Rocco—who looked spiffy in his tux, very handsome except for that horror-show pockmarked puss surrounded by skunk-streaked hair—didn't smile. That business about me kidding him, that treating-him-like-a-regular-guy routine, wasn't going to play.

His voice boomed hollowly: "You know what I'm talkin' about, Heller—I'm talkin' about you picking up my castoffs. . . . You gonna go through my garbage, too? See if there's any sandwiches I didn't fucking finish?"

Still washing up, I turned my head and said, "She's not garbage, Rocky. She's a nice kid. She's still a nice kid, even after your beatings."

More echoing footsteps—he was within arm's reach of me, now. The close-set eyes under the black slashes of eyebrow were fixed on me like twin revolver barrels.

He grinned—a grin as terrible as he was. "Maybe you don't know it yet, Heller—but that 'nice kid' is a goddamn ad—a fuckin' jabber!"

He meant an addict who used a hypo.

I soaped my hands, a regular Lady Macbeth. "Rocky, you're the one who turned her into a junkie. I'm the one who's gonna help her." I shot him another sideways glance. "I'm asking you as a friend, Rock—back off. She's not your property, anymore."

The black-slash eyebrows leapt up his forehead; his lip peeled back over white store-bought teeth. "Her ass will always be mine, you dumb fuck! All I gotta do is snap my fingers . . ." He snapped them. ". . . and she'll come crawlin' on her hands and knees, beggin' for—"

I didn't know whether he was going to say dope, or make some filthy sexual reference, but I didn't care to hear it, in either case.

Which is why I threw a handful of soapy water in his wide-open eyes.

His hands came up to his face, like I'd splashed him with acid, not harmless sudsy water, and I swung a hard right (wet) hand into his balls.

His yowl of pain echoed as he folded up and went down, and now he was the one on the floor, crawling. While he was still helpless, I frisked him, found no firearms, and then I leaned over and hit him in the face—in the right eye, in his burning eye.

And then I slugged him in his other eye, his burning left. Two shiners for one seemed a fair exchange to me. Finally rage fueled him—and perhaps the stinging in his eyes abated—enough for him to rise up off the floor and come at me.

But I'd had plenty of time to get my nine millimeter out. He hadn't seen me pull it, but he saw the gun now, and he froze—hands clawed before him, a werewolf in a tuxedo.

That was the tableau Charley Fischetti witnessed when he came in the john, looking for his brother, no doubt.

"No, Heller," Charley said, approaching tentatively, hands up and out, sending a nonthreatening message. He too was in a tux, his dyed-blond hair combed perfectly back. His elevator shoes clip-clopped, echoing. "Don't do it—let him go."

I cocked the automatic; the click echoed, too, like another footstep.

"Doesn't he know who he's dealing with?" Rocky asked his brother, flabbergasted, astounded, frustrated by my actions. Then to me: "Don't you fucking *know* who you're *dealing* with?"

I smiled at him, but my gun hand was trembling—just a little. "You're a tough man, Rock. A killer. I'd be impressed, only I killed more Japs in one afternoon than your goombah career total."

Rocco was trembling, too—whether with fear or rage or both, I couldn't say. At the same time, he seemed coiled to spring; and part of me welcomed that.

Charley stood next to us—had he moved forward two steps, he'd have been between us. "Come on, Heller—back off. . . . Rocky, back off . . . back off!" Charley swallowed, eyes flicking from me to his brother and back again. "I know what this is about—it's that girl, isn't it? That goddamn girl. . . ."

"Her ass is mine!" Rocco snarled.

I backhanded the son of a bitch.

He couldn't believe it. Rocco just stood there with his red eyes and touched the red in the corner of his mouth and couldn't believe it.

"You touch her again, you come near her again," I told him, "I will kill you so fucking slow you'll be begging me to finish you. I'll shoot your toes off and let you bleed to death out your fuckin' feet."

Rocco didn't know what to say. The skunk-haired gangster looked afraid; it did not seem to be a state he was terribly familiar with. People were, after all, supposed to be afraid of him.

"Rocky," Charley said, gently, "you put the girl out on the street with her bags—you sent her away. If Nate wants to take up with her, that's his business."

Rocco looked at Charley in amazement, searching his brother's face for some sign that these were just words meant to fool me. If he found that, I didn't sense it.

Charley turned my way, his voice gentle, reasonable. "Nate—can Rocky go now? Could you and I speak, alone, for a few moments—just the two of us?"

I shrugged. "Sure. Rock, did you need to use the facilities before you leave? Maybe you want to throw some water on your face."

Rocco's upper lip curled back, like a Doberman about to growl—or attack.

"*Go*, Rock," Charley said, and he took his brother's arm and tugged him away from where he'd stood facing me. "Go sit at the table and enjoy Frankie and stay away from our friend, Mr. Heller here . . . and stay away from the girl."

Rocco swallowed, nodded, and hurried out.

Charley, breathing hard, leaned against the sink counter. "Nate . . . Nate, are you insane? Aren't you fucking aware my brother is a very violent man?"

"I'll take those questions in order: yes I am insane; that's how I got out of the Marines. And your brother *is* a violent man—almost as violent as I am, and much tougher with women than I'll ever be."

Charley was shaking. He reached a hand in his tux pocket and found the small round silver box, from which he selected two pink pills. He popped them in his mouth, and ran a faucet and stuck his face under the water and drank. Then he used a paper towel to dry his face and turned to me, his hazel eyes tight with apparent earnestness.

"Nate . . . I will handle my brother. I will make sure this unfortunate incident is a . . . one time thing. . . . Just a sad falling out among old friends."

"I'll kill him if he touches her."

"I know! I know. . . . You made your point. What Rocco fails to understand is how . . . misguided he was in evicting Miss Payne."

"Why is that? He was tired of her—she was nothing to him but a dog to whip."

Charley drew in a long breath and let it out slowly. "This inquiry . . . with the potentially damaging publicity it could bring. . . . Miss Payne might feel sufficiently alienated from my brother to do something unwise."

"You mean, she lived in your penthouse for a long time, and saw people come and go, and probably heard things."

He nodded, once, a kind of a sideways nod. "Now. If I . . . *handle* Rocco. Keep him away from her—and from you . . . will you see to it that Miss Payne does not become friendly with the senator from Tennessee and his little tea party?"

I considered that. Then I said, "You know, that seems fair."

He sighed and beamed. "Good. Good. . . . And thank you for helping my brother, my *other* brother out, with that Mortimer character." He shook his head. "Such a lout. Such an uncouth lout."

"Some people have poor social graces," I said, holstering my nine millimeter.

Charley exited the men's room, with me right behind him; no sign of Rocco. I think Charley was as relieved as I was. He turned to me and extended his hand.

"We have a deal, then?"

"Deal," I said, shaking with him.

When Charley had headed back toward the showroom—where Sinatra was singing, "If I Loved You"—I glanced toward the ladies' room door, and saw Jackie cracking it, peeking out.

"Come on, honey," I said. "We're missing the show."

She rushed to my side, looped her arm in mine. "I saw Rocco come out! He didn't see me, but I—"

"He's not going to bother you, anymore."

"What happened?"

"I didn't kill him."

And I couldn't keep the disappointment out of my voice.

8

Washington, D.C.—the seat of political power in the western hemisphere—was also the hub of the mightiest industrial and military machine in the history of the world. The White House, the Capitol, various imposing monuments and a multitude of marble buildings swimming in seas of manicured green, were dignified symbols that imparted a stateliness, a nobility to the terrible powers certain men in this town possessed—men who charted the strategies and movements of armies and navies all over the world, who dispatched diplomats and spies to every corner of the earth, who controlled the man-made cataclysm of the atomic bomb.

I had come to our nation's capital to see two men who wielded power of a different sort—the power of information . . . or sometimes misinformation. A few well-placed words—truth or fabrication, it didn't seem to matter much which—could destroy lives as surely as any bullet or bomb . . . and without the mess.

One of those powerful men resided in a townhouse on Dumbarton Avenue in Georgetown, a quaint neighborhood of cobblestone streets, reconditioned slave quarters, and Early American shutters. This was a cool, overcast Sunday afternoon, and the well-shaded lane was alive with fall colors—coppers and yellows and oranges and reds (not the card-carrying variety).

I'd flown in this morning, arriving at the National Airport, on the Virginia side; from my window seat, as we glided over the city, the pilot executing a tourist-pleasing swoop, I'd taken in the grand obelisk of the Washington Monument and the familiar Capitol dome, dominating a distinctive skyline they and other monuments formed, no skyscrapers to compete with—buildings over 110 feet were banned by law, locally.

I had spent a lot of time in D.C. over the years—particularly on various jobs I'd done for the late James Forrestal, our nation's first secretary of defense—and was quite used to Washington's old-fashioned Southern sensibilities, its spacious avenues, tree-shaded lawns, the landscaped green (some of it dyed to stay that way year-round). What the hell—green seemed to symbolize the power in this city even better than stately marble.

At the townhouse in Georgetown, I trotted up the half-dozen steps to the landing and used the polished brass knocker. The golden-tressed young woman who answered smiled in recognition.

"Mr. Heller," she said, playfully, because in other circumstances she had called me Nate, "you are expected."

She had a perfectly delightful middle-European accent.

"Hi, Anya," I said, stepping at her invitation into an entrance hall that fed both the residential and office areas of the townhouse. "You look swell."

"You look good, also."

Anya was a Yugoslavian war refugee in her early twenties, with big blue eyes in a heart-shaped face. She wore a businesslike blue dress with white trim and a white belt, an ensemble that played down her bosomy shape. We'd had a brief fling a while back, but her boss didn't know it—because he was in the midst of a longer fling with his "secretary," himself.

Anya was the office's current "fair-haired girl," as the staffers around here dubbed them, "cutie-pies" in her employer's own terminology. Since her English was limited, her secretarial duties ran not to taking dictation but accompanying her married boss to cocktail parties and out-of-town speaking engagements.

A living room loomed straight ahead, with a formal dining room off to my left; but this was not a social call—the lady of the house, Luvie, spent most of her time at the family farm, anyway. Anya led me down the right a few steps, into the office area, ushering me—wordlessly—into a book-, paper-, and memento-flung study where her boss sat typing furiously at a stand to one side of his big wide wooden desk. Wearing a purple smoking jacket, fingers flying, the tall, bald, sturdy-looking journalist seemed oblivious to our entrance.

Beyond an open double doorway opposite the desk, a larger office area hummed with activity, a file cabinet-lined bullpen with three women and two men, typing, talking on the phone, interacting. Anya smiled and nodded to me, as she went out and joined them, shutting the doors behind her, though I could see her through the panes of glass, positioning herself at the wire service ticker, watching stories come in, doing her best to read them.

Sunday was one of Drew Pearson's deadline days—he had his weekly radio broadcast tonight and he and his staff were prepping frantically for it. (One key figure around here, legman Jack Anderson, was not present: a Mormon, he didn't work on Sundays, though he toiled his ass off on Saturday.) About twenty years ago, Pearson had gone from being a journeyman Washington newsman to a national figure by appropriating the technique of Manhattan and Hollywood gossip columnists for his "Washington Merry-Go-Round."

That syndicated column—growing out of a book not unlike the *Confidential* series by Mortimer and Lait—was an immediate smash, and Pearson was soon America's preeminent crusader for liberal causes. From time to time I had done background investigations for him, particularly those involving Chicago or California; but we had a rocky relationship—he was a cheap bastard, slow to pay his bills, plus he had an ends-justifies-the-means approach that troubled even a cynical Chicago heel like myself.

Speaking of Chicago heels, I stood rocking on mine, my

hands in my suitpants pockets, waiting for Pearson to come up for air and notice my existence. This study had dark plaster walls decorated with photos of Pearson with show business figures (Sinatra among them) and national political luminaries, including a couple presidents and Senator Estes Kefauver; a few political cartoons, lampooning Pearson and his sometimes controversial stands, were framed and hanging here and there, as well. I was thinking about what an egomaniac this guy was until I realized these reminded me of my own office walls.

This was homier than my Monadnock suite, however, cozier—snapshots lined the mantelpiece of a working fireplace, and windowsills were stacked with books and magazines and one sill was occupied by a slumbering black cat. A primitive rural landscape and an oil painting of Pearson's late father—neither very good—shared wall space with the framed photos and political cartoons.

Pearson stopped typing, heaved a sigh, and flipped the fresh page of copy on a desk lined with paper-filled wooden intake boxes. He had still not acknowledged my presence. He glided over, backward, on his swivel chair and got behind the desk, and turned to me, finally bestowing that foxy grin I knew so well.

"Must you always come by on broadcast day?" he asked, standing to his full six three, extending his hand. Just as he typed rat-a-tat-tat style, he talked the same way, having trained himself to sound like an elitist version of Walter Winchell, for the radio version of "Washington Merry-Go-Round."

Reaching across his messy desk to shake with him, I said, "Remind me—what *is* your slow day around here?"

The bustle of the bullpen provided background music.

"No such animal, as you well know." He gestured for me to sit and I took a hard wooden chair across from him.

Pearson settled back in his chair. He had an egg-shaped head, close-set eyes, a prominent nose, and a wide mouth adorned with a well-waxed, pointy-tipped mustache. Under the purple smoking jacket, a white shirt and brown-and-yellow bow tie peeked out. Gentlemanly, aloof, he would have made a fine British butler.

"Thanks for making time for me," I said.

His arms were folded; he was rocking gently in the swivel chair. Then he halted in midrock and he reached for a jar of Oreo cookies on the desk, took off the glass lid, and dug himself a couple out; then he told me to help myself.

I passed. This—and cheating on his wife, and not paying me promptly—was his only vice. He was a Quaker and did not smoke, though he took hard liquor, albeit not to excess. He also did not pepper his speech with "thee" and "thou," which would have been a little hard to take, considering his superior manner.

"I understand you're not cooperating with my friend Estes," he said.

Suddenly I felt as if I'd been summoned by Pearson, even though it had been me who arranged the appointment.

"I haven't even met Senator Kefauver yet," I said. "But I'm sure you'll appreciate, Drew, that I don't intend to compromise the privacy of my clients."

An eyebrow arched. "You won't testify?"

"If the committee calls me, I will, sure. But they won't learn anything except name, rank, and serial number. If you could pass that info along to your 'friend' Estes, that would be swell."

"Your visit does have something to do with the Crime Committee, though," he said.

On the phone, I had indicated as much, if vaguely. Arguably, I could have handled this—and the other conversation I'd come to D.C. for—over the long-distance wire; but Pearson was one of the most paranoid men in a paranoid town, and refused to talk frankly on the telephone. He had his office swept for bugs on a weekly basis, and made most of his own calls from pay phones.

I said, "Yes—I would appreciate your insights on a couple of matters related to Kefauver."

His response was to bite into an Oreo. Seeing the chunk of cookie disappear into that prissily mustached mouth was amusing, but I kept a straight face.

"I spoke to Lee Mortimer the other night," I said.

"Mortimer." He shook his head disgustedly, chewing his cookie. "What a pathetic little creature."

"Lee claims he's been shut out of the Crime Committee's inside circle. Apparently he deluded himself into thinking they'd take him, a reporter, on as a paid, government investigator . . . just because he was the guy who inspired Kefauver to look into—"

But I never finished that thought, because Pearson lurched forward, and anger glistened in his close-set eyes. "Mortimer is a self-aggrandizing liar. I am the one who got Estes interested in organized crime—how many exposés have I written over the years, anyway? Louisiana, New York, Chicago. . . . Damn it, Nathan—you contributed your investigative prowess to a number of them."

"I guess I hadn't made that connection."

He made a sweeping gesture. "Isn't it enough that Mortimer and his fat friend Lait plagiarized my approach in their trashy *Confidential* books? Must this iguana now lay claim to my efforts to help launch the Crime Investigating Committee?"

I knew Pearson was a booster of Kefauver's, and the columnist had even been talking up the Tennessee senator as a possible presidential candidate. But I didn't realize Pearson was—or anyway thought he was—a prime mover behind the mob inquiry.

Pearson was saying, "Hell, I was delighted when Estes introduced his resolution to investigate the rackets on a national scale. But then it got stalled in the Senate for lack of support—until *I* put the pressure on."

"Who was trying to block it?"

"McCarran, for one—though technically McCarran is Kefauver's boss, you know."

Senator Pat McCarran of Nevada, home of Las Vegas, was—no shock here—in the mob's pocket. McCarran was a Democrat who voted like a conservative Republican, one of the rabid anti-Commie crowd.

I was confused. "How in hell can McCarran be Kefauver's boss, particularly when he tried to stop the investigation before it even started?"

Pearson shrugged, smiled his insider's smile. "Kefauver's committee ultimately reports to the Judiciary Committee, of which McCarran is chairman."

"Christ."

Pearson shifted in his seat. "And of course without the support of the Senate majority leader—Lucas, of your home state—Estes could never have launched his probe, in the first place. And initially Lucas was dead set against it."

Pearson was referring to Scott Lucas, currently campaigning against Everett Dirksen.

"So I simply spoke to my good friend Scott," Pearson continued, "and reminded him of certain rumors that he'd received big campaign contributions from Chicago gamblers. Pointed out that it would look very bad, if he continued to block the Kefauver investigation . . . and he graciously granted his support—Mortimer my ass! He's a hack, a conniving hack."

"What about these accusations he's making about Halley?"

"Jack's investigated Halley thoroughly . . ." Pearson meant Jack Anderson. ". . . and the man is a straight arrow. A partner in Halley's law firm did indeed represent the railroad in question, the Hudson & Manhattan line, the one with the supposed gangster investors—a relationship that ended some time ago. Halley had no contact himself, and he's been a dogged investigator, a relentless inquisitor in the hearings thus far."

"What about his so-called Hollywood connections?"

"Nothing of substance there, either. His firm represents a distillery whose publicist has a few Hollywood clients. Typical Mortimer and Lait yellow journalism."

Drew Pearson complaining about yellow journalism was like an infected mosquito bitching about yellow fever.

"Drew, do you have influence with Estes?"

Tiny shrug, twitch of the mustache. "Certainly."

I nodded toward a certain photo on the wall. "Can you ask your friend from Tennessee to steer clear of our mutual friend Frankie?"

His eyes narrowed. "That might be difficult. An inquiry has to go wherever the truth leads."

"Bullshit. Drew, this investigation has all sorts of political strings, and you damn well know it. Look at the emphasis on gambling—I don't see the mob's influence on big-city machine politics coming under the microscope."

A more elaborate shrug. ". . . I can try."

I leaned forward. "Certainly you can understand it would be devastating to Frank's career right now, if he were called in front of TV cameras to testify about gangsters he met on his summer vacation."

Nodding slowly, Pearson said, "Yes. I can understand that. . . . I can but try."

"Thank you. I'll let him know—he's under a hell of a lot of pressure. You see, Frank's also got a problem with another Senate inquiry . . . courtesy of a certain old pal of ours."

Pearson knew at once who I was talking about. "I can well imagine. Frank has a good heart—and he believes in the right causes. That's enough to make him a 'pinko' in some circles. I can well imagine that 'Tailgunner Joe' might relish lining the Voice up in his capricious sights."

"No imagining necessary. Really, that's my main reason for coming to Washington . . . to try to reason with Joe McCarthy."

"Well, then you'll be the first one to manage that unlikely feat."

I frowned. "Your relationship with McCarthy has completely soured?"

"It verges on war. Even he and Jack aren't friendly, anymore."

It might seem unlikely that Pearson and McCarthy had ever been soulmates, but the archliberal columnist and the ultraconservative senator had a shared interest in weeding out federal corruption. Pearson's credentials in that arena were impeccable: he cracked the Russian spy ring in Canada; he exposed the Silvermaster Communist spy ring; and he ferreted out miscellaneous congressional skulduggery, ruining the careers of a number of powerful legislators.

Wisconsin's McCarthy—elected to the Senate in 1946, in part by courting Communist support ("Communists have the same right to vote as anybody else, don't they?" he'd asked rhetorically)—had been for several years a key Pearson source of inside info about his congressional colleagues and their secrets. I knew McCarthy because I followed leads he provided Pearson, about the so-called "five per-center" influence peddlers.

But earlier this year, after a national magazine rated him our nation's worst senator, McCarthy bragged to Jack Anderson that he had come up with "one hell of an issue." Shortly thereafter, McCarthy gave a speech to the no doubt bewildered little old ladies of the Republican Women's Club of Ohio County, declaring to have "in his hand" a list of 205 members of the Communist Party, currently operating in the State Department, with the secretary of state's blessing.

Never mind that within a day the list had dwindled to "fifty-seven card-carrying Communists" . . . or that Communist Party members hadn't carried "cards" for years. McCarthy had made himself an instant household word . . . and a feared man in Washington.

Only, Drew Pearson didn't fear anybody in Washington or anywhere else.

"Before he's through," Pearson was saying, "no one's reputation will be safe—the whole political process will be poisoned."

"He's got a real, rabid following."

"That's why he's got to be cut down now, before he becomes a walking national disaster area. Frank Sinatra? A Communist? Good Lord, where would such lunacy stop?"

"You're losing a hell of an informant."

"My best on the Hill," Pearson admitted. "A good source, but a bad man. . . . McCarthy's already caught up in the demagogue's compulsion toward escalation. He upgrades 'fellow travelers' into Communists, and pro-Communists into spies!"

"Well, your friend Estes has provided him the blueprint for witch-hunting. You have that coonskin cap to thank."

Pearson's nostrils flared, his eyes hardened. "Don't compare the two, for God's sake! Estes is a sincere, honest man, a true servant of the people. There's something . . . pathological about McCarthy, some inner demon that pushes him to take extravagant risks."

I shrugged. "Maybe he'll undo himself."

An eyebrow lifted. "Waiting until that time would be a risk too extravagant for me to take. I'll handle this in my own fashion."

"How?"

He nodded toward his battered old typewriter. "With my usual weapon—my column, my radio show. Within the coming weeks, every American will learn that their esteemed Red-busting hero has committed a laundry list of transgressions."

Pearson began to enumerate: State Judge McCarthy had sold "quickie" divorces to campaign contributors; he had violated the Wisconsin constitution by running for Senate without resigning from the bench; his disbarment had been recommended by the State Board; he'd falsely attributed lavish campaign contributions to his father and brother, who didn't make five grand a year between them; he retained his judgeship while serving in the Marines; he'd cheated on his income taxes; and he'd exaggerated his war record, a much publicized "wound" a phony. . . .

None of it seemed terribly impressive to me, frankly—McCarthy sounded like a typical politician. But Pearson knew just how to parcel this stuff out, and really put a guy through the meat grinder.

As I watched the tips of Pearson's waxed mustache rise ever higher as the columnist smiled, listing the Wisconsin senator's various sins (assembled by Anderson, no doubt)—soon to be shared with the American public—it came to me that Joe McCarthy was about to really find out what smear tactics were all about.

On this cool, quiet Sunday night in September, under a starless sky, the Mall—that wide expanse of green, extending a mile and a half up from the Washington Monument to the Capitol Building—was bathed in light by streetlamps, thousands of luminous orbs lining the pavement, crisscrossing this most accessible of parks. The Capitol Building seemed a glowing crown in this sweeping array of marble, grass, and floodlights. Unencumbered by the rush of people—save for a few tourists attending the church of their government—the Mall gave Washington a sense of pageantry, of elegance, of order. How Joe McCarthy fit into this was anybody's guess.

One of three white marble buildings facing the Capitol grounds, the Senate Office Building—inevitably nicknamed the S.O.B.—was at First and B Street, near the northeast corner. Capitol Hill was all but deserted, and even nearby Union Station—where I'd parked my rental Ford—seemed underpopulated.

I trotted up the broad flight of steps on the southwest corner, to a terraced landing, then on to the main doorway, which opened onto the second floor, depositing me in a marble two-story rotunda with a balcony, conical ceiling, and armed security guard. Fortunately McCarthy had seen to it my name was on the guard's clipboard list, and—after my ID was examined, and I'd signed in—he allowed me to clip-clop across the marble floor, creating disturbing echoes in the vast, underlit chamber. It felt wrong, being here after hours, and eerie, the long shadow I cast resembling an intruder skulking unbidden into the hallowed halls of government.

Through an arch, down a white marble corridor, I crept along, like a ghost haunting the place. I was not entirely alone, however: now and then, slashes of light at the bottom of doors indicated Senator McCarthy was not the only person taking advantage of the peace and quiet and lack of hubbub a Sunday night could afford.

But only McCarthy's office seemed to be going more or less full throttle. When I entered the anteroom, a secretary and two staffers were bustling about, much as Pearson's crew had been—typing, filing, poring over research materials.

Delores—an efficient, pleasant-looking woman in her thirties who McCarthy called "mother"—recognized me from previous visits. She smiled in a harried manner, said I was expected, and hustled me in to the senator's spacious, rather underfurnished office.

McCarthy was on the phone, seated behind his big square government-issue desk, which was piled with file folders. He was in a white shirt with the sleeves rolled up, his food-stained red-and-green splatter-design tie loose around a bull neck, the suitcoat of a double-breasted ready-made dark blue suit (he seemed to buy them by bulk) flung over a hardback chair. He was the kind of guy whose socks matched his tie only by accident.

In his early forties, McCarthy—who was chummily talking with "Dick" . . . Nixon, it soon became clear—had a blue-jowled, barrel-chested, unchiseled masculinity that was close enough to handsome for government work. His dark hair was just starting to thin, and his muscular physique seemed fleshier than when I saw him last, maybe a year before.

My host, in his nasal Irish baritone, was working on Nixon, trying to get him to share current Un-American Activities Committee files. McCarthy kept referring to the "cause."

His manner made me recall the first night I'd played poker with him. McCarthy had invited me along to the National Press Club. Sitting down with seven men he'd never played with before, he tried to bluff each one of them out of a pot; and no matter what he had—even a pair of deuces—McCarthy would bet heavily.

He also tried to bluff me, and I won a healthy pot of mostly his money; I heard whispering that McCarthy was a "sucker," and that was when I caught on. He'd been acting the hayseed, and when the cards started to run in his favor, he bet heavily and everybody stayed in—assuming he was bluffing. At one point down five hundred bucks, he wound up winning twelve hundred.

I wondered if Drew Pearson knew that this grinning, blue-jowled ape was far more resourceful than his enemies gave him credit for. Watching him twist Nixon's arm over the phone, I could see this son of a bitch played politics like he played poker—committing well-calculated highway robbery.

The office, by the way, was barren of the sort of celebrity photos and mementos that characterized Pearson's study—though McCarthy was every bit as big a public figure. The only item on display was a baseball bat on a little pedestal, on a counter at left, between file cabinets.

The bat had the name "Drew Pearson" burned into it.

McCarthy was hanging up the phone. He grinned at me, rising to his six feet, and reached a long arm across his cluttered desk, offering me a big square hand.

I shook that powerful paw, and when he told me to sit down, I did, in the hard wooden chair opposite him—next to the one with his suitcoat slung over it.

He was still grinning after he sat back down—but the grin seemed strained, almost a grimace. He said, "Should I have agreed to see you, Nate?"

"Why not, Joe?"

He nodded toward the baseball bat. "Word is you and Pearson patched up your differences."

I shrugged. "Only to the extent that I'm willing to take his money again."

Thick black eyebrows climbed his Cro-Magnon forehead. "Not to look into *my* business, I hope?"

"No. That's never happened, Joe . . . never will."

The grin relaxed into a smile; he sat forward, leaning on the file folders, brutish shoulders hunched. "I'm going after him, Nate," he said, still referring to Pearson. "I mean, no holds barred. I figure I've already lost his supporters—and now I can pick up his enemies."

"Do what you want to do."

"I'm going to break him, Nate—put him out of business."

I figured long after McCarthy was out of the Senate, Pearson would still be around, destroying careers on the Hill; but I said, "That's between you and the skinflint."

The latter made him laugh. "You know, I'd be a hero on the Hill if I could pull a few of his teeth, break his insteps, or maybe bust a few ribs. Say fifteen of 'em."

"That bat would do the trick," I said, wondering if he was kidding.

He leaned back, gestured with a big hand. "You know, you could have called me on the phone. You didn't have to come all this way."

"Some conversations shouldn't be sent through the air. Phones can be tapped."

"I guess you'd know." He scratched his nose. "A fella in your position can acquire enemies, after all."

That seemed an odd remark.

But I just said, "That's true. Not everyone loves me. Listen . . . I wanted to talk to you about a friend of mine."

"The pinko singer."

I sighed. "Joe, he's no pinko. Frank's about as political as I am."

"Is that a good thing?"

Something was crawling at the base of my neck. "Am I missing something?" I asked.

He selected a file—whether randomly or not, I couldn't say. He thumbed through it and, either referring to it or pretending to, he said, "I've been approached about you. About your background."

"What?"

"Your father was a Communist, wasn't he? Ran a Commie bookstore on the West Side of Chicago? You grew up there, among those radicals?"

I felt like I'd been sucker punched in the belly. I managed, "He was a Wobbly, Joe—a pro-union guy. He killed himself, back in '32."

"Terrible tragedy. Terrible."

"He killed himself because I wasn't like him—I *wasn't* idealistic. I just wanted to make a buck."

"That's the American way."

My head was swimming. "Jesus—what are you saying to me, Joe?"

He heaved a huge sigh; shook his head, sorrowfully. "There are people . . . powerful people . . . good Americans, like my friend Pat McCarran . . . who would like me to take a hard close look at you, and your background."

". . . Are you saying, somebody's told you to paint me with a red brush?"

His beady eyes turned into slits. "Let me say this. This fellow Kefauver, he's like a bull in the china shop. He's causing trouble for a lot of fine Americans. He's abusing the system, with these hearings of his—I can't abide seeing our fine system, the most nearly perfect system of government ever to find a place under God's blue sky, abused for personal aggrandizement. That Tennessee turncoat will never be president if I have any say in it."

The panic had been brief, but terrible—I'd had a tiny glimpse of the horror of having your world imperiled by government-sanctioned lies.

But that panic was gone.

"McCarran," I said, smiling just a little, nodding. "Senator from the great state of Nevada. As in, Las Vegas. Joe—do you have friends who don't want me to testify in the Kefauver hearings?"

He cleared his throat. "If you're called, you'll have to testify. That's the law. But what you choose to share with these witch-finders, that's another matter entirely."

I laughed; the laughter was genuine but tinged with hysteria. The great Commie hunter was mobbed up!

He folded his hands, prayerfully; he had knockwurst fingers. "Nate . . . I couldn't let this happen to you. I was so pleased when you called, and wanted to meet. After all, you were friends with Jim Forrestal . . . another great man Drew Pearson assassinated with his pen."

That was why Pearson and I had fallen out: the columnist's unremitting, merciless attacks had contributed to Forrestal's suicide.

"Jim was my mentor," McCarthy said. "He was the one who informed me about the Communists high up in our government."

Forrestal was also a delusional paranoid schizophrenic.

I folded my arms. "Joe, I've already talked to the committee, who I basically told to go fuck themselves . . . and to Charley Fischetti, and Sam Giancana, given them my assurances that I'm not talking."

"Those names mean nothing to me."

"Yeah, right. You tell McCarran I'm no problem. And Christ, neither is Sinatra. You've got to give that kid a pass, too, Joe. You'll destroy his career."

"Mr. Sinatra is also on Kefauver's list."

"Oh. Wait. . . . I think I'm finally getting this." I shook my head, not knowing whether to laugh or cry. "You'll lay off Sinatra, if he doesn't cooperate with the Kefauver Committee."

He twitched a humorless smile. "You make this sound like a quid pro quo. . . . I can tell you that Senator McCarran admires Mr. Sinatra, has enjoyed his many appearances in Las Vegas."

I raised a hand, as if I was being sworn in. "Frank won't give those guys the time of day—even if they put his ass on TV and embarrass him in front of the entire nation."

"You can speak for him?"

"I am speaking for him."

McCarthy thought about that. Then he grinned, and it didn't seem strained. "Great. Great! Jesus, Nate it's nice seeing you. You want to go out for beer and steak? I'm ready for a break."

"No thanks," I said. "Rain check."

I was the one with the strained grin, now.

I stood, he stood again, and we had another handshake, and I went quickly out. At first I was pissed off, although relieved; but then the humor of it hit me.

The other shoe had finally dropped.

I'd thought Fischetti, Giancana, and company had too easily accepted at face value my assurances not to help Kefauver. I mean, hell—I was Bill Drury's friend and almost partner! Yet there'd been no intimidation—just one bribe, from Tubbo, nothing from the Outfit itself.

Until this Sunday evening screening of *Mr. Heller Goes to Washington*, that is.

This had all been just another scam, courtesy of the mob and that poker-playing ape back there. Sinatra was a friend of the Chicago/Nevada gambling interests, after all; they wouldn't want to insult him, not directly. And me, better to keep me a friendly nonwitness.

So they had reached out to Senator Joe McCarthy, that great Red-hunting all-American boy, to squeeze Frankie and me into silence.

No silence right now: I was laughing, loud and hard, and it was echoing through the rotunda of the S.O.B., filling the hollow, hallowed halls, startling the guard.

9

The flight from D.C. took maybe three hours, the bag handlers at Midway managed not to lose my suitcase, the ride to the Loop clocked thirty-eight minutes, and I was back in my suite at the St. Clair before noon on Monday.

Unfortunately, I was alone: no sign of my new roommate.

Not only was Jackie Payne absent from my apartment, so were her things—the clothes she'd hung in my bedroom closet, her toiletries, suitcases, everything. Gone. Like she'd never been here . . .

. . . except for the lingering fragrance of Chanel No. 5., in the bedroom particularly.

I got the front desk on the phone and asked the clerk to round up Hannan, the house dick. Hannan sometimes did jobs for me, and he was supposed to have been doing me a favor, while I was away.

Leaving Jackie even for twenty-four hours had been problematic. We'd spent Saturday together, mostly at my suite, loving each other, me assuring her that I was going to get her the best help for her problem. We'd gone to a picture show—a matinee of *All About Eve*, at the State-Lake, holding hands like high school kids—and had a light, early supper at the Tap Room, back at the St. Clair. The rest of the evening had been consumed by passion worthy

of honeymooners, intermingled with bouts of doubt and
paranoia on her part, worry about me leaving even for just
a day (and night), fear that Rocco would barge in and beat
her, or worse.

"I'm afraid of him," she'd said.

We were in bed, and the only light was courtesy of the
lakefront and the moon through the window; she was nestled against me, her face against my chest. I was fooling
with her hair, scratching and rubbing her scalp.

"No need," I said, lying only a little. "Rocco's going to
have to watch himself where we're both concerned." She
looked up at me, eyes a-glimmer with worry. "Why do you
think that?"

"His brother Charley will keep him in line. Baby, Charley knows I'm capable of dishing out the same kind of . . .
medicine as his brother. And one thing these goombahs
don't want right now is bad publicity."

"Bad publicity . . . ?"

"I'm the friend and associate of an ex-cop who's going
to testify against them in this crime inquiry. The curtain on
that roadshow is going up soon—probably after the election, but soon—and the Fischettis of this world . . . the
smart ones, anyway . . . don't want the papers filled with
stuff out of an old Jimmy Cagney movie."

"You mean—they have to behave themselves?"

"That's right." If they were smart—but Rocco wasn't
smart; Charley had to be smart enough for both of them . . .
which was the catch I didn't explain to her.

So I had, seemingly, soothed her nerves and eased her
fears; but I needed to take other steps, to soothe and ease
my own.

Hannan had agreed to keep an eye on my suite and the
precious contents therein; he and the night dick—Goorwitz,
who also did occasional jobs for the A-1—would make sure
she wasn't disturbed. Both were reliable, at least as far as
ex-cops went, and could handle themselves with Rocco
should he, or any underling, come around. Hannan, in particular, was a hardcase, an ex-GI who survived the Battle
of the Bulge.

I was pacing when knuckles rapped on my door; the

peephole revealed red-headed, freckle-faced, blue-eyed Hannan, in a rumpled brown suit and brown felt fedora.

He stepped inside, saying, "She went out this morning. I saw her, and stopped her."

"Stopped her?"

"In the lobby—a bellboy paged me, to let me know what was going on . . . I mean, that she had called down to get help with her luggage."

At my directive, Hannan had alerted the staff to inform him of Jackie's movements, and he'd shown around a picture of Rocco—which I'd plucked from Jackie's wallet in her purse—so that clerks, bellboys, elevator attendants, and cleaning ladies would be on the lookout for that ugly face as well.

Hannan shrugged and held out his empty hands. "She said she was leaving, and I said you wouldn't like it, and she said to say she was sorry."

"Sorry."

"A cab came for her, and she was gone. I couldn't tail her, Nate—the follow-that-cab routine, I mean, it was out. I *am* on the job here, you know, and she was obviously skating of her own free will."

I shook my head. "Hannan, that girl doesn't have any free will—she's on the damn spike."

"And you were gonna get her off it, I suppose? Maybe that's your answer—she decided she didn't wanna get off it. You weren't trying some cold turkey number on her, were you, Nate?"

"Hell no. I'm not that fucking stupid." But I didn't elaborate: I couldn't tell the St. Clair's house detective that I had been paying for her habit to be temporarily fed, that I'd arranged a delivery of H to hold her over, here at the hotel.

"She didn't look like she was coming down, at that," Hannan said.

Maybe he was wise to what I'd done.

"Listen . . . thanks. I appreciate it." I dug into my pocket.

But Hannan put a hand on my suitcoat sleeve. "That C note you already gave me'll do just fine . . . it let me spread some around and have plenty left for me. Hey, I didn't do you much of a service, anyway, as it turns out. . . . Sorry, buddy."

The hotel operator said, yes, she'd been working the switchboard on Sunday; and several calls had come through for my room yesterday, which she'd connected. So Jackie had taken calls meant for me—or had someone called for her?

I tried to imagine Rocco calling Jackie and convincing her to come back to him. He'd been tired of her, after all . . . but could his brother, the Machiavellian Charley, have advised Rock to take this potential witness back into the fold . . . at least for now?

When I was grabbing a burger at the hotel coffee shop, I spotted two Chez Paree showgirls—in babushkas over pin curls and no makeup, unrecognizable as glamour pusses—sharing a booth. They agreed to give me a call if Jackie showed back up around there. A long shot, but one of the things Rocco could have enticed Jackie back with—besides smack—was a return to the Adorables chorus line.

At the office, Gladys informed me that Bill Drury had called, wanting to meet with me this afternoon.

"You didn't have anything in the book for four o'clock," she said at her reception area desk, "so I wrote him in. . . . I can try to contact him and cancel if you like."

"No, that's all right."

"I told him to bring back those Revere recorders, if he was dropping by."

"He hasn't returned them yet?"

"No. And he has a paycheck coming."

I doubted Drury had been doing much A-1 work in the past several weeks, but I merely nodded at Gladys and headed for my office.

A knock at my door preceded Lou Sapperstein sticking his head in; he found me sitting at my desk, leaning my chin into an elbow-propped hand.

"How was D.C.?" he said, ambling over and depositing himself in one of the client chairs.

I'd made Lou aware not only of my trip, but that the A-1 was working for Sinatra, on the singer's "pinko" problem.

"Fine," I said. "A success. McCarthy's laying off."

"Great." Lou didn't ask how I'd managed it; he'd learned a long time ago not to ask me how I pull things off. "Have you called Frankie boy, yet?"

"No. I'll do that."

"Man, is he gonna be relieved. . . . You look a little peaked, my friend. Have a rocky ride home?"

I looked at him, wondering if "rocky" had been a dig; Lou's deadpan showed nothing.

I said, "That girl I took in . . . the one Rocco threw out on her ass—Jackie Payne? She's disappeared."

He sat forward. "Shall we put somebody on it? I got two good boys sitting out in that bullpen, doing paperwork, just to keep 'em from playing with themselves."

"She seems to have left my protective custody of her own volition." I had not told Lou about Jackie's drug habit, merely that she had been a punching bag of Rocco's.

"Sometimes these masochistic dames go back for more from assholes like that," Lou said, shaking his head. "I could send somebody around to talk to the doorman and janitor at the Barry Apartments."

"Let me think on it. In the meantime, I'll call Sinatra and tell him the good news."

"I got a couple of jobs I need to talk over with you, this afternoon, Nate, if you're up to it—that banker in Evanston, looks like his brother-in-law is embezzling, all right, and—"

"Sure. Let me make my phone call."

Lou nodded, got up, and went quietly out.

I called Sinatra at the Palmer House, and filled him in, without sharing my theory that McCarthy had been rattling his cage at the behest of his mob friends. No reason to get Frank stirred up; better to let him think I was a miracle worker.

"You're the best, Nate," he said. "How did you like the new material, the other night?"

"You were great. Shave that mustache, and you just might have a career again."

He laughed. "I'll take it under advisement."

"Yeah, definitely see what Ava thinks."

"Fuck you, Melvin," he said, cheerfully, and hung up.

For maybe the next half hour, I sat and tried to think if there was something I could do about Jackie—do *for* Jackie. And I couldn't come up with a goddamn thing.

So I went back to work, and dealt with the matters Lou Sapperstein had for me, and a couple of other things. Then at four o'clock, Bill Drury was shown into my office, his usual natty self, blue suit and gray homburg.

"I'm not alone, Nate," he said, the homburg in hand, exposing his thinning dark hair. "Someone's with me—this is business. Can I have him come in?"

"Sure." I hadn't got up to greet Bill—I was still sitting behind the desk.

Drury turned to the open doorway and crooked his finger. A rather fleshy man in his mid-forties stepped in—six foot, hatless, with a square head, dark alert eyes high lighting strong features, and black, gray-at-the-temple hair, wearing a dark gray vested suit with a gray-and-blue tie. His name was Marvin J. Bas, and he was an attorney and Republican politician, in the Forty-second Ward—the turf of notorious saloonkeeper/alderman Paddy Bauler.

I stood up as Bas approached, smiling anxiously; we shook hands across the desk, said hello—using each other's first names, though we didn't know each other well, at all.

A folded newspaper tucked under his arm, Drury—who seemed uncharacteristically edgy—shut the door and came over and sat next to Bas, the pair filling both client chairs across from me at the desk.

"I'm a little surprised, Bill," I said. "I thought you were coming around to settle up—return equipment, collect a paycheck. I hope Marvin's presence doesn't mean you plan to sue me."

I'd said that with a smile, but anything was possible.

"No," Drury said, with his own small smile, the newspaper in his lap like a napkin, "I realize I've taxed your patience, and took advantage of our friendship, these last few weeks . . . putting you on the spot, thoughtlessly."

"If you're expecting an argument—"

"No. I returned the tape recorders, and I'll forgo any

further paychecks from the A-1. Frankly, I've really been working for myself, for a good month now . . . longer, but prior to that I did earn my agency paycheck."

"Fine. Is that why you're here—to apologize? Patch up our friendship? And does that take an attorney?"

Bas, who had a resonant voice, sat forward and said, "Actually, we're here to seek your help—not to ask a favor, based upon your long-standing friendship with Bill . . . rather, to hire you."

"Really. To do what?"

Drury said, "I have a witness—a new witness—to an old crime."

"And what crime would that be?"

"A murder, Nate." Pouchy as those dark blue eyes of his might have become, they had lost none of their unsettling penetrating power as he fixed them on me like magnets seeking metal. "A murder you and I tried to solve together in 1946."

". . . You have a new witness to the Ragen shooting. Another eyewitness?"

"Not an eyewitness," he said, but nodded and kept nodding as he continued, "a witness who will testify to Yaras admitting being one of the assassins—and that Tubbo Gilbert himself covered up the murder. That the witnesses who recanted did so due to Tubbo using a prostitute to—"

I held up a hand. "I know the story, Bill—each of the witnesses admitted to the same chippie that you told them what to say and who to identify."

"Which was pure utter horseshit," Drury said.

"It was enough to invalidate them as witnesses . . . and get you suspended." I turned to Bas. "You're working for Babb's campaign?"

Bas had intense eyes, as well, and his courtroom orator's voice gave him further weight, as he said, "That's right. But I'm also working for the Chicago Crime Commission. Virgil Peterson and I are old college chums. I share his enthusiasm for cleaning up this—"

"The idea being," I said, "expose Tubbo for the corrupt, mob-connected bastard he is, and your man Babb wins the race for sheriff."

Bas winced. "That's an oversimplification, but . . . yes."

"So why do you need me?"

Drury said, "We have to meet with this witness, tonight—our first face-to-face."

Bas said, "It's strictly been intermediaries and phone calls . . . till tonight."

I shrugged. "So meet with him."

Drury said, "That is where you come in, Nate—you and your Browning. I'm hot right now—never hotter. We need backup. The address is at Orchard and Frontier . . . near the El."

"That's a rough neighborhood. Edge of Little Hell."

Drury raised an eyebrow. "You can see why we need help. This could be a setup."

A guy didn't need Drury's list of blood enemies for this meeting to be dangerous—you could get killed without trying, in that part of town.

"I really want to stay out of this," I said.

Drury seemed almost jittery—I'd never seen him this way. "Nate—please. If this is a trap, I need somebody with your balls, and your savvy. You can handle yourself, if the lead starts flying. . . . Nate, who else can I ask?"

"How about your new friends on Kefauver's advance team? They have their own private investigators working for them—a couple ex-FBI agents, or so I hear."

Drury reddened; he tossed the newspaper he'd been cradling in his lap onto my desk. I opened it up—today's *Chicago Daily News*.

"I thought maybe you'd seen that already," Drury said.

"No," I said softly, as I quickly scanned the story (by-lined Hal Davis), which announced that Drury would soon be meeting with the Kefauver staff to arrange a date for his testimony. It also mentioned his new "bombshell" witness which would require the Crime Committee to "retry the entire Ragen case," and that Drury would be turning over his voluminous notebooks and personal diaries detailing mobster activities.

"Here I am," Drury said, "ready to spring a surprise witness, and it's plastered all over the front page. What are they trying to do to me?"

"This is the kind of advertising you don't need," I admitted, "but, Bill, other than mentioning the witness—Fischetti and company knew all this stuff, anyway."

"That's not the point, Nate." Drury sat forward. "All of the information in that article is a direct paraphrase of a letter my attorney sent to Chief Counsel Rudolph Halley, marked 'confidential.' "

Now I understood why he didn't want to go to the committee for his bodyguard.

"There's a leak on the staff," I said.

Drury nodded. "Ultimately, that doesn't affect my ability to present Kefauver with testimony and information. I haven't lost any of my confidence in Kefauver himself . . ."

"Lee Mortimer has doubts about Halley," I said. "But I just saw Drew Pearson yesterday, and he pooh-poohed that."

"Whether it's Halley or some underling," Drury said, "I can't trust them for this kind of help . . . the kind of help you can give me, Nate."

I thought about it. Then I shifted in my chair and said, "Bill, did you stake out Fischetti yesterday and today? At the Barry Apartments?"

Drury studied me—not sure what I was after. "You told me to clear out."

"Yeah, but I notice you didn't bring my Revere machines back till today. The truth."

He shrugged—he knew better than to con me. "I was there today—I've shut that operation down, but earlier, I was there."

"Did you hear anything or see anything of that girl of Rocco's?"

"The former Miss Chicago?"

"That's right."

"No."

"You didn't hear any talk about her—or hear her come in at the apartment today? Or see her . . . ?"

"No. Nothing interesting involving Rocco, at all today. Of course, I only ever had rooms at Charley's pad bugged—that's the nerve center of the Outfit, you know, Charley's penthouse. Anyway, if I'd rigged Rocco's place,

I'd just have a bunch of train whistles and chugga chugga. . . . Why, Nate?"

"Personal matter. Never mind."

Drury glanced at Bas, then turned his penetrating gaze back on me. "Okay, Nate—I've said my piece, and answered your questions. . . . Now—will you do it? Will you back my ass up? He was your client—Ragen. They murdered him on your watch."

"I can wait while you go rent a flag to wave, if you like."

He shot to his feet and leaned his hands on my desk and looked right at me. "Nate—Ragen was your friend. . . . Peggy's uncle. Jake Guzik and Charley Fischetti and Ricca and Accardo . . . they had him killed. Jim Ragen wasn't an Outfit guy! He ran a wire service . . . he sold information to mobsters, but he wasn't a mobster. And they killed him to take over—to grab what was his and make it theirs. It's an old, old story, Nate."

". . . You just want a bodyguard."

He backed away from my desk, but did not sit. "That's right."

Leaning forward, Bas said, "Mr. Heller, we'd be very grateful. You'd have powerful new friends in Cook County."

I glanced at Bill. "Marvin here does know that I was also Cermak's bodyguard, doesn't he? And Huey Long's? Jim Forrestal, too."

Bas looked somewhat alarmed.

Drury, amused, sat back down, saying, "Don't pay any attention to him, Marvin. That's just his way. . . . Nate? Will you?"

"When is this famous meeting?"

"Tonight—seven o'clock."

"Okay," I said.

Drury grinned and Bas smiled tightly.

The lawyer stood and said to us both, "I'll meet you there a little before seven—I have to make a stop at my office, over on Clark."

I shook his hand and Bas went out, with a spring in his step.

Drury, still seated, said, "Why don't you follow me home, and I'll drop my car off, and you can drive us over."

"All right." I checked my watch. "We have a little time. . . . Want to get a cup of coffee, first?"

"Sure," Drury said, and stood. "You're, uh—already packing, aren't you?"

I patted the nine millimeter in the sling under my left arm. "Oh yeah."

"That's not like you—you hardly ever wear that thing."

"I had a little dustup with Rocco Fischetti the other night. At the Chez Paree."

Drury's eyes tightened. "Over Miss Chicago?"

I nodded.

"Well, Nate . . . all of us have our Achilles' heel. Yours is just a little higher."

In the St. Clair coffee shop, as we both drank coffee, I said, "Tell me about this witness."

"I can't give you the name, Nate."

"Don't you trust me, either?"

"No—I don't have a name."

My eyes almost fell out of my head and into my coffee. "You don't have a name for your surprise witness?"

Drury shrugged, embarrassed; he knew this was half-assed. "I told you—we've been going through intermediaries, and we've been talking on the phone. Our witness is nervous, understandably so."

"How did you find this anonymous witness?"

"That attorney, Kurnitz, has a client at Joliet, who's unhappy with the warden there. Our witness is a friend of the unhappy inmate, who's been our chief intermediary."

"What's the inmate get out of it?"

"Kurnitz is going after the warden for mistreatment of prisoners and misappropriation of funds."

Actually, that rang a bell: I'd seen stories in the press about this unlikely lawsuit.

The dark blue eyes were no longer penetrating; they had turned soft, and even sentimental. "Nate—I appreciate this. I didn't know who else I could turn to."

"It's okay."

"I know you don't want to buck these Outfit guys. I know I'm imposing on our friendship. . . ."

"Shut up, Bill. Drink your coffee."

He flashed a chagrined grin, and drank his coffee.

So I followed Drury home. He was driving a blue Cadillac—a new model—which sure didn't reflect his A-1 earnings; apparently he'd been paid well by journalists Lait & Mortimer and Lester Velie for his insider's views on Chicago's gangsters and the crooked cops who served them.

Funny, if you think about it—Drury despised police officers who took the mob's money . . . yet he'd been making good money off the mob himself, lately.

Traffic on the Outer Drive was heavy—rush hour—and the going was slow; dusk was already darkening into night. When Drury's Caddy and my Olds rolled past the Fischetti penthouse on Sheridan, I wondered if Jackie was sitting up there with Rocco, an engineer's cap on her pretty blonde head, her lovely brown eyes glazed with horse.

Drury lived on Addison, a mile west of Wrigley Field, which we passed on our way. I knew this area well—the United States Marine Hospital, where I'd had outpatient treatment after the war (for my recurring malaria, among other things), was just three blocks northeast of here. And Riverview amusement park, for whom the A-1 provided security consulting, was less than a mile northeast.

This was a typical Chicago middle-class/working-class neighborhood, an amalgam of two- and three-story apartment buildings with an occasional single-family home. Some buildings, particularly on corners, housed apartments on the upper floor or two, with stores at street level. Town Hall Station—where in another life, not so long ago, Bill Drury had been in command—was just ten blocks away.

Drury's block was dominated by the looming twin towers of nearby St. Andrew's Church and, of course, the Ravenswood El tracks and the Addison Street Station. Most Chicago Els went from the North to the South Side, but the Ravenswood went nowhere, really, starting a couple miles further north and west, going down to curl around in the looping fashion that gave the Loop its name, then heading back from whence it came. The El ran along the trestles at the end of Drury's block, curving east along Roscoe Street; the thunder of its trains was omnipresent.

Bill needed to park his car in the garage behind his

house, before joining me in the Olds to drive over to Little
Hell for our mysterious appointment with the Lone Ranger
of surprise witnesses. We rolled past the Drury homestead,
a narrow brick two-story with a spacious, open porch with
brick pillars and white trim—a two-flat, though the entire
building was filled with Drury and his extended family—
and I followed Bill as he turned left on Wolcott.

I pulled over and waited with the motor running as Bill
turned into the narrow alley, off of which was his garage.
He would have to get out and unlock his garage door, climb
back in the car to drive it in. So I wasn't surprised that it
was taking a while, and with a train roaring across the
nearby El—at the other end of that alley you had to drive
under the elevated train tracks—I didn't react immediately,
when I heard the two booms and the sharp crack.

For a couple seconds I tried to make them be part of
the El racket, or maybe backfiring cars . . . a neighborhood
service station was a block away, after all . . . and then I
shut the car off, jumped out, and ran down the alley, filling
my hand with the nine millimeter, trenchcoat flapping, my
fedora damn near flying off.

I slowed to a stop at the garage, off the alley. The over-
head door was swung up and open—Bill had backed the
car in. Nobody was in sight, including Bill, but the Caddy's
windshield had four baseball-sized holes punched in it—in a
neat row. As I approached the vehicle, the smell of cordite
hanging in the air like foul factory smoke, I was careful not
to step on the four shotgun casings on the cement . . .
twelve gauge . . . and the single ejected shell from an automatic handgun . . . seemed to be a .45, but I didn't bend
down for a closer inspection. I was busy looking into the
car, through the passenger window.

Bill was slumped in the front seat, still sitting behind the
wheel, but the top of him draped across the rider's seat.
His well-punctured homburg was beside him, where it had
fallen (or been blown) off. He might have been going for
his glove compartment, where I knew he kept a .38, or
maybe he'd just ducked down seeking safety when the
assassins . . . two were indicated . . . stepped out of the
garage where they must have been hiding, moving right

around in front of his windshield, to start blasting, one with
a shotgun, the other a .45.

But Bill Drury hadn't made it to his revolver, or to
safety—riddled with slugs as he was, blood streaming from
a dozen nasty wounds in his face, chest, arms, and the
reaching hand, the seat already soaked with glistening crim-
son. His eyes were wide and empty, but the surprise and
fear were frozen on his pellet-ravaged face.

Probably the decent thing to do would have been to go
up to the house and break the tragic news to his wife, so
she could be spared discovering the body.

But in the few seconds I'd taken in the murder scene,
I'd already decided to try to catch the sons of bitches, before they made their getaway from the neighborhood,
and—nine millimeter tight in my fist—I ran back out of the
alley, to where I'd left the Olds on Wolcott.

It's what Bill would have done.

For me.

10

Since no getaway car was in sight down the alley, I figured the shooters had jumped a backyard fence to cut over to either Addison or Eddy, where their vehicle would be parked, possibly with a wheelman waiting.

As I backed out into Wolcott—catching a break: no cars in either lane—I craned around looking left and right, checking both streets and saw a maroon coupe, a Ford, go flying east on Eddy, the driver hunkered forward, like he was in a goddamn stockcar race.

That was good enough for me.

I swung the Olds around and took pursuit—twilight had faded fully into nighttime—but when I turned onto Eddy, the maroon coupe was not in sight. That was no surprise—after going under the El, Eddy dead-ended just half a block off Wolcott. I could see taillights glowing like red eyes in the darkness, about a block down Ravenswood, a deserted-looking street to my left, and that had to be the coupe, although I'd have to get closer to find out for sure.

I took the left onto Ravenswood, and followed the taillights, warehouses and factory lofts to one side of me, an embankment on the other. The maroon coupe—if that was the coupe up ahead—had slowed down, and I stayed back; unless I wanted a full-blown chase, I needed not to attract

their suspicion, which on this desolate stretch wasn't easy.
I cut my headlamps.

Three blocks down Ravenswood, the vehicle turned right
on Roscoe, as if tracing the path of the El tracks; in doing
so, the coupe revealed itself definitely as the maroon Ford,
gliding under a streetlight. The driver wasn't sitting forward
now, and the car was moving along at a legal twenty-five
miles per hour. No sign that they'd spotted me. . . .

Soon the coupe had turned right onto Lincoln Avenue,
and we were no longer alone, or in the dark—this was a
busy shopping district, rich with German bakeries and small
shops of every stripe, dominated by a huge Goldblatt's department store, the sidewalks crowded, the streets clogged
with traffic. I put the lights back on, though I hardly needed
them. This wide busy thoroughfare allowed me to put several
cars between my Olds and the maroon coupe—they still
hadn't made me, it appeared—but when we approached the
Lincoln/Belmont/Ashland intersection, I got worried.

This was one of Chicago's patented crazy three-way in-
tersections, with Lincoln cutting diagonally across Ashland
and Belmont, the kind of crossing that can give a tourist
an instant nervous breakdown . . . and even a veteran Chicago driver the shakes. . . .

The coupe did not take the sharp left onto Belmont, but
the easier, saner one onto Ashland. That made my life easier, too, if not saner—this was a four-lane boulevard, sharing space with the streetcar line, and gave me more
maneuvering room. I was now having no trouble main-
taining a tailing distance of almost a block, keeping cars
between us. Most of the time I was driving one-handed, as
I had never let loose of the nine millimeter in my fist; and
no other drivers had noticed—on those occasions I used
both hands on the wheel—that I was juggling a Browning
automatic.

My hope was that the assassins were on their way to
report in to their boss; but even if they weren't, following
them to a destination, any destination, would be better than
turning this into a Wild West guns-blazing car chase. Somewhere along Ashland, I took time to put down my Browning for a moment and fish a pack of Camels out of my

glove box, a pack Lou Sapperstein had left behind last week; matches were conveniently tucked in the cellophane and I lit up, sucking the smoke into my lungs greedily. The tobacco craving was rare, but when it came, it really came.

The drive down Ashland took us up onto the overpass across the north branch of the Chicago River. For a moment I thought the maroon coupe's driver had finally made me, when he took a quick left onto Courtland; but I had a feeling it was just a turn he almost missed, and—not wanting to lose him—violated proper surveillance technique and, rather than continuing on straight through the intersection and doubling back, took the Courtland left, myself.

I'd been expecting them to hit Armitage, another busy commercial street, but then I saw the coupe take a right, sliding onto Kingsbury, a dreary rutted road cutting through a canyon of factories, with a railroad track running down the center, to feed the concrete tongues of loading docks on either side. This solitary stretch was all but uninhabited—save, presumably, for the odd night watchman— and the streetlamps were minimal, throwing occasional pools of light into the shadow-soaked world.

Had they spotted me? Were they leading me to a lonely section where they could deal with me, unseen? I had cut my headlights again, as soon as the coupe turned down this tunnel-like passage. I dropped back, a block and a half; they weren't slowing, or speeding—just proceeding at a legal twenty-five to wherever the hell they were going.

It then occurred to me that we were heading—or at least could be heading—to where Drury and that lawyer Bas were supposed to be meeting the surprise witness, in . . . I checked my watch . . . fifteen minutes. Was Bas the boss to whom the hitmen were reporting? Had the lawyer suckered, and betrayed, Drury, with his unlikely story of a witness without a name?

At North Avenue, the coupe turned left; I followed, and almost missed noticing that—two blocks down—they'd taken a fast right onto Orchard. I made a last second turn and got honked at by a startled, pissed-off driver—I'd forgotten my headlamps were off.

But I left the lights off, despite the irate motorist's bleat, because traffic was sporadic now, as I crawled behind the coupe into the outer circles of Hell. From where we were, and southward, lay Little Hell, the roughest slum of the Near Northside; this had been a Sicilian area, not so long ago—Little Sicily, they'd called it, proud home of Hell's Corner, the location of more gangland slayings than any other spot in the city.

Though the fringe blocks we were creeping through were still home to a few handfuls of Sicilians, and white faces were not completely unknown in these parts, the area was eighty percent colored, now. At the south end of this nasty neighborhood was some new public housing—the Frances Cabrini Homes, several blocks of tidy row houses—intended for the colored residents of the area, but filled with Sicilians and other whites who moved into the projects, bequeathing to the blacks the truly decrepit slum dwellings of Little Hell—a mix of dilapidated paint-peeling frame houses and crumbling brick tenements, dating back to the Chicago fire.

Little Hell was an apt phrase, except perhaps the "Little" part. These tenement apartments were usually shared by two families, and most buildings were without functioning bathrooms or running water. Sections of the vaulted sidewalks—often used to store coal—were cracked and unsafe, fissures in the cement that might have been the aftermath of an earthquake. Rats the size of small dogs ran these streets and sidewalks as if they owned them—and I wasn't about to argue with them.

It was five till seven when the maroon coupe pulled over and parked near the corner of Orchard and Scott. I continued on, pulling over half a block down. I sat and smoked and watched in my sideview mirror as two men got out of the front seat of the coupe, leaving it running. Despite that, no driver could be spotted behind the wheel: seemed only two men had been in that coupe after all; hadn't been a wheelman waiting for them. That might explain why their getaway had been slowed enough for me to catch sight of their escape from Drury's neighborhood. Nine millimeter in my fist, cigarette in my mouth, I turned in my seat and looked out the back window.

From across the street from where the maroon coupe was parked, where he'd been sitting in his own parked car, a six-foot figure in a dark gray suit under an open raincoat stepped out and crossed to join the two men on the corner, under a streetlamp, one of the few around here that was working.

They were talking—smiles all around, a friendly confab. All three men were an anomaly in this neighborhood: well-dressed white men, lawyer Bas and the two assassins, neither of whom (at this distance, anyway) looked familiar to me. The man who'd been driving the maroon coupe—small, round-faced, mustached—wore a light gray suit, no topcoat, and a darker gray fedora; his lanky partner, also mustached, wore a dark blue topcoat and a lighter blue fedora.

So that fucking Bas *was* their boss—he'd set Drury up for these natty assassins. But why was the lawyer meeting them here, where the meeting with the (I now assumed) imaginary witness was to have taken place? He did represent some taverns and clubs in this part of town, but still. . . .

I was just realizing, with a shudder, the faultiness of my original thinking, and reaching for the door handle, thinking that Bas might be innocent, and in danger, when the taller mustached assassin swung something out from under that dark blue topcoat—a shotgun.

Even from half a block away, I could see Bas's wide-eyed shock, and he turned to flee down the sidewalk, away from them (and me) when the guy opened up—shotgun all right . . . no doubt the same one that had nailed Drury—and the night exploded. Bas seemed to pause in midair before he pitched face-forward to the cement, his splattered back a modern art study in charcoal and red, worthy of Charley's penthouse wall.

I was long since out of the car, and running down the street, hat flying off, cigarette trailing sparks into the night, gun tight in my fist, when the guy in the topcoat got in behind the wheel of the parked, motor-running coupe—he'd traded jobs with his partner, who had trotted down to where Bas had belly-flopped onto the cracked cement. The .45 in the round-faced assassin's hand blasted down at the supine attorney, once, twice, blossoming orange in the darkness.

The round-faced guy ran back to the coupe, climbed in on the rider's side, and they took off, heading straight at me, though neither had noticed me yet; the glare of their headlights made me squint, but I'd anticipated it, and I saw them, both of their mustached faces (the tall one had a harelip scar), and they saw me too—their expressions as saucer-eyed as Bas's—as I pointed the nine millimeter at their oncoming windshield and fired.

The shot rang through Little Hell, echoing, and the bullet spiderwebbed the windshield, but I didn't think I'd hit either one of them, goddamnit, and I dove and rolled as the driver swerved, first to try to run me down, second to take a right that would take them toward and under the El tracks, toward Ogden Avenue.

I was barely back on my feet, when they were gone, out of my view, and—gun still in hand—I ran down to the fallen Bas, knowing it was hopeless, but checking him out, anyway.

Kneeling down to take a closer look, I figured the shotgun blast in his back had probably killed him; but the coup de grace pair of .45 shots in his head made taking his pulse a worthless procedure. I did it anyway.

Now that the shooting had stopped, people were coming out of their houses and tenements, colored faces filling doorways and windows, eyes wider than Willie Best's and shouts of "Call the police," and "Buncha white men shootin' at each other," and such like, from either side of the street, surrounding me, an accusatory gospel choir singing skyward in the night.

Before the cops or Jesus responded, I ran back to my car and got out of there, hoping to hell we all looked alike to them.

The same red-uniformed doorman as on my previous visit to the Barry Apartments—paunchy, fiftyish George with the drink-splotched face—was on duty; and he remembered me . . . and my name.

"Oh yes, Mr. Lincoln," he said, accepting another of my green business cards. "How can I help you tonight?"

"I just want to go up and see my friend Joey Fischetti."

George shook his head. "I'm not sure any of the Fish family is in, this evening. I came on at four, and the other guy said they've all cleared out."

"Yeah? Vacation?"

"Not sure. They winter in Florida, y'know, but I never saw 'em go down this early, before. You could ask that girl who lives with Rocco. She's back."

The corner of my left eye twitched. "Is she?"

"If you can get past Pete, she is," he said, with a shrug.

"Pete?"

George nodded toward the lobby. "The elevator operator. He's sort of the guardian at the gate. I work for the Barry Apartments; but Pete works for the Fischettis."

"I appreciate the information, George."

"Any time, Mr. Lincoln."

I had a clear head and I had that cool, detached limbo state of mind that I'd experienced in combat on the Island—Guadalcanal, that is. A distancing that keeps men under fire from going mad.

I clopped across the marble floor of the narrow, mirrored, fern-flung lobby. Over my arm the London Fog was draped, which hid the nine millimeter in my fist; I wasn't wearing a hat—it was somewhere in Little Hell, having blown off my head when I was running down the street, trying to help Bas, fucking up yet another bodyguard assignment.

Nice thing about bodyguard work is, the clients who survive will write letters of reference; and the dead ones never complain.

Stepping on the elevator, I said, "Ten, please."

This was the same blue-uniformed, blue-five-o'clock-shadowed thug as before—with the same bulge under his left arm. He glanced at me—maybe he recognized me, maybe he didn't—but he just did as I asked him. After all, I wasn't going up to the penthouse.

When the doors slid shut, I pretended to drop my London Fog, and as I was coming up, I slapped the bastard along the side of his head with the Browning barrel. He stumbled into the side wall of the elevator, his ear bleeding, his eyes doing a slot-machine roll; I reached into his coat, withdrew Pete's .38 revolver from its holster, and stuck it in my waistband.

He lurched at me, grabbing at me like I was a ladder he was trying to climb, and I slapped his other ear with the Browning; now he went down on his knees, like he was praying, or preparing to blow me—neither image appealed to me, so I pushed him all the way to the floor with my left foot, and—now that he was unconscious, or pretending to be—tied his hands behind him with my necktie.

The door opened on ten and, when nobody got on or off, the doors closed again, and I drove myself up to the seventeenth floor. Pete had come groggily around; he was on his side, looking up at me—he seemed puzzled and like maybe his feelings were a little hurt.

"What did *I* do?"

"Nothing," I said. "Which is what you're going to keep doing. You got a passkey?"

"Fuck you!"

That meant he did. I searched him and found it in a shallow slanty pocket of his blue uniform's jacket.

"Are they here?" I asked. "The three Fish brothers?"

"Fuck you," he said, with no enthusiasm.

That meant they probably weren't—that George the doorman had been right . . . goddamnit. At that moment, fresh from the murders of my two clients, I would have loved to return the favor to Rocky and Charley— slowly. . . . Rocky because he was a sadistic son of a bitch, and Charley because he was the brains, and undoubtedly had ordered these hits.

I parked the elevator, flicking the OUT OF SERVICE switch, stepped past Pete, who was on his side, scowling at me, and got off at the entryway, where the golden Egyptian settee and sunburst clock awaited. Using the passkey, I went in, nine millimeter still an extra appendage growing out of my fist—I didn't think the Fischettis were here, but I might be wrong. My track record tonight wasn't that great, after all.

Or some other watchdog or two might be present, more competent than the McCarthy-jowled elevator operator.

But I was barely inside when I heard music, coming from the living room.

Someone was playing the piano—"They Say It's Wonderful," Irving Berlin, *Annie Get Your Gun*—and someone was singing, a clear, sweet soprano . . . exquisitely feminine, and not Ethel Merman.

Jackie Payne was sitting at the grand piano in the spacious living room, near the terrace-style balcony, the curtains open, revealing the sky with its stars and the moon with its glow that was turning the endless lake shimmering silver. Accompanying herself (she played fairly well), Jackie sang with delicacy and feeling, and she looked fine—no black eyes, just those lovely big brown ones; she wore a white short-sleeve blouse and sky-blue pedal pushers, her feet bare, toenails painted blood red.

Nine millimeter still in hand, I began to clap; the first of the claps—echoing off the slate floor—made her jump, and stop in midnote, hands frozen over the keys.

"Please," I said, the gun lowered, "don't stop on my account. You sound fine."

She just sat there and looked at me, her face as expressionless as a Kewpie doll; then her lip began to tremble and tears rolled down her face. No sound of sobbing, though.

I sighed, walked over, sat next to her on the piano bench, gun in my lap, in my hand, limply now.

"Why?" I asked her.

"I'm not going with you, Nate."

"Why?"

"I don't deserve you. You were wonderful, you believe in me, but I'm not ready to kick."

"Why?"

"I need it—I need the stuff. I can't get through the day without it."

"Why?"

"Rocco called—he was crying. I know . . . I know you can't believe that, Nate. But he does have a good heart, a soft side. He said he missed me, he couldn't live without me, and he would never harm me again. He said, if ever he touched so much as a hair on my head, I could leave him forever, and he'd never bother me again. I had to come back to him."

"Why?"

"He needed me."

"Why?"

"I love him."

"Why?"

"He's good to me. Look at this place. Look around you. And now he's promised to let me have my career—starting at the Chez, then, eventually, opening for acts in Vegas. Joey owns part of a recording label, you know. And . . . I can't do that, any of that, without my . . . without help, you know—medicinal help."

"Why?"

"Because I'm just not strong enough without it. Maybe . . . maybe someday I can shake it. But not now."

"Why?"

"Stop it! Stop it! Stop it!"

She covered her face with her hands and she wept. I let her do that for a while.

Then I asked her, "Where are they?"

Her voice seemed tiny; so did she. "Gone. They've let all but a skeleton staff go. Rocco put me in charge of the apartment here. He didn't want to take me with him."

"Why?"

The brown eyes, red from tears, flashed at me. "Are you going to start that again? He said he and his brother Charley—I think Joey is in Florida, at his house there—but Rocky and Charley are sort of . . . on the run. Incommunicado, until this thing, this Kefauver thing, blows over."

"And Rocky left you here? Knowing if you changed your mind—if I talked sense to you and you changed your mind—you could be a witness against them?"

She shook her head, shrugged. "What could I testify about?"

"You could tell them, for example, just how many times Tubbo Gilbert came calling in recent months."

"No, I couldn't."

"You couldn't? Two men died tonight, Jackie—I saw it. But I couldn't stop it."

She frowned and looked at the piano keys. "Oh, Nate . . . don't. I don't want to hear this. . . ."

"Bill Drury, a cop—maybe you read about him in the papers. He saved my life once. He was an honest cop—in Chicago, can you buy that? He and an attorney named Bas . . . they both have wives who probably love them, and families to support . . . were trying to get the goods on Charley and Tubbo. And they were murdered, just about an hour ago—Bill in his own garage, that attorney on a public street. Executed. Cattle at the stockyards die with more dignity."

She swallowed, looked up, stared right at me. "Nate, I couldn't testify against Rocky, and I don't know anything about Charley."

"You couldn't testify against Rocky? Listen, if they subpoena you, and you're under oath—"

"Nate! You don't understand. Listen to me: I can't testify against Rocky. A wife can't testify against her own husband."

I just looked at her. Finally I said, almost spitting at her, "What?"

"We were married this afternoon, at City Hall. Rocky pulled some strings, to get past the waiting period. He has connections."

"No kidding."

She was looking at the keys again. "I saw him off at O'Hare. Our honeymoon will have to wait."

"Where are you and Rocky and your hypodermic planning to go?"

The brown eyes fixed themselves on me—they were soft, even loving; she touched my hand—the one that didn't have a gun in it.

"Nate . . . I'll always love you, you'll always occupy a special place inside of me. Our few days together—the things you did for me, and tried to do for me—I'll never forget them. I'll cherish that memory—like a flower pressed into a book."

"Swell. I get the honeymoon, but Rocky gets the bride."

"Please, Nate. . . ."

I sat there, wondering if I should search the penthouse.

I couldn't think of a reason to; and the brothers were long gone. Probably I needed to get out of there—the cops would be coming to talk to the Fischettis, as soon as the Drury and Bas murders went past the crime scene stage. Of course, Tubbo Gilbert would probably be in charge of the investigation.

"Wait here," I said, standing.

"What are you . . . ?"

"You're going to hear some noise. Don't worry about it. Just stay put. Okay?"

"Why?"

I grinned at her. "You don't get to ask that question, baby. Just sit tight and shut up."

Five minutes later, breathing hard, I came back in the living room—my arms ached. Jackie had a startled-deer look—she had to have heard the racket I made; but she had stayed put.

"What on earth—Nate, what did you do?"

"I threw each and every one of them against the wall," I said. "I broke every goddamn precious fucking train."

Then I went over and grabbed her by the shoulders and kissed her on the mouth.

And got the hell out of there.

11

St. Andrew's Church—a stone's throw from the Drury home, just beyond the rumbling El—was more than just the biggest cathedral on the Northside: it was a tribute to the fund-raising savvy of Bishop Bernard J. Sheil. The sprawling complex of Catholic activity, including a school and a gym, took up three of the four corners of the Addison/Paulina intersection, and the formidable brick cathedral spanned a city block, with twin bell towers, a massive round stained-glass window between them, and a trio of solemn wall-sconce-enshrined concrete statues, one of them depicting St. Andrew (don't ask me which or who the other two were—it was my mother who was the Catholic).

The vast ornate sanctuary, with its high vaulted plastered ceilings, was filled almost to capacity for the funeral of William Drury, the fallen Watchdog of the Loop . . . though noticeably absent were the high-ranking city and county officials, who—in the days since Bill's murder—had been badmouthing the deceased in the press.

Bishop Sheil himself was sending Bill off, with a requiem high mass, and a dramatic sermon worthy of the fat-cat Catholic industrialists and politicos who had made this cavern of Christianity possible. Of course, Catholics do love a good martyr, even a poor one.

"Bill Drury was a man who gave his life for things he thought were right and just," the prelate said. "Now we have men elected to a high public office who have thrown innuendos at this hero, and sullied his name, and attempted to tarnish his character."

This didn't bode well for Captain Dan "Tubbo" Gilbert and his boss, State's Attorney John S. Boyle, who were the unnamed public officials the powerful priest was referring to. And the reporters, scattered amidst the mourners in the pews, were scribbling down every word.

"I am prevented by the canons and ethics of my office from saying things burning now within my heart and body," the bishop said from his pulpit. "I will say them on another, not so sacred occasion in the near future."

Another service, in a modest chapel at Erie and Wabash, was also under way this morning: Marvin J. Bas was being laid to rest, before a smaller but no less indignant group of mourners.

Bas, like Bill, had been the object of Tubbo and the State's Attorney's afflictions, in the days since the twin murders. To reporters, Boyle asked the tactless rhetorical question: "Who says Bill Drury was a brave, heroic crime-fighter? We don't know how he made his living, the last two years. He had six hundred dollars in his pants when he was shot—in his new Cadillac!"

As for Bas, Tubbo's boss proclaimed that the attorney "worked the wrong side of the fence. Bas was always getting a habeas corpus for persons we arrested. And he represented a lot of honky-tonks and hoodlums."

According to Boyle, "good, law-abiding citizens" had no fear of being "shot down on Chicago's streets—no one tending to his own honest business is in any danger in Chicago."

Which meant, of course, that Drury and Bas were not good, law-abiding citizens tending to their own honest business.

Tubbo—who abandoned his leave of absence to take command of the Drury and Bas investigations—proclaimed that the slayings were unrelated, though he offered no theory on the murder of either man. And a statement from

Gilbert's campaign manager made it clear that "we can see no connection between these slayings and the candidacy of Captain Gilbert."

No connection, that is, other than Drury and Bas working together to gather evidence against Tubbo to hand over to his opponent in the sheriff's race.

Tubbo's investigation consisted of issuing an "arrest on sight" order for "every hoodlum in town"; and making an accusation to the press that, while on the force, Drury had "shaken down" bookies. Then, the day after the killings, without a warrant, Tubbo raided murder victim Bas's office, seizing the attorney's papers and records.

John E. Babb, Tubbo's opponent for sheriff—who was among the mourners at Drury's funeral—told the press, "It's a new twist in law enforcement that the officers in charge are devoting more time to maligning the murder victims than to catching their murderers."

And the widows of the two men stuck up gamely for their husbands, Mrs. Bas decrying Tubbo's gestapo tactics in confiscating his private papers, while Mrs. Drury said, "I'll sue any public official—State's Attorney Boyle and Captain Gilbert included—who makes dirty statements about my husband."

Petite, pretty Annabel Drury—who'd been married to Bill for twenty-one years—had had a rough time of it from the start. And I'd made that inevitable, when I'd bolted the crime scene to pursue the assassins, leaving Mrs. Drury the most likely person to make the ghastly discovery.

Around six-thirty that evening, she'd heard three loud reports, which she took to be cars backfiring at the nearby neighborhood service station. She and Bill lived on the second floor, and a kitchen window looked out on the garage.

"I had a strange feeling about those noises, though," she'd told me last night, at the funeral home. Her dark silver-streaked hair in a fashionable bob, she wore a black suit and white gloves as we sat, holding hands. "I kept thinking about those noises. . . . They seemed . . . different. But when I looked out the window, I could see down below, and the garage lights weren't on—Bill always turned the lights on when he came home."

I knew she wanted to talk—had to talk—so I let her; she couldn't know how goddamn lousy she was making me feel, for my role in making her ordeal even harder.

"I knew Bill said he had an appointment, at seven, but he also said he'd stop at home, and grab a bite to eat if there was time. I was preparing a little something in the kitchen, just a sandwich he could take with him. . . . Then when it was almost seven, I thought—maybe he'd gone on to that appointment. . . . Still, something seemed wrong, and finally I got a little flashlight and went out to the garage."

She had found Bill there, sitting in the Caddy, covered in blood, torn by bullets, and her scream had summoned Bill's seventy-six-year-old mother, and several other family members—all of whom were subjected to that terrible scene.

"I'm sorry," I said.

"You have nothing to be sorry about, Nate."

Well. . . .

She looked at me with weary, dazed eyes. "Bill thought the world of you. But I want you to know—I don't expect you to do anything about this."

"Annabel—"

"Please understand—I anticipated this. I feared it for a long, long time. But Bill had absolutely no fear. I never pried into his business affairs. That's why we had a happy married life. I let him tell me only as much as he wanted to."

The trimly attractive, fortyish widow was calm, tearless—a mix of shock and resignation . . . and probably a weird sense of relief. In a way, a long personal siege of terror had finally ended.

"Annabel—Bill kept diaries, notebooks."

"I know."

"Do you have them?"

"No. He kept them in a desk in his den—they filled a whole drawer. I have no idea what was in them, and he took them with him on the day . . . on that last day."

"You don't know where they are, where he took them—who might have them?"

"No. No idea." She looked at me, searchingly. "Nate—you're not going to get involved, are you?"

"I am involved. Why, should we leave this to Tubbo Gilbert and the police department?"

A tiny bitter smile etched itself in one corner of her mouth. "They won't find his killers. They won't even look. But, Nate—how can you even know where to start? Bill was a one-man crusade, and he made a lot of enemies in his twenty-six years on the force."

Annabel didn't know I'd been at the scene of her husband's death, not to mention the shooting of Bas on that desolate street, half an hour later. No one but me did, except those two assassins . . . although since I hadn't recognized them, perhaps they didn't know me from Adam, either.

I had told no one, certainly not Tubbo when he came around to the office to question me the day after the shootings, not even Lou Sapperstein and certainly not anyone connected to the Kefauver staff. A few colored witnesses in Little Hell had seen a white man leaving the scene, but no one reported my firing at the maroon coupe, and no one contributed a description of my Olds, much less its license number. My fedora had been found, giving the crack sleuths of the Chicago P.D. and the State's Attorney's office my hat size to go on.

I was the little man who wasn't there—a role at which I'd become adept. But who the hell were those mustached assassins? They had been young—mid- to late twenties, well dressed—but nonetheless cold-blooded pros who knew their way around firearms and were unperturbed about the notion of pulling off back-to-back hits. Out of town talent, almost certainly—hired by Charley Fischetti, who had skipped in anticipation of the heat the two murders would stir up.

The day after the news got around, just about every other major hoodlum in town had skipped, as well. In the papers the morning after the murders, Kefauver—in Kansas City holding hearings—was quoted as saying the Drury and Bas hits "showed the savagery of Chicago gangland. There is no doubt that the slaying of our key witness, former police lieutenant William Drury, is a brutal attempt to thwart our investigation."

Kefauver—who rejected Tubbo's claim that the Drury and Bas murders were "unrelated"—retaliated by turning over more than a dozen subpoenas to the U.S. Marshal's office in Chicago. But the small army of servers discovered that the mansions and penthouse apartments of such Outfit luminaries as Jake Guzik, Tony Accardo, Paul Ricca, and (of course) the Fischetti brothers contained only servants and the occasional wife.

Even the relatively modest yellow-brick bungalow of Sam "Mooney" Giancana, in Oak Park—well, it did take up a corner lot and had a lavishly landscaped lawn—had been bereft of Sicilians. With the exception of a handful who had already been served, the local mobsters had flown the coop.

After the funeral, out in front of the massive cathedral, the fall breeze had teeth that made me turn up the collars of my London Fog. Lee Mortimer—in a charcoal suit and silk light blue tie, under a lighter gray topcoat with a black fur collar (a coat that cost no more than a good used Buick)—had no babe on his arm this time, as he picked his way through the milling crowd and planted himself in front of me, like an unwanted tree. Make that shrub.

"My condolences, Nate," he said. He produced a deck of Chesterfields and offered me one—I declined—and he lit up . . . no cigarette holder, this time. The smoke curling out his mouth and nostrils seemed about the color of his grayish complexion, while his hair was more a silver gray. He looked like he hadn't seen the outside of a nightclub since 1934.

I hadn't replied to his expression of sympathy, which seemed about as sincere as a Fuller Brush salesman's smile.

"I mean," he said, with a lift of his shoulders, "I know Bill was your friend. You went way back, right?"

"Right."

He raised an eyebrow, cocked his head. "I tried to call your office, last week, and you weren't available. We were going to talk, remember? Maybe do some business? Hope you're not ducking me."

"Why, do you bruise easily, Lee?"

"Not really." He blew a smoke ring, which the wind caught and obliterated. "I have a tough enough hide—but you're a public figure, these days, with your Hollywood clientele. You don't want to alienate a nationally syndicated columnist, do you?"

I started walking toward the parking lot, edging through the crowd, and Mortimer tagged along. I said, "Actually, Lee, I looked into that Halley matter for you—the chief counsel's so-called Hollywood connections? A great big pound of air."

The hard, tiny eyes slitted and he shook his head, as we moved through the mourners. "Then you didn't look into it hard enough—there's a major leak on the Crime Committee, and I swear that clown Halley is it. . . . You going out to the cemetery?"

"Yeah."

"I'm gonna pass. But we can still do business, you know."

"Yeah?"

He put a hand on my shoulder and I stopped to look at him. His grin was wide and ghastly, like a skull's—this was a man who smiled only when he was wheedling or threatening.

Mortimer whispered: "Bill Drury has ceased to be a source for me—as you may have noticed. I need a new one. His murder gives you the perfect 'in' with the Crime Committee. . . . Halley's turned Estes against me, and—"

I removed his hand as if it were a bug that had settled on my shoulder. "You really think this funeral's a good place to recruit Bill Drury's replacement?"

The hearse was gliding by, cars falling in line for the procession to Mt. Carmel cemetery.

"I mean no offense to the dead," Mortimer said, "but you're smarter than my previous source. You know what his motto was?"

Actually, I did.

But Mortimer said it: " 'A coward dies a thousand deaths, a brave man only one.' A man who sees himself as a hero is a fool, Nate. You, on the other hand, are one tough, shrewd, manipulative son of a bitch."

"Stop. I'll blush."

"In short, you could have been a newspaperman." And he gave me that ghastly smile again. "Tah tah." And he pitched his cigarette, trailing sparks into the street, and moved through the thinning crowd to go hail a taxi.

I slipped away, heading toward the parking lot. Lou Sapperstein—brown topcoat over a dark suit, his bald head hatless—was waiting at my Olds, leaning against a fender, having a smoke. He and I had been ushers; the pallbearers had been relatives but for ex-captain Tim O'Conner, Bill's fellow railroaded-off-the-force police pal. I knew O'Conner had taken it hard—he'd been crying, and more than a little drunk, at the funeral home last night.

I had avoided him—I'm half-Irish, and that was enough to be embarrassed by Irish drunks who felt famously sorry for themselves.

At the immaculately landscaped cemetery, after the graveside service—which was also overseen by the bishop, and well attended—I was walking with Lou along a graveled drive, heading back to my car when O'Conner came striding up alongside me.

"Got a minute, Nate?" the lanky ex-cop asked. With his black suit and tie under a black raincoat, O'Conner might have been the undertaker, not just a pallbearer; he looked like hell—his blue eyes bloodshot, his pockmarked face fish-belly pale, but for a drink-reddened nose.

Somehow I kept the sigh out of my voice. "Sure, Tim."

His sandy blond hair riffling like thin wheat in the bitter breeze, the wind turning his black tie into a whip, O'Conner turned to Sapperstein, and, a little embarrassed, said, "If you'll excuse us, Lou—"

Since Lou had also been a cop, and a friend of Drury's, as well as a member of our poker-playing cadre, this seemed a vaguely insulting exclusion; but Sapperstein just shrugged and nodded and walked over by an oak tree, leaning against it, while O'Conner led me off between rows of headstones with their elaborate carvings and statuary.

"I know this shouldn't be a surprise," O'Conner said, hands dug in his raincoat pockets, his eyes hollow, "but somehow I thought Bill was . . . above anything anybody could do to him."

"Nobody's above a shotgun, Tim."

He was shaking his head, staring at the earth, across which a few stray leaves were dancing. "I . . . this is fucking hard, Nate. Ever since I lost Janet . . ."

"She didn't die, Tim. You fucked around on her, and she divorced you and took the kids."

Now he looked right at me—his eyes tight with surprise. "Are you really this hard?"

"I see in the papers where you barely knew Bill."

"Oh. That."

O'Conner had been quoted as saying he'd had no business association with Drury in recent months—that in particular he hadn't been part of his late friend's journalistic endeavors. His comments had seemed designed to keep the heat off him with the Outfit.

Embarrassed, looking at the ground again, he said, "That was all true—I just didn't mention that Bill and I had been working together, cooperating with Kefauver's staff. I mean—that was confidential stuff."

"Really? And are you still planning to spend your spare time, Tim, pouring Cokes and coffee for the Crime Committee?"

Chin up, now. "I'm still working for Kurnitz, and he's still working with Robinson and Halley, yeah. I was hoping you'd come aboard."

I laughed, once. "You think that's the way to make this thing right?"

"You know there's no way to make this right. Bill's gone forever . . . and we let him down."

"Bullshit. Bill was a grown-up. He knew the risks. He relished them."

He was shaking his head; he looked like he was going to start crying again. "I just don't want him to have died for nothing. I'm going to stick with the committee and see if I can help them bring these bastards down."

"You really believe that? That Fischetti and Tubbo Gilbert and Ricca and the rest, that some out-of-town senators trying to make themselves look good politically can change the way life's always been in Chicago?"

The wind shook the trees around us; the brittle brown leaves might have been laughing.

His chin was trembling as he withdrew a hand to point a finger at me, like a gun. "I'll tell you this—if Tubbo was involved, he shot himself in his foot, this time. Halley says Kefauver is furious about these killings. Apparently, the senator says, to hell with waiting till after the election for the hearings."

Maybe Kefauver's outrage in the press wasn't all talk.

But I wasn't convinced. "I'm supposed to believe Kefauver's not going to wait a little over a month, to protect the local Democratic machine? That he'll screw over the same people he'll have to turn to, if he runs for president?"

"It'll be in the papers, any day now. Kefauver takes these murders as a personal attack on him and his committee, and he's upping the ante."

"How in hell?"

"The hearings have been moved up to October fifth."

I frowned in disbelief. "Next week?"

"Next week. Right across the street from your office, in the Federal Building, Nate. And the senator's got another couple dozen subpoenas ready to go. Not just the gangsters, this time—politicians, race wire operators, liquor dealers, jukebox distributors, even the wives of the big boys."

"Why bother with the wives? They can't testify against their husbands."

O'Conner shrugged. "Halley says they can. Rules are different with congressional hearings than the usual courtroom procedure."

If that was true, where did that leave the former Jackie Payne?

"Come work with us," O'Conner said.

"No."

He found a sneer for me. "Is that it, then? Bill's in the ground, and you're just going to walk away?"

"Did I say that?"

Now the leaves seemed to be whispering, but I couldn't make out what they wanted with me. . . .

"Nate . . . you're not thinking of handling this . . . some other way. Your *own* way . . . ?"

"I don't remember saying that, either."

The bloodshot blue eyes seemed steady, suddenly—looking at me with a fresh focus. "You have a reputation for . . . sometimes people who have problems with you have been known to disappear."

"Is that right?"

Car engines were starting here and there; the mourners leaving Bill Drury behind—they were just visiting, after all; he lived here.

O'Conner leaned close to me; surprisingly, he didn't have liquor on his breath. "Listen—listen to me carefully, Nate. I would do anything to get even for Bill. *Anything.*"

"Yeah?"

Those blue eyes were hard as marbles, now. "Are you listening? Do you hear me?"

"I'm listening. I hear you."

"Promise me—if you do decide to try something . . . I don't give a shit how crazy . . . you call me. And I'm there."

"Be careful, Tim—"

"I know what I'm saying. I know what I'm offering. Don't try to do this alone."

"Are you sure?"

That pale face was deadpan, now—the softness of self-pity replaced by something hard and cold and resolute. "Dead fucking sure," he said.

"I'll keep that in mind."

I rejoined Lou, who was starting a new cigarette.

"What did he want?" Lou asked, exhaling a wreath of smoke.

"Absolution," I said, as we headed back down the graveled road.

Lou smirked. "Boy, did he come to the wrong guy."

12

The phone call seemed more than a little mysterious. I didn't take it myself—it came in during the morning, when Lou and I were at the Drury funeral. When I drifted in after lunch, Gladys gave me the cryptic message: "Silver Palm, Bas client, come alone, 3 P.M."

I *almost* went alone—the nine millimeter in the shoulder sling came along. The Silver Palm sounded like an obscure military medal; but it was a Northside strip club, a somewhat notorious one, and since the late Marvin Bas had been a Forty-second Ward politician, an attorney whose clients included a number of tavern and nightclub owners, that part of the message made a sort of sense. After all, Bas—despite his efforts to expose the incredibly corrupt Tubbo Gilbert—had been a protégé of flamboyant alderman Paddy Bauler, whose well-known slogan was "Chicago ain't ready for reform!"

What disturbed me was that someone was connecting me to Bas—my former affiliation with Drury was well known; but Bas had only hired me a few hours before he was killed . . . a new record among A-1 clients.

I found a parking place for the Olds a block and a half away, and walked to the Silver Palm, which nestled under the El on Wilson Avenue near Broadway. My trenchcoat collars were up again—it was cold and drizzling, sending the streetwalkers and dope peddlers into the recesses of doorways for cover. This once respectable stretch had, during World War Two, developed into a war zone of burlesque houses, room-by-the-hour hotels and tattoo parlors, designed to service the servicemen from Fort Sheridan and the Great Lakes Naval Station, taking advantage of the Wilson Avenue express stop on the North Shore Electric railway.

The palm tree motif promised by the neon sign in the smeary window was half-heartedly maintained inside the surprisingly high-ceilinged room, with its faded South Sea hula-girl murals, fake thatched-hut roofing, and velvet paintings of topless native babes. The joint was crowded with chairs and little tables, with plenty of seats to furnish views from every angle, if you could see through smoke thick enough to slice and sell as bacon.

On a raised stage behind an endless bar, a slightly overweight/overage henna-haired stripper in pasties and G-string was bumping-and-grinding for the benefit of an exclusively male audience running from mouth-breathing dirty old men (whose raincoats weren't as nice as mine) to sailor boys whose wide-eyed expressions indicated naked jiggling female flesh in the raw may have been a new experience for them.

On a Friday, in the middle of the afternoon, the place was maybe half-empty—call it half-full, optimist that I am. Strippers between their onstage stints, wearing diaphanous robes, joined slatternly B-girls to filter through the small crowd, conning customers into buying them watered-down drinks, while almost-attractive waitresses in frayed aloha shirts and tight slacks provided mixed drinks, bottled beer, and bored expressions. Most of the seats at the bar were taken—as this provided the best view of the Silver Palm's cut-rate pulchritude— but I managed to find one toward one end.

I ordered a rum and Coke from a bartender who looked like he doubled as a bouncer, and watched as the henna-haired broad gave the crowd a flash of pasty-less bosom and bounded off, pleased with herself.

A bleached blonde of about fifty, weighing in at maybe two hundred pounds at five foot three, strutted out in a red-and-yellow muumuu and growled wisecracks into a microphone—"Big Mary, your mistress of ceremonies, but don't get any ideas." She worked blue enough to get a few laughs, and stayed on only a minute before introducing the next stripper, wisely not wearing out her welcome.

A slender brunette minced out overdressed in a Southern hoop skirt affair with Scarlett O'Hara bonnet, and she was down to her petticoats when I got the may-I-cut-in tap on the shoulder.

A thug with a flat nose, dead eyes, and broad shoulders— all wrapped up in a double-breasted blue suit with a blue-and-gray tie and a pearl gray fedora—was standing there like a potted plant with a shoulder holster.

"Yeah?" I said.

Suddenly I realized the thug was looking past me at the brunette, who was taking off her bra to reveal perky little titties with tasseled pasties. For a second I thought the guy wanted my seat; then he blinked and looked at me and remembered why he'd come over.

"Table toward the back," he said, thickly. He gestured with a bratwurst of a pointing finger.

Through the smoke I could make out a table with a small man seated at it, way in back, off to the side—one of the worst seats in the house. Even the tables nearby were empty, affording this diminutive patron of the arts a modicum of privacy.

I thought I knew who it was—you might even say, I was afraid I knew who it was—and the thug accompanied me as I approached the little guy in the green snapbrim, who wore a gray tailored suit with a pale yellow shirt and darker yellow tie, his oval face dominated by a lumpy schnoz and close-set eyes and a blank impassivity.

Sam Giancana looked up at me and said, "Sit, Heller. . . . Join me here in my office." To the thug he said, "Sally— a little breathing room."

As the thug faded toward the bar and the stage, I sat across from Giancana at the postage-stamp table; the lighting was nil—a glass-and-candle centerpiece remained unlit, the only light near us coming from a bulb placed under a wall-hung velvet painting of a native girl with breasts the size of coconuts . . . not exactly *National Geographic* material.

I'd brought my rum and Coke with me; Giancana was drinking coffee—he needed a shave, giving him a scruffiness at odds with his natty apparel.

"This is where Satira started, you know," Giancana said.

"That stripper who killed her married lover?"

"Yeah—down in Havana Harbor, remember?"

I did—it had been page one stuff.

He was saying, "We paid for her defense, and the cunt paid us back by working for the competition across the street, when she got out. We trumped the bitch, though."

"How's that?"

He snorted a laugh. "We hired the widow of the guy she murdered. Booked her in and she out-stripped Satira."

"That's showmanship, Sam."

"That's nothing—I tried to book both of them. Wouldn't that have stood Chicago on its ear? The murderer and the widow of her murder victim, peeling side by naked side."

"That's entertainment," I said. "Little surprised to see you, gotta admit. The feds who tried to serve your subpoena think you're in Florida somewhere—that's what your gardener told them."

Giancana shrugged facially, and had a sip of his coffee. "A few of us have to stick around and tend to business. I got a couple rocks left in this town I can crawl under."

"That message you left at my office was a little vague, Sam. How did you know I'd show?"

"I know what makes you tick, Heller. You're a fuckin' snoop. Curiosity is in your blood."

"And my blood is still in my veins, inside my body. I'm hoping to keep it that way."

Giancana flashed a sick-looking grin; like Lee Mortimer, he had a gray pallor—I didn't figure Sam for many camping trips . . . except maybe to bury an occasional stiff in a field.

"This is a friendly meeting," Giancana said. He placed both his hands on the table, palms down, fingers spread. "Friendly on my part, anyway. Your friend Drury—that little scuffle we had at the Stevens . . . you tell anybody about that?"

"No."

"You think you could keep that unpleasantness to yourself?"

"Yes."

"That thing, that was nothing. Drury was like that—he saw anybody remotely Outfit, he went off on them. You know that."

"I know that."

"He rousted Guzik, Fischetti, even Accardo, tons of times."

"I know."

Both eyebrows raised. "You don't think I had anything to do with what happened to him, do you now?"

I chose my words carefully. ". . . I think it was Outfit. I don't make it as anything to do with you, Sam."

He was studying me like a scientist studies a slide under a microscope. "And why is that your opinion?"

"Because you're smart, Sam. You have a temper—you've been known to lose your head, if you get pissed off . . . no offense."

"None taken."

"But this was stupid. This is bringing heat, these killings. St. Valentine's Day Massacre type heat. Jake Lingle type heat."

He was nodding.

I continued: "The Crime Committee hearings are getting moved to next week, you know. Kefauver is tossing fucking subpoenas over this city like advertising leaflets out of a plane."

"You're tellin' me. You know, he's going after our wives next, the prick."

I wondered where he heard that.

Shifting in my hard seat, I said, "I figure this is like when Dutch Schultz wanted to hit Dewey, and the rest of the New York boys said no fuckin' way. You don't hit a cop; you don't bump off a public figure."

Giancana's expression was blandly friendly; but he was still studying me. "You're not just sayin' this, Heller. This is how you see it."

"Sam, this is how I see it. I'm not just trying to talk my way out of a tight spot."

"This ain't a tight spot." He nodded toward his hands, still spread on the table. "It's a public place, Heller. That's why I arranged to meet you somewheres like this. Specifically, this joint 'cause Bas was the lawyer for the management . . . and, after you sort through all the holding companies, I'm the management."

All of this was news to me. "Bas was your attorney?"

"Only where certain businesses, like this one, was concerned. And Drury had no knowledge of that. Don't get thinking Bas was dirty, 'cause he wasn't—he was just a lawyer with various clients . . . like a private eye can have various clients."

"Right. Would I be overstepping if I suggested you might have been helping Bas in his efforts to unseat Tubbo?"

He twitched a grimace. "I'd rather not say. Tubbo has been a friend to Outfit interests for a lot of years—one-stop shopping, a fixer who can help with both the cops and the State's Attorney's office. But a guy that's been around as long as Tubbo can get . . . too powerful. Too full of himself."

For a guy who'd "rather not say," Sam had said a hell of a lot.

I sat forward. "Was Tubbo involved in the Drury hit? The Bas hit?"

"Heller, I don't know the answer to that question. But I know you—and know how you can go off on these . . . little rampages, now and then. You wouldn't talk to the Kefauver Committee, but you might decide to settle some scores in your own way. You've done it before."

I just shrugged.

He leaned forward, and lifted his right hand off the table, to gesture. "Now . . . there's something you need to know, Heller: neither of these hits was . . . what's the word? Approved—authorized. Just the opposite—Charley Fischetti asked to have this done, and was told not to. In no uncertain terms."

"But he did it anyway."

Giancana leaned back, raised another eyebrow. "Charley claims not—swears up and down, stack of Bibles, mother's grave. This was a meeting at the highest level, understand—Ricca, Accardo, Guzik. . . ."

"Do they believe him?"

"Fuck no. But Charley hasn't been challenged over this. He's still a powerful guy, Heller—Al's cousin, remember. And a smart guy—knows the business side. Understands the politics. Which is why you'd think he'd know better. . . ."

"So the boys are letting this slide?"

He shook his head, folded his arms. "Don't think there isn't a lot of displeasure. Don't think guys like Ricca and Big Tuna like having to pack their bags in the middle of the night and beat ass out of town, like common punk crooks."

The back of my neck was starting to tingle. "You're not saying. . . . You're not giving me permission to. . . ."

Tiny shrug. "I'm not saying anything. I might be implying that if you wanted to do something, personal, about Charley Fischetti . . . there would be no repercussions from certain circles. You know, when you might expect there to be."

". . . And just how would I find Charley Fischetti?"

"At a hotel in Mexico."

I blinked. "What hotel in Mexico?"

Giancana reached inside his coat, almost as if he were going for a gun; but I wasn't nervous, anymore. He just handed me a small piece of paper with quite a bit of writing on it.

"That hotel in Mexico," he said.

I slipped the piece of paper in my pocket without looking at it. "I saw Bas go down."

Giancana's eyes flared; this really was news to him. "No kidding?"

"No kidding. . . . Obviously, not in time to stop it. I got a shot off at the torpedoes—cracked their windshield. Got a good look at the bastards."

"Anyone you know?"

"No." I described the mustached pair. "Anybody *you* know?"

His expression gave away nothing. "Maybe. . . . Maybe."

"What aren't you telling me, Sam?"

With his folded arms, and his tiny smile, Giancana seemed guarded, to say the least. "Heller, like you, I have to be discreet. I'm limited in what I can say. But I will say this—those two gunmen are almost certainly from out of town . . . just not very far out of town."

"Jesus, Sam—what does that mean?"

Another tiny shrug. "That's all I can say. That slip of paper I give you?"

"Yeah?"

"The number at the bottom—that's a local number. You have any problems—need any . . . assistance . . . you call that number. If I don't answer, somebody will, who can get me in a hurry."

"You're not going to Florida?"

"Not right away."

"You, uh—mentioned Kefauver going after the wives of Outfit guys. Where did you hear that, Sam?"

"I just heard it, is all."

"You have somebody on Kefauver's staff, don't you?"

"Now you're asking too many questions, Heller."

"Just tell me—is it Halley?"

"Fuck no! That vicious, slandering son of a bitch. If he was ours, would he make so many lives miserable?"

I kept pressing, though my tone seemed casual. "You know Rocco married that girl—from the Chez, Jackie Payne? Married her the other day so she couldn't testify against him."

Giancana smirked. "Yeah—little Miss Chicago. But word now is, Rocky was wrong . . . that canary *can* be made to sing, or sent to the slam for contempt. And you know what's gonna happen then, don't you?"

"What, Sam?"

"She'll talk. She'll sing her lungs out. I mean, shit, she's a junkie. . . . The feds will own the keys to her." He shook his head. "Fucking Rocco—he's a chowderhead, anyway, a real shit-for-brains. And *he* put her on the junk!"

"Maybe you wouldn't mind if something bad happened to him," I said.

His face was blandly expressionless again. "I'd get over it."

Feeling like I was trying to put the pin back in a grenade, I ventured, "Sam—the girl. Miss Chicago?"

"Yeah?"

"She's a friend of mine. I don't want to see her hurt."

He frowned—almost scowled. "Listen up, damnit: my friends and I are not trying to attract attention, right now. Drury and Bas getting splattered is the worst fucking thing that could have happened—bumping off a beauty queen, recently married to a Fischetti, is just as bad. Gimme a little credit, Heller, for Christsake!"

"Sorry, Sam."

Smiling, he sat forward and patted my arm. "Hey—you and me, we have no problems. You *need* somebody like me, in my circles, to be your guardian angel. Like Nitti used to be. We aren't in the same exact racket, but we can be helpful to each other. Do each other favors."

Like have me bump off your fellow gangsters, when they've rubbed you the wrong way? is what I thought . . . but sure as hell didn't say it.

"For example, a favor you could do me, Heller . . ."

"Yeah?"

"Introduce me to your pal Sinatra, sometime." Giancana stood. "Listen . . . it's going to start getting busy in here, Friday night, I need to be scarce."

"Yeah—sure."

"But you can stay, Heller—run a tab on the house. Some decent girls are comin' out. You see anything you like, just tell Fred . . . the bartender."

"Well, thanks, Sam . . ."

"But they're not hookers, understand. Lay a double saw-buck on 'em in the morning, as a kind of gift, and you'll have a friend for life."

Giancana walked toward the exit, and his bodyguard—Sally—scampered after him, like a two-hundred-fifty-pound puppy. It was still daylight out there, and a slice of it knifed into the smoky joint, as the gangster and his thug slipped out.

I finished my drink, but I didn't stick around, and I sure as hell didn't take him up on his offer of my pick of the girls. It wasn't that I was above that sort of thing; but I wasn't sure I wanted a friend for life.

Particularly one named Sam Giancana.

13

My neighbor the Federal Building (which was also the United States Courthouse) was a cross-shaped eight-story structure perched on Dearborn, between Adams and Jackson, extending to Clark, with an octagonal domed central tower adding another seven imposing stories. The grim splendor of the building's ornate Roman Corinthian design seemed an apropos setting for dramatic trials of national note, like the $29 million judgment against Standard Oil and the Al Capone tax case . . . both matters of big business, after all.

In addition to the impressive courtrooms—with their William B. Van Ingren murals depicting the development of law over the ages—the Federal Building was also a rabbit's warren of hearing rooms, offices, and conference chambers, as well as cubbyholes where distinguished lawyers and jurists could cut their sleazy deals.

Kefauver had been given one of the cubbyholes: a modest, windowless room to set up his temporary office, with space for a desk, a few hard chairs, and a bookend-style pair of file cabinets, with cardboard boxes of file folders stacked precariously along the plaster walls. It was as if the senator had been assigned a storage room that happened to include a desk.

I was sitting across from the Democratic congressman

from Tennessee, who—when I'd stuck my head in the open door of his cubicle—had stood behind the file-cluttered desk, rising to an impressive six foot three or maybe four, extending me not only his hand but a wide, ingratiating grin.

In his rolled-up shirt sleeves and suspenders, his blue-and-red patterned tie loose under a prominent adam's apple, Kefauver gave an immediate impression of unpretentiousness, a tall, angular, lanky individual with searching eyes behind round-framed tortoise-shell glasses and a beaky nose that swooped to a peak; facially, he struck me as a cross between Abe Lincoln and Pa Kettle.

"Mr. Heller," he said, in an easy, drawling, soft-spoken manner (he didn't have to be wearing his coonskin cap for you to guess he came from the South), "I am very grateful to you for agreeing to see me at such short notice . . . and on a Saturday."

I'd received the message toward the end of business, yesterday—Kefauver was arriving from Kansas City that night, and requested a one-on-one meeting with me, Saturday morning.

I was sitting with my raincoat and fedora in my lap. "That's all right, Senator—my office is just across the street, and I was planning to come in, anyway. I often save paperwork and letters for Saturday mornings, when the phone doesn't ring."

"And I wanted to speak to you without my staff present," he said with a gesture of a frying-pan hand. "They're great people, but you know, lawyers—particularly prosecutors—are sometimes, well, deficient in social skills."

"I don't think we could pack your staff in here, if we tried."

Kefauver chuckled once, but his grin was endless. He gestured with both big hands. "I know—beggars can't be choosers, I guess. I never did figure to be popular in Chicago. . . . But we do have the use of a conference room, and we'll have hearing room space, as well."

"I understand you're getting started soon."

"Next week. . . . And *I* understand you're reluctant to testify."

I shrugged, grinned back at him. "Let's just say I'm not anxious—on the other hand, I haven't come down with a case of Kefauveritis."

A nod and another wide smile. "Ah yes—that mysterious new ailment . . . the most pronounced symptom of which is an irresistible urge to travel."

"But I do know my constitutional rights, Senator—I can decline to answer on the fifth amendment; and I can protect my clients on grounds of confidentiality."

He nodded some more; his goofy-looking combination of hayseedish and professorial qualities was oddly appealing. "That's true—as I understand it from my associates, your standard operating procedure with criminal cases is to work for the attorneys of the client, not the clients themselves."

"That's right."

"Well that's a very clever approach. You're serving your clients effectively, and that's exactly what you're supposed to be doing. . . . You can't be faulted for that. And I wouldn't dream of asking you to betray your profession's code of ethics."

I tried to find sarcasm in that, without success.

"Senator, if I might explain myself further . . . ?"

"Certainly."

"I don't mean to be a hostile witness. It's just that I don't approve of your committee's methods. Your traveling circus rolls into town, you make a lot of noise, cause a lot of trouble, and move on, leaving the rest of us to clean up after the elephants."

He was sitting back in his swivel chair, arms folded; friendly though his expression was, he was clearly appraising me. "I can understand your point of view, Mr. Heller— but you need to understand mine: my aim is to expose the influence of the underworld on American life."

"That simple, is it?"

"And that complex. This is the fullest, most public investigation of organized crime ever attempted in America— and we have captured the attention, and more importantly the imagination, of the press and the public. By the time we hit New York—the climax of our 'circus'—we will be fully televised. The average American, for the first time, will be aware of the national crime syndicate—thanks to our efforts, the word 'Mafia' is already entering the national vocabulary."

I sighed. "I don't mean to knock you off your high horse, Senator—but if you really meant that, you'd be going after more than just gambling."

Sitting forward, he fixed a penetrating gaze on me. "Let me tell you something, Mr. Heller—it's the tie-up between crime and politics that most makes me sick . . . the rottenness in public life. But from what I hear and read about you, you're a pragmatic man . . . and you'll understand that I have to start somewhere."

"Plus you don't want to alienate these political machines that you're gonna depend on when you run for the presidency."

He grunted a humorless laugh. "Oh, I already have alienated them—and will further, here in Chicago, by moving the hearings up before the election."

"Well . . . I have to admire your balls for that, Senator. If you'll excuse the crudity."

"I appreciate the compliment. Also, that you seem to understand what's at risk for me, personally."

I shrugged. "You may do fine without the political machines—after all, the public dearly loves a gangbuster."

That seemed to amuse him, and he leaned his elbow against the desk and his chin against his hand. "Would it surprise you, Mr. Heller, to find out I'm a gambler myself? I do relish a good horse race."

"I've heard that, Senator." I didn't mention I'd also heard this father of four had an eye for the skirts.

"So you might think I'm a hypocrite." He leaned back in the chair again, rocking a little. "But it's a bit like the situation your friend Eliot Ness was in, back in Prohibition days. Mr. Ness, I understand, likes to take a drink now and then."

These days, Eliot was damn near a lush.

But I just said, "You could say that."

"Still, Ness knew the Mafia underworld was tied up in bootlegging . . . and that every other sin that can be marketed to man, from prostitution to dope peddling, was part of the same vile syndicate. So he went after the bootleggers. Here in Chicago—do I have to tell you?—you have the national race wire, the manufacture and distribution of coin-operated machines, including slots, and the numbers racket and every other manner of illegal gambling you can think of, flourishing openly."

"That's Chicago, Senator. Do you really think you're going to change it?"

He shook his head. "I can't change human nature . . ." But then he began to nod. "We can, however, expose these vicious, homicidal thugs . . . who think murders like those of Bill Drury and Marvin Bas are just the price of doing business."

Now I leaned back, folding my arms. "What if I were to tell you that those murders were hired by Syndicate renegades? That Accardo and Ricca and the rest had expressly forbidden those murders—but Charley Fischetti hired them done, just the same."

The eyes behind the round lenses widened. "Are you providing me with information, Mr. Heller?"

"If you want to call it that. And this . . . right here . . . is what you should be doing, if you really want to investigate the Outfit. You want help fighting this war, Senator? Then don't put guys like me on the stand, where we embarrass ourselves and get added to the same hit list as Drury and Bas. Talk to us behind the scenes, on the q.t. But no—you want to play Ed Sullivan, and put on a show."

"I think you misconstrue our motives—"

"Maybe I do. But can you seriously think putting some mobster on the stand will result in a meaningful dialogue? The revealing of new, key evidence? I know you're just campaigning for president, Senator—I mean, don't kid a kidder."

His smile settled in one cheek. "I'm surprised at you, Mr. Heller. I understood you had a highly successful office in Hollywood—I assumed that you understood show business."

"I don't follow you."

He leaned forward again. "Most of what we're gathering *is* from confidential sources. Frankly, if Bill Drury hadn't been so intent on clearing himself, and pursuing his crusade in so public a fashion, he would have been more useful to us—and might still be alive."

"Go on."

"Most of our leads are from private, unofficial sources. Newspaper reporters on local crime beats . . . private eyes like yourself . . . honest cops caught in the middle of crooked administrations . . . smalltime hoodlums who want to get quietly even with their bosses."

"And these people never get called as witnesses."

"That's right; we protect them, keep them behind the scenes. We put the information these confidential sources have provided us in front of the American people, by posing embarrassing questions of gangsters who invariably respond by pleading the fifth."

I was starting to get it. Kefauver was shrewder than I'd given him credit for. "And you guys can't get sued for libel, 'cause you're a congressional committee—legally privileged."

"That's right. Very astute, Mr. Heller. We can put sensitive facts on the record, by the questions we pose . . . even though those questions invariably go unanswered. 'Isn't it true that . . . ?' We can put what we've uncovered on the record—and reveal the corrupting influence of organized crime on American society. . . . That's the purpose of our traveling circus."

The son of a bitch was close to having my vote. "I gotta admit it's good show business, at that."

"Thank you."

"But you've set a dangerous goddamn precedent—Senator McCarthy is protected from libel suits by that same privilege."

Now, as if a switch had been thrown, his expression turned troubled. "I know . . . the potential for witch-hunting is great . . . and grim. To misuse this tool, as McCarthy is bound and determined to—"

"That's what he feels you're doing, Senator. He thinks you're the witch-hunter."

"Is this something you've gathered, following the press . . . ?"

"No, I talked to Joe McCarthy last week, in D.C. I've done my share of work in your second home."

Nodding, he said, "For Drew Pearson. Yes—and he speaks well of you."

"And he of you—he's your most ardent cheerleader."

Kefauver heaved a deep breath, seemed to be searching for words. Finally, he found them: "Mr. Heller—I would like to ask you about a certain matter . . . confidentially."

"You can ask."

"You were Bill Drury's friend—and he worked for your detective agency, in his last months. He promised us extensive materials—notebooks, diaries, files, tapes . . . do you have them?"

"No."

"Do you know who does?"

"All I know is Bill took them with him, the day he was murdered. They're gone by now, anyway."

"Gone?"

I nodded. "If that stuff's in Outfit hands, it's been destroyed."

He frowned. "What if Charles Fischetti got hold of those books, to keep his Mafia brethren from finding certain things out?"

"Then Fischetti's burned them. But I *can* give you another tidbit of confidential information."

"Please."

"You have a leak on your staff."

He said nothing; he tented his fingers and his eyes tightened behind the circular lenses. "Are you certain of that?"

"Oh yeah—it comes from an Outfit source. A high-up Outfit source. Lee Mortimer also suspects as much."

Kefauver worked up a smirk. "I'm afraid Mr. Mortimer is something of a spurned lover, where this committee is concerned."

"Nonetheless, the guy knows his beans. He suspects Halley—"

"Ridiculous!"

"I tend to agree with you, Senator. But you would be dismayed if you knew how quickly your confidential information is getting into the hands of the competition—the Outfit, I mean."

He just sat there, mulling that over for a minute; then he said, "I do appreciate this, Mr. Heller. I'll try to quietly locate the leak on my own. Thank you."

"That's okay, Senator. Just don't say where you heard it."

He managed a smile; halfhearted though it was, it was still a mile wide. "That's the nature of confidential sources, Mr. Heller."

"Swell . . . and I might be able to help you regarding another matter."

"By all means."

"Charley Fischetti."

Kefauver lifted both eyebrows. "Mr. Fischetti is a witness we would very much like to have sit before our committee. We're very interested in his brother Rocco, as well."

"Rocco doesn't know much—he's just a thug with an important brother. But I might be able to put Charley's ass in your chair, so to speak."

"Really. And how would you manage that?"

I didn't tell him that I was trying to angle a way to cause Charley trouble, without doing what Giancana strongly implied I should do—flat-out killing the bastard. Which I would have relished, at this point, but was uncomfortable doing Mooney's dirty laundry. I'd had a feeling I was being played, last night, at the Silver Palm. . . .

I asked, "Does the United States have a friendly relationship with the Mexican government, where extradition is concerned?"

He shrugged matter-of-factly. "If we knew Fischetti's whereabouts, and those whereabouts happened to be in Mexico, we could get him brought home to us, yes."

"I know where he is. At least I think I know."

His eyes narrowed; he again sat forward. "Would you like to share that information with the committee?"

"Would the chairman of the committee like to assure me I won't be called as a witness?"

Kefauver chuckled. "You are everything you're cracked up to be, Mr. Heller. . . . What do you have in mind?"

"Maybe you'd like to hire me . . . confidentially, of course, by which I mean only you and me and your government checkbook would know."

"Continue, please."

"You fund my jaunt South of the Border, where I confirm the whereabouts of your witness. I'll wire you that information, keep Charley and Rocco under surveillance until the *federales* take over."

"I like the sound of this. When would you do it?"

"Right away. Soon as I can book plane tickets . . . next few days."

Kefauver shook his head, grinned the infinite grin, and stuck his hand across the desk. "Mr. Heller—welcome aboard the Special Committee to Investigate Organized Crime in Interstate Commerce."

I shook with him, but said, "Yeah, well, let's skip the office welcome wagon. . . . No one but the two of us are hep to this, remember."

"Hep . . . ?"

"Are in the know about my role."

"Fine." The endless grin—a toothless version—seemed to crinkle across his face; then he added, "Always room for another talented performer here at the circus."

I stood. "Let's hope I'm not just another clown."

"It could be worse, Mr. Heller."

"Yeah, Senator?"

"Try not to get shot out of a cannon."

Thinking that was good advice, I nodded and went out.

That afternoon around two, in the lobby of the St. Clair Hotel, red-headed Hannan, the house dick, caught me just as I was about to go up on the elevator.

"I need a moment, Nate," he said, kind of edgy.

"Sure, Hannan," I said, walking with him over to one side. "What cooks?"

"Not my goose, I hope—listen . . . I let a dame in your room."

"Yeah? Anybody you know? Anybody I know?"

"She says she's a friend from Texas."

"Texas? I don't have any girl friends from Texas."

He gestured with open hands. "Nate, I'm pretty sure you're not gonna mind. This is one of the best-looking babes I ever saw, built like a brick shithouse and then some . . . and she was real tired, just got off the bus. She had luggage with her, and no money. I felt sorry for her."

What the hell was this about?

"Jesus, Hannan—have you seen the papers lately? I'm kind of hot right now. You might have just let some Outfit bimbo lay a trap for me."

His eyes showed white all around. "This is a trap I'd give my left nut to lay. Look, she's clean—I made her let me go through the suitcase, and her cosmetics case, and then she stood for a frisk." He grinned and his eyes narrowed and kind of glazed over. "And what a frisk. . . . Sometimes this is a great job."

I shook my head, not knowing whether to smack him or tip him. "Does this Texas girl fresh off the bus have a name?"

"Sure—Vera something."

Vera Jayne Mansfield, née Palmer—in a short-sleeve white blouse with gaucho collar and black pedal pushers ending over nicely curving calves and red-painted toe-nails—was asleep on my sofa in the living room of my suite, her powder blue suitcase next to her, a matching train case too. On her back, her cute face to one side, the brunette pageboy tousled, her magnificent bosom rising and falling, Vera was lost in a deep sleep, clearly exhausted.

I sat on the edge of the sofa and wondered why I wasn't irritated with her. For some stupid reason, I was glad to see her. Maybe that she was a gorgeous girl of nineteen or so, asleep in my apartment after driving cross-country to see me, had something to do with it. Maybe if I couldn't have the former Miss Chicago on my sofa, the almost Miss California would make a sweet substitute.

She didn't wake till after dark. I'd been sitting in my easy chair, with a lamp on, reading the afternoon papers, when she purred and, moving sinuously, stretched and yawned and cracked her neck this way and that. Blinking a few times, she finally noticed me and beamed.

"I'll bet you're mad at me," she said.

"Furious."

"I bet you wonder what I'm doing here."

"Visiting?"

She touched her breasts, eyes doing an Eddie Cantor. "I must look a fright."

"Horrible."

"I was on the bus most of last night and a lot of today." She tasted her mouth and didn't like it. "I'll be right back."

She snatched up her train case, scampered off into the bathroom, and fifteen minutes later emerged with fresh makeup and brushed hair and a big white smile. Returning to the couch, she patted the cushion next to herself with one hand, while crooking the forefinger of her other hand. It was insulting, really, even demeaning—like she was summoning a child, or maybe a dog.

I obeyed at once.

"Thanks for not being angry," she cooed. "I didn't call because I thought you'd try to talk me out of it."

"Out of what?"

"Coming to Chicago to see you. To get you to help me. You know—to get work, modeling assignments, maybe some nightclub thing, in a chorus line. Doesn't that make sense? Starting here, sort of small, and working up to Hollywood?"

This girl—who was nineteen or at most twenty—had something almost scarily intense in those wide-set hazel eyes; beneath those soft curves and that sweet face was a ferocious drive, a willingness to do whatever was necessary. Most girls who went after show biz careers were ready to settle for a husband or a sugar daddy; this girl wanted to be in show biz for one reason, and one reason only: to make it big. To be a star.

I asked, "What about Paul?"

"Paul—my husband, Paul?"

"Yeah—that Paul."

"He's at Camp Gordon in Georgia. Intense training for a month—no wives allowed—before he goes to Korea."

"What does he think about you coming to Chicago?"

She shrugged, batting the big hazel eyes. "He doesn't know. Nate, you have to understand something. . . . Back in high school, some boys at a party got me high and raped me, or anyway took advantage of me, I don't really remember the details, too out of it . . . I just know I got pregnant. Paul was a decent-looking guy, president of his class, and he always wanted to date me. So we got secretly married my senior year and he gave my daughter a name . . . and a father."

"Sounds like you got yourself a nice guy. A good catch."

"Paul really helped me out—but he doesn't understand my ambition."

"Why don't you divorce him, if you're unhappy with him?"

"I'm not unhappy. He's going to Korea—when he gets back, if he's willing to go out to Hollywood with me, I'll give him a chance. I owe him that much. In the meantime, I have a dream to pursue."

I shook my head. "Vera, I don't know if Chicago's the best place to do that."

"What about modeling jobs?"

"Well. . . . The Patricia Stevens agency I have an in with; I've done some security work for them. And there's no denying you would make a swell swimsuit model."

"Oh, Nate—you're wonderful."

"I can't guarantee anything, Vera . . ."

"Thank you . . . thank you . . . thank you for not being mad at me."

She put her arms around my neck and kissed me with those soft full lips. The only light on was the lamp by my chair, and I got up and switched it off, and returned to her on the sofa, where she was already unbuttoning her blouse.

Vera was a married woman—sort of—and I was still in the throes of an emotional attachment to another beauty queen. And I should have either thrown this one out on her pretty behind, or just been a friend to her, helping her make some connections in the big town.

About two minutes later, she was naked on my lap, her hips churning, my pants around my ankles, and I was deep inside her, my face burrowed first in one generous breast, then the other. Her devil-may-care, giddy sexuality was infectious, but she noticed something different about me, and—slowing but not stopping the motion of her hips—she placed a soft tender hand against my face and her eyes were caring as she stared into me, saying, "You're hurting, aren't you, Nate? Why are you hurting?"

"Nothing . . . it's nothing. . . ."

"Vera Jayne'll make you forget . . . or die trying. . . ."

I was the one who almost died—we did it on the kitchen table next, after I'd fixed us sandwiches, and eventually we even got around to the bedroom. It was close to midnight, with Vera curled up against me, her full lips smiling in slumber, when the phone on the nightstand rang.

Catching it on the first ring, hoping not to disturb my guest, I said, "Hello."

"Nate . . . Nate. . . ."

It was Jackie! . . . and she sounded strange . . . out of breath . . . was she crying?

"What is it, baby?" I said into the phone.

Vera, half-awake now, looked up at me, propping herself on an elbow.

"Nate," Jackie said. "Please help me . . . you have to help me. . . ."

"Where are you?"

"Riverview. A lad . . ."

"A lad? Baby, what—?"

Now another voice came on the line, a male voice, rather high-pitched but gruff. Was this the "lad" she was referring to?

"She's hurting, Heller. She needs a fix."

"Who the fuck—"

"Bring those notebooks to Aladdin's Castle."

"Notebooks?"

"Don't play dumb. We know your pal Drury gave 'em to you—notebooks, diaries, tapes, the works. Come alone. Before one a.m., or the next injection this junkie slut gets is forty-five caliber."

And the phone clicked dead.

Sitting up in bed, clutching the receiver, eyes and mouth wide open, I must have looked like a madman, because Vera backed away as she said, "What's wrong?"

"I have to go somewhere." I swung over and sat on the

edge of the bed; then I was using the phone again—dialing this time. "You'll have to stay here, Vera."

"Where are you going?"

"Riverview."

"What's Riverview?"

"An amusement park—the world's largest."

"Well that sounds like fun! Take me along!"

"They're closed for the season, Vera."

"Then why . . . ?"

"Quiet," I said, as the party I was phoning responded.

"Yeah?" the sleep-thick male voice said. "Who is it? You know what the fuck time it is?"

"Tim," I said to Bill Drury's ex-cop partner. "This is that call you asked me to make."

14

Riverview amusement park—bordered on the north by Lane Tech high school, on the east by Western Avenue, on the west by the Chicago River, and on the south by Belmont Avenue—had been a fixture of the Northside as long as I'd been alive. In fact, one of its rides—the Pair-O-Chutes—loomed over that part of town like a Chicago Eiffel Tower; actually that's what it had originally been called—the Eye-Ful tower, an observation deck that had been condemned by the city and cannily turned by the Riverview management into a freefall parachute drop. From miles around, you could see the oil well–like structure, crosshatched against the sky.

Some of my earliest and fondest childhood memories were of the so-called "world's largest amusement park"— free entrance passes were routinely mailed out all across the city, and the park refunded the two-cent streetcar fare for kids (a big table of shiny pennies awaited inside the front gates), encouraging customers for what was already a bargain-packed extravaganza.

When I was a kid, I'd held onto my stomachful of cotton candy and popcorn through the wild ride that was the Jack Rabbit roller coaster, only to be defeated by the Crazy Ribbon, with its barrel-shaped cars rolling and twisting back and forth down an inclined track. Dreams during my adult life on occasion had returned me to the funhouse called Hades, a hell of a ride through dark passageways filled with flashing figures and unearthly noises.

And my memory still tingles with other vivid images of Riverview: the freak show with the Tattooed Lady, the Rubber Man, and Pop-Eye (not the sailor but a guy who could force his eyeballs to jut from their sockets); midget fire eaters; hootchie-kootchie dancers; the African Dip (colored guys dressed like jungle warriors who taunted you into hurling baseballs at them—"Hey man, that ain't the gal you was here with *las'* night!"); and of course every kid's favorite, the Monkey Races, where you bet on the driver of your choice among the tiny terrified creatures "steering" cars of various colors, cute little critters but if you petted them you'd get nipped—don't say you weren't warned.

I hadn't been a stranger over the years, and Riverview in full sway—especially at night—remained a wonderland unparalleled in the western world, or anyway on Chicago's Northside. Ablaze with neon, flickering with banjo lights— pop-tune-blaring sound-system horns in dishes ringed by tiny flashing white lights on lamp poles—the midway was a twisty, turny paradise of sleazy nirvana. With a doll on your arm (with a doll under her arm that you'd won for her), you wound through two and a half miles of bright loud midway crammed into a three-block-by-two-block area. Frequently, the air would be torn by the shrill horrified screams of plunging patrons enjoying the park's legendary roller coasters, sounds of terror giving way to the clanking of chains as more victims were dragged up steep wooden slopes to their delighted doom.

Like most Chicagoans, however, I hadn't ever set foot inside Riverview in the off-season, much less after midnight. Having parked on Western, I approached the front gates—a white wide pillared archway trimmed patriotically in red and blue. Had I been here just a few weeks ago, that archway would have radiated with neon; now, in ivory-tinged light courtesy of half a moon and a scattering of stars and few streetlamps, the night reluctantly gave up dark shapes beyond the gates, like massive slumbering beasts, and the filigree outline of trees losing their leaves. I could also make out the lettering RIVERVIEW PARK on the ticket booth inside the six-foot fence, which I scaled without any problem, dropping to the cement without hurting myself or making a racket.

While the park was dark—not even security lighting of any kind—the sky glowed off to my left, strangely enough, as if a small sunrise was taking place in the midst of the night. Looming over everything, the steel lacework of the Pair-O-Chutes tower dangled its metal cables like weird tendrils. The air was crisp, almost cold; I was dressed for a night at Riverview, particularly a night I wanted to blend into—a pair of dark slacks, black gum-soled loafers, and a black horsehide jacket over a navy sportshirt.

The jacket was unzipped, to make it easier for me to get at the .38 in the shoulder holster . . . I had left my nine millimeter Browning at home, preferring to use this gun, which I'd taken from that elevator operator at the Barry Apartments, the night Drury and Bas were killed. Using someone else's gun has its benefits.

Wearing black leather driving gloves that fit like a second skin, I was carrying a duffel bag I'd packed with some old catalogs and newspapers, snugging in an extra revolver, a .32 that also couldn't be traced to me. Whoever had abducted Jackie—assuming she had been abducted and wasn't just party to some Fischetti scheme—was under the mistaken impression I had Drury's notebooks, tapes, and papers; so the duffel bag seemed a necessary prop.

Riverview struck me as a good choice for the bad business my adversaries were up to—in the midst of the city, the abandoned sprawl of the off-season park provided a large, deserted landscape with many vantage points for positioning lookouts (and snipers) and countless possibilities for hiding, as well as numerous opportunities for hasty exits on all sides.

That these apparent kidnappers had chosen Riverview as a drop point made me suspicious of Fischetti involvement. For one thing, this was Charley's turf—we weren't that far from the Barry Apartments, in fact—and only a few blocks away from where Drury had been murdered in his garage.

Also, gambling was Rocco's sphere of mob influence, and it was well known that the Outfit got a cut of the games of chance at Riverview, in some cases ran them.

Just to my right inside the gate, lovely in the moonlight, a vast flower garden—one of numerous landscaped areas scattered throughout Riverview—seemed to be surviving the cold snap just fine. Behind the garden yawned the wooden scaffolding of the Silver Flash roller coaster, its silver-shrouded cars no doubt stored away in one of the numerous sheds and warehouses of the sleeping grounds.

What separated Riverview from a carnival or fair were the permanent buildings, from shuttered wooden carny stalls to the ornate, overgrown-gazebo affair straight ahead, housing the Tilt-a-Whirl; beyond it, to the left, the lagoon was barely visible through the thickness of trees surrounding. Train tracks ringed the lagoon, though the tiny streamlined engine and its cars were probably in storage; but the miniature railroad made me think of Rocco . . .

. . . *Had he turned on Jackie, when he and his brother learned that wives could be forced to testify against their husbands, or face imprisonment? Had the lovely addicted Miss Chicago become a liability good only for bait, to lure a chump like me to her rescue?*

That unlikely sunrise was off to my left, and I was moving in that direction anyway, since I'd been summoned to Aladdin's Castle, which had taken the place of Hades, after the previous funhouse had, yes, burned down. Duffel bag in my left hand, my right hand poised near my unzipped jacket, I walked down the paved path, with the park-like lagoon area and its benches and miniature railroad tracks to my right. To my left were the various rides and attractions—the Dive Bomber with its two capsule-shaped cars on either end of a suspended arm; the sprawling Spooktown with its elaborate cartoony facade of ghosts and skeletons; an enormous ferris wheel, the spokes and wires of which threw shadows on me as I approached the source of illumination in the otherwise gloomy park.

Aladdin's Castle was alive!

Alive, that is, with sequential moving lights—as if this attraction alone in the park were open for business. Bookended on either side of the gigantic face and shoulders of a turbaned, bearded (and crudely drawn) Aladdin—his robe brightly striped red, a golden lamp in his massive hand—were the mosque-like towers of an Arabian castle. Somebody inside had thrown a switch—or two, or three—and the neon trim of spires and minarets and the progressive blinking light-bulb "jewels" of the giant's turban and lamp were burning in the night. Even the wide-open eyes of Aladdin were moving side-to-side in their creepy trademark fashion.

Standing before the garish display—that childishly drawn yet vaguely fiendish Aladdin face, with its lumpy nose and prissy mouth, towering over me—I felt like a child again, a child too young to handle the bizarre thrills of Riverview. That the immense park lay shrouded in darkness had not been as disturbing as seeing this one attraction aglow in the night. . . .

The door in the fence beside the minaret ticket booth stood open, and I lugged my duffel bag down a cobblestone path through Aladdin's overgrown front yard to the stairway that lay flat against the facade and led up past the pointing beard to a doorway in Aladdin's right shoulder. This door was open, too—and nobody asked for a ticket. Hadn't had a bargain like this since I got those shiny pennies.

I'd been through this place with a date, a time or two, but didn't remember the layout. Immediately I was in a maze of screen doors; all the damn things looked identical and I hit dead end after dead end, until finally I was in a hall of mirrors—looking skinny and fat in various ones, and not particularly intelligent in any.

Soon I was passing through a room with a slanted floor, having to hold on with my free hand to a railing to keep from pitching onto my ass. Then I was in a dark corridor, and tinny speakers emitted snake charmer music, telegraphing the lighted-up wall recess in which a fake cobra lunged at me; I didn't even react to that cheap shit, but I flinched when a scimitar-wielding dummy Arab appeared on the other side of me . . . damn near went for the .38. . . .

This corridor emptied me into one of those rooms with

a floor of round metal disks that rotated as you stepped on them. I had to use all my concentration to make it across without a tumble, and when I entered the adjacent corridor, another dark one, somebody grabbed me from behind, one arm looping powerfully around me, while the other arm came around and a hand deftly fished the .38 out from under my shoulder.

I didn't have time to struggle—I was simply dragged bodily through a doorway into a little bare room with unpainted wooden walls and slatted flooring, and nothing in it but a big switchbox on one wall. The cubbyhole was barely big enough for all three of us: me, the guy behind me with his arms looped around my chest, and Jackie Payne, who was tied into a wooden chair, a handkerchief gag in her mouth.

She was conscious and her eyes were wide with alarm and concern and a hundred other things. The rope—greasy carny cord—cut tightly against her pink sweater and matching slacks . . . it was the same outfit she'd been wearing when I picked her up off the street corner on Sheridan . . . the ropes making smudgy stains, and obviously hurting her, her wrists behind her, her ankles tied together, not to the chair. Her feet were bare, which led me to think she'd been snatched out of her apartment. Her left sweater sleeve was yanked back and the tracks and bruises on her slender white arm were painfully apparent.

The guy shoved me past her, into a corner of the shack-sized room, and positioned himself opposite me, with Jackie in between, giving me my first good look at him—actually, my second good look, because not long ago I'd had another memorable view of him, when he and his partner were heading right at me, about to run me down in that maroon coupe in Little Hell.

This was the tall, lanky one, with the harelip scar through his mustache. Hatless, he had neatly combed longish brown hair, his eyes brown and cold, his cheek bones rather sharp—he was like a pale Apache; I put him in his late twenties, though there was experience in that hard face. He wore a glen plaid brown suit that had a tailored look and a silk green-and-brown striped tie; he was a natty son of a bitch, for a guy training my own .38 on me. Well, the elevator operator's .38.

"You don't have to die," he said.

This was not the voice I'd heard on the telephone: so there was at least one more of them . . . probably the other mustached assassin, the smaller, round-faced one.

"Sooner or later, we all do," I said.

That snake charmer music was still playing, distantly, over scratchy speakers.

The mustache curled into a small smile. "Well . . . it can be sooner, if you insist. You got what I want?"

He meant the Drury notebooks. I hefted the duffel bag.

"That's it?" he asked, eyebrows raised.

"It's not gym clothes," I said. Truthfully.

Her eyes agonized now, Jackie—tied tight in her chair—was looking back and forth between us, as if she were following a tennis match with life-and-death consequences. Maybe she was.

As he pointed the .38 at me with one hand, he reached his other hand into a suitcoat pocket. Then he tossed something, which clunked on the wooden floor at Jackie's feet. A pocketknife—a good-size one.

"You give me what's in that bag," he said, "and I'll just go. And by the time you cut the little junkie loose, I'll be long gone. You'll have what you want, I'll have what I want."

"Where's your partner?"

A tiny shrug. "He might be anywhere. Maybe he's up on top of the Pair-O-Chutes. Maybe he's sitting in a ferris wheel car."

"Somewhere he can shoot me from, you mean."

But the pale Apache was shaking his head. "We don't want to shoot you."

Fuck him—I'd witnessed him and his partner killing Bas. I hadn't come forward about what I'd seen, but the threat of my doing so still hung over them—which was part of why we were here at Riverview tonight, besides the fun and games of Aladdin's Castle. To remove that threat.

The only thing keeping me alive was their need to get what they thought I had: the Drury papers.

"All right," I said to him, as Jackie looked at me with affection and desperation in those big brown eyes. "I suppose if you wanted to shoot me, I'd be dead by now."

"That's right," he said, accepting that as my actual line of thinking.

"You mind if I ask you who you're working for?"

"Just give me the damn bag, okay?"

I held out the duffel bag, assertively—right out in front of Jackie's face. "Take it, then. Fucking take it!"

The pale Apache winced in thought. Too much thinking is bad for some people. But it was clear he now figured I'd booby-trapped the bag somehow . . . maybe put a real cobra in it. After all, we had snake charmer music playing in the background. . . .

He sneered at me; natty as he was, that mustache could use a trim. "You open it—slowly. Show me everything that's in there, one item at a time . . . make a pile on the floor."

"Okay." I pretended to be trying to juggle the bag into a workable position. I gave him a frustrated look, saying, "Can I put the bag down?"

Sighing with impatience, he nodded.

I crouched and unzipped the duffel bag; he was watching me carefully, the gun poised to blow me away at the slightest sign of treachery. My hand found the .32 and I fired it up at him through some newspapers and the canvas of the bag itself, which muffled the sound almost as well as a silencer, and the son of a bitch never had time to realize what had happened, much less squeeze the trigger of the .38.

He just stood there for a moment, with the little blue hole in the middle of his forehead, like a third eye, and his other two eyes weren't seeing any better than the new one; reflexes severed, his body flopped like a stringless puppet right about where I was supposed to pile the notebooks and tapes. The splash of blood and brains on the wooden wall behind him would have looked fine in a frame at Fischetti's penthouse.

Jackie had an astonished expression—not as astonished as that dead mustached fucker, but astonished enough. He fell at her feet, so I shoved him aside to get at that pocket knife, and flipped it open and started cutting her loose—the guy had played fair, providing a nice sharp blade, and I was able to free her within a minute . . . though that minute seemed like an eternity, since I couldn't be sure the shot . . . however muffled . . . might not have carried well enough for the partner to hear.

With the ropes in a pile at her bare feet, Jackie stood—she weaved for a moment, put a hand to her head; she seemed groggy.

"You okay?" I said, slipping an arm around her waist; I'd already retrieved the .38 from my late host, the .32 consigned to a jacket pocket. "Can you make it, baby?"

She nodded, tugging her sleeve down over the bruises and tracks, and I went to that control box and found a switch in the OFF position labeled HOUSE LIGHTS, and another in the ON that said MASTER GIMMICK; I hit both switches, and when I walked her out of there, occasional bare work bulbs unmasked the mysterious corridor of Aladdin's Castle as unpainted plywood. With my arm still around her waist, we moved down a sloping ramp that I seemed to remember would take us out.

The exit awaiting us was one of those big rolling barrels so awkward to navigate without falling comically ass over teakettle; but it wasn't rolling now. Before we could duck through it into the night, I paused, kissed her forehead, looked into those dazed-looking brown eyes, and said, "His partner's out there, somewhere."

She nodded. "Yes—he's smaller."

"Round face, also has a mustache."

"Yes! They just showed up at the apartment . . . came into the den and grabbed me. I don't know how they got in. . . ."

"That can wait. But here's the plan."

I told her that right behind Aladdin's Castle—separated by one knee-high fence and another somewhat higher one—was a parking lot; beyond that parking lot, and another fence, Western Avenue, along which my Olds was parked, in front of the quiet clapboard houses of the residential neighborhood in Aladdin's backyard. I would go

out first—to see if I drew any fire (but I didn't say that)—
and when I signaled her, she would join me, we would duck
around the side of the building, and she was to climb the
fences first as I covered her with the .38.

"Got it?"

She nodded; but she seemed woozy.

"Jackie, you have to get ahold of yourself."

She nodded again, more assuredly. Then she touched my
face and looked up at me with a longing expression. "You
really do care about me, don't you?"

It sounded childish—and both absurd and slurred—yet it
was so tender my heart broke, a little. She was another
man's wife . . . and I suspected that man had sent her here
to die.

"You know I do," I said, and I kissed her—a short,
sweet kiss.

Then, .38 in hand, I ran through the barrel, and exited
into the crisp, somewhat breezy night; I was on a platform
that, if I followed it to some stairs, would present another
round of adventures in the other wing of the castle. I would
pass on that privilege.

I slowly scanned the landscape—the thickness of trees
surrounding the lagoon, empty benches, the idle railroad,
the empty expanse of paved midway, curving around the
lagoon at left and right. The tower of the Pair-O-Chutes
adjacent to the castle seemed to me an unlikely spot for a
sniper—no elevator went up there, after all, only those dan-
gling chains (whose chutes and harnesses were in storage),
and I doubted my round-faced adversary was hanging up
there by a chain or two, waiting to get a good shot off.

I looked at the castle's next-door neighbor on the other
side—could someone be up in one of those ferris wheel
cars?

I hopped off the platform, motioning for Jackie—waiting
on the other side of the barrel—to stay put. Moving as
silently as possible, I stepped out into the castle's lawn, one
slow step at a time, listening for any sound that might give
movement away.

Nothing.

Nothing but the wind rustling the tarps and rattling the

shutters of Riverview in hibernation, the scaffolding of various roller coasters whining and creaking; and the occasional honking car horn and other late-night traffic sounds of the nearby streets.

Where was the son of a bitch? Had he heard the shot and panicked and fled? Had he positioned himself elsewhere in the park—was he roving the midway, to see if I'd enlisted backup, despite warnings to the contrary?

If he'd seen me, he'd had plenty of opportunity to take a potshot.

I turned toward the barrel—which was positioned as if at the end of one of the giant Aladdin's sleeves—and waved at Jackie to join me, which she did. At my direction, she took the lead, as we ducked around the side of the castle, and I moved in circles, gun fanned out, trying to be ready whatever direction the shit might fly from.

We were approaching the first, shorter fence, when the shot split the night open, a gun blossoming orange from just behind the castle building, across the fence—near the damn parking lot! The bastard had anticipated my move, was waiting for me.

I caught a glimpse of him, his pale round face like a mustached moon in the night, as he ran right at us, his dark suitcoat flapping, his hat flying off, and I yanked Jackie down off the fence, onto the grass, another round blasting, the bullet flying over us as the little man charged toward us.

I took her hand and almost dragged her away from that fence, back toward the park. Our pursuer had to climb that smaller fence and that would slow him down. Then I turned back toward where he was coming, with Jackie in front of me, and without taking time to aim threw two shots in his general direction, just to give him something to think about.

Then we ran again, Jackie stumbling, but I pulled her along as we fled down the midway, cutting to the right, in front of Aladdin's, then rounding the lagoon, heading down the midway, back toward the looming roller coaster scaffolding and the front gates.

But Jackie wasn't making it—she seemed about to collapse, sweating, tottering, and finally I had to duck with her between two shuttered stalls, a Skee-Ball and a penny arcade, and I knelt at the mouth of the little grassy alleyway, while she leaned against the side of the stall, next to me. I was watching the midway for our pursuer, but also sneaking side glances at my fading companion.

"I'm . . . sorry," she whispered, out of breath.

"Shhh," I said, .38 poised.

"They . . . they gave me a fix."

"What?"

"Be . . . before you got here . . . so they . . . could handle me better . . . didn't want one . . . didn't need one. . . ."

I knew I should keep my eyes on that midway, but I turned to her, and she looked terrible—ghostly white, perspiration pearling her forehead, despite the breeze. "Christ, Jackie—had you already shot up?"

She nodded, swallowed, her breath heaving; she seemed dizzy, as if about to pass out.

Had she overdosed? Surely that would have taken more immediate effect; but perhaps not—perhaps what she'd been put through . . . and was being put through . . . had taxed her system, her heart. . . .

And who the hell knew *what* they'd slammed into her?

"I'll get you out of here," I said to her.

She summoned a weak little smile. "I'll be . . . all right. I'll be . . . all right."

"I'm getting you help, baby." And I didn't mean just tonight.

"I'll be fine . . . just let me . . . let me catch my breath."

I heard movement and snapped my attention back to the midway and saw him—my round-faced assassin.

He wasn't running—he was prowling, staying low, fanning his gun out now, as if it were a flashlight in the darkness, walking close to the trees, not on the midway itself, rather on the grass, behind the benches, near the train tracks.

If he would just keep coming, keep that same pace and direction, stepping into that shaft of moonlight, I could get a good shot at the son of a bitch. . . .

The night cracked, like a whip, and the bullet stood the little assassin up straight, as if he were coming to startled attention—and then dropped him on his face.

From in back of the fallen assassin, Tim O'Conner came into view, his expression as stunned as if he had been the one who'd been shot . . . not the one doing the shooting.

I left her propped against the side of the booth, whispered, "Stay put, baby," and she nodded, as I scooted out into the midway, .38 in hand.

I wasn't sure whether Tim had seen me or not—I guessed not, because he seemed in a sort of trance as—*damn!*—he fired again, his revolver belching orange as he shot down into the figure already sprawled across the little train tracks.

"This is for Bill Drury, you lousy cocksucker," he said, and then he put one in the back of the dead assassin's skull; the sound was like a ripe melon hitting cement.

O'Conner stood there, his revolver limp at his side now, the acrid smell of cordite heavy in the air.

"Are you all right?" I asked him.

He blinked, swallowed, looked up at me with that stunned puss. "Are *you*? I heard the gunshot, and came running."

Tim's job had been to scope out the park, even as I was entering it, and take care of any sniper in the woodpile, or shut down any other sort of trap that might have been laid for me; after that, he was to position himself on the other side of the lagoon, close enough to Aladdin's to maneuver himself no matter what took place. Shooting one of Bill Drury's two assassins in the back was his own idea.

O'Conner seemed almost embarrassed, as he nodded down at what he'd done. "Jeez, Nate . . . I hope you don't mind."

"Not at all," I said. "You through?"

O'Conner nodded, and I kneeled over the corpse, turning it over just enough to get at the guy's wallet. I flipped it open and the metal of a badge caught the moonlight and winked at me.

"What the hell," O'Conner said, leaning down. "Is he a cop?"

I nodded, reading the ID card. "Calumet City. I bet his dead partner's got the same kind of tin in his wallet."

This made an awful sort of sense: Tubbo Gilbert—the State's Attorney's investigator running for sheriff—did business with crooked cops all around Cook County, and the state for that matter. The Calumet City P.D. was a handy place to recruit a pair of contract killers whose faces would be unknown in Chicago.

O'Conner was saying, "His partner is dead, too?"

Distant sirens announced we had outworn our welcome at Riverview—the gunshots and the lights of Aladdin's Castle had attracted neighborhood attention.

"Fill ya in later," I said, trotting over to where I'd left Jackie, but she wasn't leaning against the stall now—she lay prone on the ground.

"Shit!" Kneeling over her, I saw awful signs: the brown eyes were open and empty, a trail of spittle ran down her cheek. And she was motionless.

O'Conner was right there. "What is it? What's wrong with her?"

I was trying to find a pulse. "I think she's overdosed—help me with her! We have to get her to a hospital!"

He was bending beside her now, taking a closer look, touching her throat. "Nate—I don't think . . ."

"Help me carry her!"

O'Conner's hand gripped my shoulder. "Nate! She's dead! We have to get out of here, unless you want to explain all of this—maybe to the State Attorney's investigators? Leave her!"

I could have knocked his teeth down his throat for that, except for one thing: he was right.

She was dead.

"No helping her," I said.

"What?"

"No helping her—not now."

I kissed her forehead, and O'Conner and I went over a fence behind Spooktown, cutting through a parking lot over to Western Avenue. Blinking through tears, I was heading south on Western when the two police cars came zooming north, sirens screaming like riders on the Silver Flash.

15

We took a morning flight—six hours from Chicago to Mexico City on Mexicana Airlines—and rented a Jeep for the drive to Acapulco. My companion—a certain model and aspiring actress named Vera—was a cooing delight, her enthusiasm for the trip and bubbly personality going a long way toward rescuing me from the funk I'd been in for the last several days.

Arrangements for the trip had been simple; no passports were needed—just tourist cards, furnished through my travel agent—and I had press credentials, supplied by Drew Pearson, who had paved the way for me with the Associated Press office in Mexico City. As for Senator Kefauver, he made calls to the embassy in Mexico City, to arrange for a Narcotics Bureau agent stationed there to transfer temporarily to the consulate office at Acapulco. It seemed bureau director Harry W. Anslinger—unlike J. Edgar—was backing up the Crime Committee, all the way.

What I had in mind—and in due time I'll let you in on it—would benefit both Senator Kefauver and my perennial journalistic employer Pearson, meaning I could hit them both up for paychecks and expense accounts.

Even in a funk, I looked after business.

But I had been depressed, no question, sick with sadness

and shame. I had not managed to rescue Jackie Payne, though perhaps she was past rescuing: a girl who could go back to the likes of Rocco Fischetti, for drugs and show biz, might well have been past salvation. In time I would see that, but in the days—and, at times, during the weeks and months and even years ahead—I would suffer a gut-wrenching guilt thinking about abandoning that overdosed beauty queen in the grass at Riverview.

The worst of it would come late at night, when I convinced myself she may not really have been dead, and I had left her there, to die in the cold, fleeing to cover my own ass. . . .

Other than remorse, however, repercussions for the carnage at the park never came. I never knew exactly how it was done—although I could easily guess who accomplished it—but the deaths of Jackie and those two Calumet City cops were covered up in a fashion both imaginative and thorough.

Jackie's body was found in Lincoln Park, and the papers reported the tragic demise of a Miss Chicago turned showgirl turned drug addict. Hal Davis at the *News* uncovered her connection to Rocco, but no one came forward with the information that she and he were married. She was merely a "former flame" of the notorious Northside gambling boss. Her holy-roller parents saw to it she got a "Christian" burial back in Kankakee, and for about three days she achieved one of her goals: Jackie Payne was in the limelight, a star of sorts, albeit the tabloid variety.

The two cops were found in a ditch along the roadside in that stark industrial stretch north of Calumet City, in the shadow of a grain elevator. The chief of police pledged an around-the-clock search for the prime suspects, a stolen-car ring the brave detective duo had been closing in on; their records as cops were immaculate and they were buried as heroes with full honors. Their deaths were a further indication, said the press, of the peril faced by honest cops like these late Calumet City heroes and Chicago's own William Drury.

Only a few spoilsports in the press—Lee Mortimer for one—pointed out that Calumet City was an Outfit stronghold of wide-open gambling, prostitution, and narcotics, a state of affairs only possible with police cooperation. "Putting their names in the same sentence as Bill Drury," Mortimer wrote, "is a kind of blasphemy."

I couldn't help but admire the ability of Captain Dan "Tubbo" Gilbert to stage-manage these deaths, when he had to deal with whatever officers happened to catch the call out to Riverview. Impressive. Of course, as chief investigator of the State's Attorney's office for these many years, he had developed remarkable clout on all levels of state and local law enforcement.

Somebody needed to do something about the son of a bitch, but as Drury's friend and "partner" (not really an accurate designation, but that's how the press termed our business relationship) I would have been a prime suspect should a public-minded citizen put a bullet in Tubbo's beer-keg head.

Anyway, I had other fish to catch.

Vera and I, enjoying the warm wind stirred up by the open-air vehicle, tooled across a mere dozen or so mountain ridges along the superhighway thoughtfully provided by President Alemán, who'd been pumping Acapulco as a tourist spot. I was in sunglasses, a straw porkpie, a blue-and-tan Hawaiian aloha shirt, chino shorts, and sandals; I'd given my reddish brown hair a blond rinse. Vera was in a pale yellow shirt with flaring collar and cuffs, knotted at her midriff above canary yellow shorts; she too was in sandals and wore sunglasses. She had her hair ponytailed back and it was streaming behind her.

"I've been in Mexico lots of times," Vera the Texas girl said, eyes as wide as Orphan Annie's, "but this is something else."

My busty companion was right. The drive to Acapulco displayed itself in green breeze-stirred grass on rolling land that occasionally jutted rock and even grew terrifying precipices above tan beaches flecked with foamy white; sleepy little communities of houses and huts of pastel stucco and tile roofs; snarls of coral vine and fields of bougainvillea, mango clumps and banana trees and tropical flowers; boats with sails of white and pea green on a sapphire sea glimpsed beyond piers and wharves with silver nets drying in the sun. I could identify with the latter—I was fishing, too, remember?

But for the fringes of beach and a flat grassy patch just big enough for a landing field, Acapulco itself was an up and down affair—a land-locked harbor of cliffs and promontories and white-gold beaches, a tropical paradise of orchids and coconut palms and parrots. Radiating out of the unpretentious plaza, with its nondescript church, were humble residential streets, while on the heights above perched the seasonal villas of the well-to-do, like pastel stairsteps climbing the hills. Between the two worlds of everyday locals and wealthy foreigners—spread out on their different levels—pockets of shantytown, like fungus, infested hillsides.

La Mirador was the first of the luxury hotels built in Acapulco, back in the early thirties, followed by maybe a dozen more; some of the shiny highrise hotels had mob investors—Moe Dalitz, from Cleveland, for one—who'd got in on the ground floor, back when Repeal was around the corner. Like Havana and Vegas, Acapulco was the kind of resort area mobsters loved—for business and pleasure.

Built on Quebrada Cliffs, La Mirador was no highrise, rather a rambling affair, rich with patios and terraces, and very open, starting with a lobby that had no walls. The beach—though it was late afternoon when we arrived—was scattered with sunbathers, taking in the declining sun, and swimmers, splashing in the foam; Vera and I saw this from a terrace above, the yellow and red and blue of beach umbrellas like polka dots on the creamy sand. Our room, however, opened onto the swimming pool area, which overlooked a magnificent waterview, white waves emerging from the vivid blue Pacific to crash on enormous ragged rocks.

We'd arrived after the daily siesta, just in time for cocktail hour. We didn't even change our clothes—the atmosphere was almost pretentiously casual; resorts like this, after all, were where the international set came to lounge in open-neck shirts and shorts and sandals. There wasn't a coat or tie to be seen in the entire Mirador bar.

Which, as bars went, was an unusual one, hewed in the side of a cliff. We sat in our booth, as if in an opera box in a theater, watching the stage the lack of a wall presented, providing a full view of the setting sun using its entire paintbox to color the sky as waves dashed against the rocks a hundred and fifty feet below.

Vera had a *coco loco* (coconut milk, gin, and ice) and I sipped rum out of hollowed-out pineapple, a treat called a *pie-eye*. We also both popped quinine capsules, as a precaution against malaria . . . a real must in my case, since I still had recurrences from Guadalcanal.

Vera's face had a wide-eyed, youthful innocence, as she drank in not only the gin but the magnificent sunset, and I dared to hope the almost Miss California's ambition to make it in show business wouldn't destroy her, as it had the late Miss Chicago.

Throughout, I'd been wearing my sunglasses, but soon my doing so would seem affected and might attract attention—the opposite of my intention. The blond hair, the dark glasses, the typically touristy clothing, and the context of La Mirador and Acapulco itself would keep me—I hoped—from being made by Charley and Rocco Fischetti, who were also staying in this hotel.

In fact, they too were in the Mirador bar, at this very moment, sharing a booth with two Latin dolls who I figured to be showgirls in the hotel's nightclub, La Perla. In short-sleeve linen sportshirts, slacks, and the tans they'd developed, the two brothers were ignoring the dying sunset and the twinkling harbor lights coming alive. Charley, smoking a cigarette in a holder (like his adversary Lee Mortimer!), seemed to be enjoying himself, chatting up his date; Rocco sat sullenly, a cigar going, the smoke bothering the girl beside him, not that he gave a shit.

The way the booths angled around, I had a good view of them from across the room—and my dark glasses allowed me to gawk without seeming to. Neither Charley nor Rocco (nor their showgirls, for that matter) seemed ever to glance at us, which meant they'd been distracted when we came in, because every other normal man in the bar had noticed bosomy Vera.

Which was another reason to slip out of there.

I drove her over to La Riviera Hotel, a newer hotel with a nice layout, all roof garden and terrace; the food was a fancied-up but tasty version of Mexican, and—despite the business nature of our trip—we found ourselves flirting and acting like honeymooners. Vera could do that to you.

When we got back, I checked the bar and the Fischettis were not present—which was no surprise. They would almost certainly be in the nightclub, which provided a great view of the Mirador's main attraction: the famed local boys who took heroic dives into the shallow inlet from the hotel's high rocky cliff, risking their lives—nightly . . . four shows.

Vera and I caught the ten-fifteen show from a little spot of our own on the rocky hillside, below the balustrade that was down several sets of steps from the parking lot. We sat on the grass, hand in hand, watching as the boy—bearing a torch, and guided by newspapers set afire and adrift below—hurled himself forty feet into a breaker. Then he climbed the opposite, higher cliff, diving a good hundred feet into a narrow ravine lined with jagged rocks.

This went on for a while, and later the boys came around up on the balustrade, where tourists were watching, to collect coins and sometimes even paper money. Vera urged me to go up there and give them something, which I did— a buck—and Vera squealed at my generosity and gave me a big kiss.

She had her hand in my hair, looking at me like I was as beautiful a man as she was a woman—deluded girl—and she said, "I think I like you blond."

"Thanks. Maybe you oughta try it."

"Like Jean Harlow?"

"Yeah. Sure."

"Maybe I will."

We necked there on the hillside for quite a while; it was overwhelmingly romantic—I don't think I'll ever forget it, not the glimmering ocean in the moonlight, the crashing waves against the jagged rocks, or that incredible blow job.

That night we had room service bring us several *coco locos* and *pie-eyes*, and in our simply but nicely appointed room, the drapes to the pool area shut tight thank you, we drank and played pretend honeymoon and when we woke up the next morning, it was approaching eleven. Both of us felt remarkably good, considering how much we'd had to drink last night. We showered—one at time, which I feel showed remarkable restraint—and I got dressed in another aloha shirt, shorts, and my sandals, getting the Speed Graphic out of my suitcase.

"How do I look?" Vera asked, spreading her arms.

She was in a bikini, a couple of blue scraps that together might have comprised a decent handkerchief.

"Even my tongue is stiff," I said.

That made her ooze delight, and she came over and hugged me and kissed me and put her Pepsodenty tongue in my mouth.

"Not now," I said, incredibly enough. "We have work to do."

I was registered under the name Joe Samuels. The hotel management had been alerted to the fact that I was a pin-up photographer, and (we'd been told ahead of time) they had no objection to my taking photographs of my model, around the pool, down on the beach, anywhere around the hotel, in fact.

"You really think my picture will be in the papers?" she asked, batting her lashes over those big hazel orbs.

"Oh yeah. This will make Miss California look like a footnote in your portfolio."

"You know, I can splash around in the pool, and lose my top. I can make it seem real natural."

I savored the image for a moment or two, then said, "That I can't get in the papers, sugar. You understand, this man . . . these men . . . they can be vicious."

"But they do like girls."

"I wouldn't say they like them exactly. They like fucking them—and, later, they like batting them around."

She was nodding. For all her cartoony sexiness, this was not a dumb girl.

"Nate, I understand—they're dangerous. But you're right there with me. My protector."

That gave me a twinge. I hadn't been much of a protector

for somebody else, where the Fischettis had been concerned. . . .

I peeked around the closed curtain, onto the pool area. Bright, sunny, beautiful—just another day in paradise. Beyond the little fence at the far end of the pool, enormous waves threw themselves on massive rocks, followed by massive waves throwing themselves on enormous rocks. Just for variety.

And out on that patio area around the pool—two of several dozen hotel guests either sitting around the water or down splashing in it—were Charley and Rocco Fischetti, in deck chairs.

I released the curtain, backed away, saying to Vera, "We just got lucky."

"Really?"

"They're out there—right now."

"It's showtime?"

"It's showtime."

We exited through the sliding glass doors of our room out onto the patio around the pool. The Fischettis were down to the left, sitting under a yellow umbrella. The showgirls were not with them; a pair of burly bodyguards, however, were. The bodyguards—an interchangeable pair of flat-nosed, cauliflower-eared, dead-eyed dagos—sat on either side of the brothers, but back a few feet.

Rocco wore a white sportshirt and gray slacks and canvas shoes; he was smoking a cigar and leafing through *Ring* magazine. He seemed bored, glum. The umbrella shaft was stuck down through a small round table, which had drinks and ashtrays on it and separated him from his brother.

Charley—his hair was blond, like mine, also a dye job— wore gray shorts and a white blue-checked shirt which hung open revealing a tanned hairy chest and small paunch; he was stretched out in a lounge chair, smoking his cigarette-in-holder, watching pretty girls in swimsuits, of which there was no shortage.

But pretty girls in swimsuits was one thing, and Vera Jayne Mansfield in a bikini, that was a whole other thing.

In my sunglasses and tourist attire, the camera blocking my face, I shot picture after picture of Vera, in and out of the pool, preening, posing, sticking out her chest, pushing out her bottom, peeling those lush lips back across the white teeth. I was whispering photographer type things at her, complimenting her, directing her; but she didn't need any direction. She knew just how to handle herself in front of a camera.

Every man around that pool—and this included young men, old men, married men, single, even guys on their honeymoons—watched the brunette babe in the bikini like they'd just heard about sex for the first time, and were really, really impressed. . . .

And in many of those shots, I caught Charley and Rocco Fischetti on film. Neither one of them—nor their bodyguards—thought a thing about it.

The problem was, the brothers were under that umbrella, sitting in shade, and I didn't have what I needed, not yet. We had talked about this, Vera and I, and as she climbed from the pool and I helped her into a hooded terrycloth robe that ended midthigh, I whispered, "We haven't got it yet."

"He's leaving," she said, looking past me.

"What?" I said, but Vera was on the move.

I turned to see Charley and Rocco getting up, their two thugs falling in line—it was almost noon, so this was simply lunch, most likely. We could have waited for another time, but she was going right up to him . . .

. . . and I moved in—clicking.

"Excuse me, sir," she said, in that Betty Boopish voice, "I hope you don't mind my saying how elegant you look." She was standing in front of him, the robe open onto all that bikini-bound, water-pearled flesh of hers, and Charley smiled, tightly.

Her smile radiant, she said, "I mean, that cigarette holder—you just look so . . . continental."

This gibberish was holding Charley hostage. Rocco was gazing at her suspiciously, but neither he nor his brother—or their idiot retinue—seemed to have noticed me, moving in ever closer, snapping photos.

"Thank you, my dear," Charley said. "You're a lovely girl. Are you in show business?"

"I want to be."

And now Rocco stepped up to the plate, his suspicions gone. "We have business associates in that field," he said. "Ever hear of the Chez Paree?"

"Oh yes!"

"We own a piece."

I faded back—I had all the photos I needed, but she was still talking to them. Finally, she beamed at them and said something—I was out of ear range, now—and bounced over to me.

"I think I made a good impression," she said.

"They're making impressions in their pants right now," I said, taking her gently by the arm and walking her over to our room. I unlocked the sliding doors and we stepped in.

She jumped up and down, jiggling in all the interesting places. "They liked me! They said they'd give me an audition."

"Vera. Sit down."

She sat on the side of the bed and I told her about Jackie Payne. I gave her a fairly detailed version, starting with the religious parents in Kankakee and ending with death by overdose. When I was finished, Vera wasn't crying or anything, but her expression was sober and her eyes melancholy.

"You didn't have to tell that story," she said. "I know they're gangsters. I don't want anything to do with them."

"I know. But you're just starting out—and I saw today the effect you have on men."

"It's just my body."

"No, lots of girls have big tits, kiddo. You have confidence, and stage presence. You'll go somewhere. Just try not to do it by getting in bed . . . literally or figuratively . . . with the likes of Charley and Rocco Fischetti."

She grinned up at me. "Hey—I wouldn't care if that was Darryl Zanuck out there . . . I'm here with Nate Heller."

"Actually, you're here with Joe Samuels . . . who has work to do."

I dropped the Kodak rolls in a packet off at the front desk; arrangements had been made for my film to be taken by courier to Mexico City and delivered directly to the

Associated Press office, where it would be developed and the best shots of the Fischettis wired to Washington . . . where both Drew Pearson and representatives of Senator Kefauver would receive them.

From our poolside room I made two calls: room service, to bring us lunch; and the American consulate, where a lanky, well-tanned Narcotics Bureau agent named Dennison was waiting to hear from me.

"The photos are on their way," I said.

"Good," the agent said. "First thing tomorrow morning, I should have the proper warrants. I won't pull in the local *policía* till the last moment."

"Smart. Outfit guys have a piece of this town."

"You haven't been made?" Dennison asked.

"No. I'll lay low till tomorrow morning."

After I hung up, Vera looked at me with what pretended to be innocence and asked, "You'll lay how?"

She was a handful. Two, actually.

I took her to another hotel to spend the evening—Los Flamingos, a hotel whose modernistic architecture stretched along the edge of an orange-and-slate-blue cliff three hundred and fifty feet above the ocean. The dining room had no outside walls, only a high-beamed roof; but we sat under a roofless section with the moon and stars as our ceiling, while in nearby papaya trees, yellow-and-blue macaws tried to make conversation with us.

Out in the ocean, under the moonlight, on the silver waves, a whale was spouting, and flying fish were leaping from the depths, huge creatures that looked like minnows from our high perch. We both ate charcoal-broiled red snapper, drank wine, and danced to a rumba band well into the night.

When we slipped into our room, back at La Mirador, just after one a.m., we were both a little tipsy and neither of us expected skunk-haired Rocco Fischetti to be sitting on the bed waiting for us, with my nine millimeter Browning in his hand.

"Go in the bathroom, honey," Rocco said. His eyes were like dark stones close-set in that pockmarked face; the black slashes of eyebrow angled down in a scowl that his mouth was participating in. My suitcase was open on the floor—that's where he'd found the gun.

Vera was clinging to my arm, shivering with fright. Like me, I had the feeling she was sober, suddenly.

"Honey," he said, just a little louder, "in the damn bathroom."

"Do it," I told her.

She ran in there, glancing back at us, framed in light.

"Shut the door," Rocco said.

She did.

I stood looking at him. Wearing the same white shirt and gray slacks as this morning, he was seated on the edge of the bed, the gun in his hand draped casually in his lap.

"This is the rod you waved in my face, in the Chez crapper, ain't it?" he said.

"She's an innocent, Rock. Let's go someplace and do whatever we have to do. And leave her out of it."

"Those shiners you give me—they're almost gone." He laughed hollowly. "I looked like a fuckin' raccoon."

"Rocky—we were friends once. Let's settle this another time, in another setting—with this girl out of the picture. She's an innocent kid."

Rocco swallowed. Something was weird about him. Was he drunk?

"Jackie was an innocent kid, too," he said.

"Yeah . . . yeah, she was."

"What are you here for?"

"What do you mean, Rock?"

"What the fuck are you *here* for?" He hefted the nine millimeter. "To kill me? To kill Charley?"

Standing there casually motionless, I was nonetheless looking for the moment to jump him. The weird state of mind he was in might help—*might. . . .*

"I'm not here to kill you," I said. "You'd already be dead, if I were."

"Or you'd be dead. Why *are* you here, Nate?"

". . . you saw me."

"Playing photographer. Yeah. You snapped me and Charley."

"Yes. And those photos are on their way to Washington."

I thought that might get a rise out of him, but he just sat there, zombie-eyed. Finally, he said, "That means, unless Charley and me clear out . . . tonight . . . we'll be in cuffs tomorrow. On our way back home."

"That's pretty much it, yeah."

"He's fuckin' ruined me, you know."

"What? Who? *Charley*?"

Rocco sighed, nodded. He kept thumping my gun against his thigh, nervously. "He and Tubbo went against the Outfit."

"Arranging the Drury and Bas hits, you mean?"

"Yeah. They had inside help, y'know."

"I do know."

And I told him who I figured it was.

He confirmed my suspicions with a shrug and a nod. "You don't buck Accardo and Ricca or even old Greasy Thumb. You either die, or if you're real lucky, you lose damn near everything. Giancana, that crazy bastard, he'll be sitting where the Fischetti brothers was sitting."

"Because your brother bucked the Outfit."

"Yeah. Drury had all sorts of tapes of Charley and Tubbo talkin'—'bout the election and shit."

"You haven't told Charley about me, have you?"

"No—no, Nate, I ain't told him, and Charley ain't made you. He was too busy today looking at Little Miss Big Titties. I saw you, though. You kinda look like my fuckin' brother, with that blond hair."

"If you don't tell him now, Rock, you'll be arrested tomorrow, along with him. You know that, don't you?"

"What the fuck's it matter? Maybe I go back and plead the fifth, don't cause the Outfit no trouble, and the boys see I'm a stand-up fella."

"You *want* Charley to get dragged back to the States?"

"Oh, yeah. 'Cause if he does, they'll either kill him . . . or his heart will. He's a sick man, you know."

"How sick?"

Rocco coughed a laugh. "Sicker than he fuckin' knows."

"What do you mean?"

A shrug. "Maybe somebody switched his little pink pills with, whaddyacallit . . . playsee what's-it's."

Was I hearing this?

"Placebos, Rock? You switched your brother's pills?"

"You tell him, Nate, and I *will* kill you."

I looked at him for a long time—the depression I'd seen lately in my own face was in Rocco's, only deeper, like a mask that wouldn't come off.

Then I came over and sat next to him. "You loved her, didn't you?"

"What, jus' 'cause I slapped her around, you don't think I loved the little bitch? She could get under your skin. She was so goddamn sweet, and pretty. You ever hear Jackie sing?"

"Yeah."

"How could you kill that? How could you kill something sweet like that, when you know your brother loves her?"

"You married her to protect her."

"Of course. Then Charley found out that wouldn't do no good, in this Kefauver thing . . . and he and Tubbo. . . . Fuckers."

"I tried to save her."

"How?"

All Rocco knew was Jackie had turned up in Lincoln Park, overdosed. I told him the whole story—about Riverview, and how Tubbo had covered it up so masterfully.

"Somebody's got to bring that fat bastard down," Rocco said.

"Somebody will. She was a great girl. I can see how she'd be easy to fall for." I didn't say I knew as much because I'd fallen, too.

He was slumped so far over now, it was like he was doubled up with a cramp; he was rocking a little. "She died, all cold and scared . . . overdosed. It's my fault . . . I got her hooked on that fuckin' junk. I thought I could . . . handle her better, that way. She wanted a career, I wanted a wife."

Only in Rocco's world would you try to accomplish that by putting your fiancée on junk.

But the guy loved her, all right, in his twisted way. He

was sitting there, slumped in half, and I reached over and took the gun from his fingers, and slipped my arm around his shoulder. He put his head against my chest and he wept. He wept for a long time.

Then he got up slowly and swallowed thickly, wiping his face with his hands, saying, "Nate . . . don't tell anybody."

"Don't tell anybody what?"

"That I blubbered like a baby. I will kill your ass, you do."

"I cried for her, too, Rock. I just got it out of my system, already . . . and anyway, you loved her longer . . . and more."

He sighed, nodded, straightened his shirt. "Nobody can know about Charley, neither."

"Obviously."

"But with a little luck, that bastard'll keel over dead, any day now." He smiled to himself, savoring his brother's imminent demise, as he headed for the door. "Any day. . . ."

Around ten the next morning, Charley was sitting by the pool again, with his brother next to him, the thugs playing bookends. Charley was wearing a bathrobe and swim trunks; and Rocco was in a loud sportshirt and quiet slacks.

I had left Vera in our room, but she was watching out the glass doors. She saw me as I pulled up a deck chair and sat next to the broad-shouldered, oval-faced gangster, who was smoking his black-holdered cigarette.

"How you feeling, Charley?" I asked pleasantly. "You look a little peaked to me."

The cigarette in the holder fell from his mouth, and hot ashes hit his chest; quickly he brushed them off, his eyes wide with surprise and alarm.

"What the fuck are you doing here, Heller?"

"Today, just relaxing. Thanks for asking, Charley. Yesterday I was taking pictures—your pictures. You don't know it, but you made the papers all over America, this morning. Drew Pearson has quite a story."

His eyes were huge and filled with rage under the same sort of black slashes of eyebrow Rocco wore. "You dumb son of a bitch! I was your friend—don't you know what a bad enemy I can make?"

"No, but I bet Jackie Payne does. . . . Charley Fischetti, this is Agent Dennison . . . Agent Dennison, Charley Fischetti."

And Agent Dennison, in a tan tropical suit that blended well with the uniforms of the *policía* backing him up, stepped forward.

Charley began to swear at me, and shake his fist; then he froze, his eyes popped out a bit—reminding me of Pop-Eye at the Riverview freak show—and he clutched his chest, heaving heavy breaths.

Acting quickly, Rocco went to his brother's aid, helping him with his little pink pills.

16

After a few days of legal wrangling, Charley and Rocco Fischetti were flown from Acapulco to the Miami Airport, where—barely having stepped off the plane—they were served with subpoenas to appear in Chicago in front of the Kefauver Committee. Custody was transferred from the Narcotics Bureau agents to federal marshals, with whom Charley got into an argument.

One of Charley's residences, after all, was in Miami—actually, a mansion on Allison Island—and he demanded to be able to return there, to speak to his wife, and to call his attorney, and generally make arrangements. Even the United States government should have the simple courtesy to treat a taxpaying American citizen with a little goddamn fucking dignity.

The refined collector of modern art, that bon vivant whose nickname not so long ago had been Trigger Happy, blew his top when he was informed he and his brother would be transported directly to the county jail, in "protective custody." He ranted and raved, and was hauled into a waiting van. The affront of subjecting a connoisseur of the finer things to ride in a paddy wagon was simply too much: Charley exploded.

So did his heart.

And Charley Fischetti got his way: he never had to set foot in that county jail, having died of a heart attack, en route.

Which meant he also avoided testifying in front of the Kefauver Committee, and avoided the wrath of the Outfit, for having disobeyed their collective ruling not to hit Bas and especially Drury.

Brother Rocco did testify—saying "I refuse to answer that" so many times he may have set the record in all of the Crime Committee hearings. (Joey was not called.)

An all-star rogues' gallery testified in a hearing room at the Federal Building, and I—as a paid investigator on staff, now—heard a lot of it, one of a select handful of insiders allowed to sit in on the hearings, including Virgil Peterson and a few other civic leaders involved with the Chicago Crime Commission, as well that lawyer Kurnitz, who'd been working with the senator's staffers.

"Why aren't you up on the dais," I asked Kurnitz, in the hallway between witnesses, "with Kefauver and his other lawyers?"

The handsome if bug-eyed Kurnitz replied in his courtroom baritone, "Well, of course you understand I'm not really a part of the senator's staff."

"I understood you were working for the committee."

"*With* the committee, Mr. Heller—not *for* the committee. I'm a sort of liaison between them and a number of my clients. Friendly witnesses—and confidential sources. Like your friend Bill Drury, rest his soul."

"And Jack Ruby?"

"Yes, him too."

The mob all-stars (and in many cases, their lawyers) were kept in a little room fourteen foot square, blue with cigarette smoke, off a hallway that echoed with the chatter of typewriters and office machines, an unsettling symphony for the unlucky witnesses, who had been casually informed by a U.S. marshal that this was the IRS checking their tax records.

The straightback wooden chairs, primly lined along all four walls, were filled with some of the most celebrated criminal backsides not only in Chicago, but America. Because most were ex-cons, two chairs were left vacant between the parties, since associating with one another would be a parole violation. Short, square-shouldered Louie Campagna—a minor hoodlum from Capone/Nitti days who'd risen to some power—sat next to (that is, two empty seats away from) big, silver-haired, movie-star handsome Johnny Rosselli, the former's baggy, slept-in-looking suit contrasting with the latter's natty Hollywood threads.

Rosselli—and major L.A. mob boss Jack Dragna—were flown in from the coast, because of their connection to the race wire racket.

A small radio was playing the World Series—and the rapt attention of these sports fans was fixed upon the action of the Yankees clobbering the Phillies . . . almost as if money were riding on the outcome.

For the several days of the hearings, the room—littered with cigarette butts, candy wrappers and newspapers—was mostly filled with men, and famous ones at that: Paul "the Waiter" Ricca; Tony "Joe Batters" Accardo; Al Capone's brother Ralph; Murray "the Hump" Humphries; Charlie "Cherry Nose" Gioe. The lone woman was Mrs. Charles Fischetti—Anne—a slender, pretty blonde flown up here from Miami; wearing widow's weeds, she appeared with an attorney, and she rivaled Rocco in the number of times she said, "I refuse to answer that."

Though these were closed sessions—excluding the public and press . . . no TV this round!—Kefauver himself would brief the press at the end of the day, giving them a thumbnail description of the testimony. An exception to this procedure, however, was part of the unusual courtesy paid to one witness, Captain Dan "Tubbo" Gilbert.

Under fire from Senator Lucas and other Democratic bigwigs, Kefauver agreed not to subpoena sheriff's candidate Tubbo—merely extending an invitation to him to appear, on the eve of the election, to give him an opportunity to address the press feeding frenzy over Gilbert's questionable finances and dubious police practices.

But Kefauver was not entirely caving in to political pressure, because he announced the invitation to the press, which put pressure on Tubbo to comply, though at first the esteemed chief investigator of the State's Attorney's office refused the invite.

Then, one afternoon, unannounced, wearing a three-piece tailored brown tweed suit, silk gold-and-yellow tie, and his ruby stickpin, the jovial Tubbo—without an attorney at his side!—just showed the hell up, and expressed a willingness to answer questions. The decks were cleared, and a seat at the witness table made available.

The hearing room was wide and narrow, the gallery consisting of a dozen seats on one side with an aisle and another dozen seats on the other—very few filled, just Peterson and a couple of his people, and Kurnitz and myself. A courtroom atmosphere prevailed: the witness table faced a long bench on a dais in a room made somber by the institutional green plaster walls with dark-oak wainscoting and gilt-framed prints of Washington, Jefferson, Lincoln, and FDR (other than Illinois's own Honest Abe, no Republicans, of course—maybe next administration).

Behind the bench on the dais, framed by windows with their blinds drawn, Lincolnesque Kefauver was flanked by his youthful, moon-faced chief counsel, Rudolph Halley, and fiftyish, professorial George Robinson, their associate counsel. All three men wore dark suits and ties and glasses, quite a contrast to Tubbo's jaunty, dapper attire. No microphones were necessary, and a court recorder sat off to one side, a businesslike young brunette with dark-rimmed glasses and flying fingers.

From private conversation with him, I knew the senator was embarrassed and, well, pissed-off that the other members of the Crime Committee—even Senator Charles Tobey, a Republican who relished castigating thugs for their immorality and misdeeds—had chosen not to come to Chicago and share the political risks.

"Let the record show," Senator Kefauver said, "that Captain Gilbert was not subpoenaed to come before this committee. You came of your own free will and accord, is that correct?"

"Yes, and let me say at the outset," Tubbo replied cheerfully, his chin held high (anyway, his first chin), "that I will cooperate one hundred percent. My reason for appearing is the fact that the press has been carrying some malicious stories about me . . . and, of course, as chief investigator of Cook County, I felt as though I would be doing my duty to come here."

For several minutes, Kefauver posed background questions—about Tubbo's age (sixty-one), his family (grandfather of four), his rise to power in law enforcement (swift), and the nature of Captain Gilbert's job (buck-passing). Tubbo was relaxed and breezy in his responses. When Kefauver shifted gears, it wasn't immediately apparent.

"The man you work for, State's Attorney John S. Boyle, has described you as . . ." Kefauver adjusted his glasses on the bridge of his nose, as he read from a yellow pad. ". . . 'one of the hardest-working police officers I have ever known.' "

Tubbo shrugged, smiled contentedly. "That's generous of him."

Halley was already smirking, as he introduced the voluntary witness to his high-pitched, lispy, sarcastic vocal style: "Mr. Boyle also admits you have a reputation as a gambler, and of playing the stock market heavily."

Another shrug. "Well, I guess you'd say I'm a gambler at heart."

Robinson chimed sternly in: "And what do you think about a sheriff being a gambler, Mr. Gilbert?"

"I don't feel it's any violation of my oath of office—if a fellow wants to bet against me, I am willing to bet."

"What sort of bet?"

"Well, I bet on football games. I bet on prize fights . . . but mostly on elections."

"Elections," Halley cut in. His upper lip twitched in a sneer. "And how big are these election bets?"

"Oh, in 1936 I think I won around $10,000 or $12,000. In the last presidential election, I picked up around $1,500 by taking odds of seven to one that President Truman would be reelected. . . . I haven't lost an election bet since 1921."

The three men on the dais were clearly amazed by the pride of the last statement.

Finally, Kefauver said, "Your income tax returns, Captain, indicate considerable yearly profits from gambling."

Yet another shrug. "I never denied doing a little honest gambling on the side."

Halley leaned forward. "What would you say is your net worth today?"

"Oh . . . I would say if I sold everything, half a million dollars, something in that neighborhood."

"Half a million dollars," Kefauver said, staring at the witness, as if having trouble bringing the chubby, well-dressed cop into focus. "Working as a law enforcement officer on a ten-thousand-dollar-a-year salary—half a million dollars."

Tubbo seemed neither embarrassed nor defensive—just matter of fact, as he replied, "Mostly it was done through investments—in stocks, bonds, from market tips that friends give me."

"Friends. Could you give us an example of these friends?"

The big man leaned back in his chair, folding his arms, searching the ceiling for facts. "Well, let me see. . . . I believe I got my first important stock tip from George Brennan—I was his chauffeur, and a kind of bodyguard, oh, twenty-five, thirty years ago."

That was Boss Brennan, who had then controlled the Democratic machine in Chicago.

Halley's shrill voice sliced the air like a scalpel. "Captain Gilbert, getting back to your net worth—can you understand how difficult it is to comprehend how a public servant like yourself got hold of all that money?"

Gilbert then explained, in some detail, how he was trying to invest for his son, how he was worried that on a public servant's salary he couldn't provide well enough for his family . . . and how he had "pyramided" his holdings to $100,000 in the bull market, losing all but $15,000 in the crash of '29. But he had rebuilt—speculating in grain, diversifying by purchasing shares of Pepsi Cola, Union Pacific, and AT&T.

Halley seemed spellbound by this recitation of financial

legerdemain, but finally blurted: "Captain Gilbert, may I ask a question?"

"Certainly, sir."

"When do you find time to take care of your law enforcement duties?"

"Why, every day—sometimes twenty-four hours when we are working cases."

"To me, you have quite an active financial business that would have to be watched very closely."

Shrug. "The telephone is all that does it. The broker I'm dealing with will call me up."

Halley's expression might be seen at a car wreck—a bad one, involving fatalities. "You don't think this interferes with your law enforcement duties?"

"No."

"It hasn't cut in on your time and energy?"

"Not whatsoever, no, sir."

Halley's eyes behind his round lenses were huge. "You've been able to amass this fortune in just your spare time—a hobby, so to speak."

"That is right."

"But you also find time for betting."

"That's the telephone."

"That's the telephone, too?"

"All I do is pick up the phone and make the bet. Doesn't take five minutes."

"When you're betting on sporting events, Captain, where do you place your bets?"

"With a handbook at 215 North LaSalle."

"Is this legal betting?"

"Well . . . no sir, it is not. Not in the strictest sense, not legal, no."

"In your job, as the chief investigator for the State's Attorney, would one of your duties be to raid handbooks—bookie joints, like the one you frequent?"

"Yes."

"Have you ever done so?"

"Certainly!"

"When was the last time?"

". . . 1939, I believe."

As Halley was digesting that juicy tidbit, Robinson asked, "Do you think a person with a 'gambler's heart' can take the right approach in putting down bookmaking?"

"Yes."

"And other forms of gambling?"

"Yes."

"What is the difference between your betting on sporting events and elections, and betting on a horse race in a handbook?"

"Well . . . of course I don't know what the difference is."

"Then how can you make a distinction on whether to raid a place or not?"

Tubbo thought about that; then he offered, in what sounded like a question, "If you make a bet in a gambling place on a horse race, it is against the law."

That one left Robinson reeling, as Kefauver leaned in and took over the questioning, starting with: "Do you know these so-called gangsters, Captain? The Fischettis and Guzik and Accardo?"

"Yes, I know them from seeing them."

"I mean, have you ever had any relationship with them?"

"No sir. I never did."

"No business dealings whatsoever?"

"No, sir. None whatsoever."

"Are you under any obligation to them?"

"No. I am not."

"Well, what do you think the problem is, here in Cook County? Our own investigators have noted numerous gambling operations running unimpeded."

Tubbo held his head high. "There are no gambling operations now in the city of Chicago. There have been some in the county, of late, but I am satisfied, should I be elected as sheriff, that we will drive that evil element out, the same as we have driven it out of Chicago."

Halley—properly astounded by having so outrageous a load of horseshit dumped before him—cleaved the air with that whine of his. "The charge has been made that in all your time as chief investigator, Captain Gilbert, you have not sent any major gangster to jail."

Tubbo seemed hurt by this suggestion. "That is simply

not so—besides, there is no other officer who has done that, either."

Not bothering to stop to make sense of that, Halley pressed on. "And of course there are numerous unsolved murders in Chicago."

Another shrug. "There's numerous unsolved murders all over the United States."

Halley nodded, as if that were a reasonable response. "Then, Captain, let's talk about one unsolved murder in particular."

"All right. If I know anything about it."

"What can you tell us about the murder of William Drury?"

"Terrible. A terrible thing."

"You've been investigating this murder. Have you uncovered anything?"

"Mr. Halley, there is no police officer gifted with a supernatural mind. . . . You have to understand, when these gangsters go out and kill they are as precise and detailed in their work as an architect. If a murder is committed by a mobster or gangster element, they leave no traces."

Halley answered that speech with one of his own: "Wouldn't the man in the street say to himself, if only Captain Gilbert weren't concentrating on whether or not to buy and sell stocks and bonds, wouldn't he have given just a little more thought to finding out who killed Bill Drury?"

The chin went up again. "Any time a crime is committed in the city of Chicago and I work on it, I give my whole-hearted effort."

"And that includes the murder of William Drury?"

"Mr. Halley, I have done good work. I have sent thirty-one men to the electric chair, thirteen for killing police officers. In none of those cases was one finger of criticism pointed at my conduct, other than the fact some would say, he has a lot of wealth. . . . Well, I haven't bought a car since 1918, and I have no maids."

The stupidity of that caught Halley off guard.

But Kefauver, referring to a file, picked up the thread. "We have a letter written by the late Mr. Drury, in which he makes certain charges against you to John E. Babb, your opponent in the upcoming election."

"I've seen that letter. Pack of lies."

"In it, you are described as a 'menace' to law enforcement. Is it true that during the period Lieutenant Drury served under you from 1932 to 1937, many topflight gangsters he arrested were speedily released or dismissed in court?"

"With all due respect to the deceased, that's nonsense, Senator. It just shows that arresting these alleged 'gangsters' without any evidence to convict them is irresponsible law enforcement."

Kefauver sighed; his long droopy face seemed very tired indeed. "Captain Gilbert—would you acknowledge that it would be natural for the public to lose confidence in a police officer who amassed such great wealth?"

Tubbo shook his head, sadly. "The failure of human nature, Senator, is that we are prone to believe evil about our fellow man . . . especially about a police officer."

That gem of folk wisdom seemed to stun his inquisitors, and after a few more questions, the executive-session interrogation of the World's Richest Cop came to a close.

As disingenuous as he'd been, Tubbo—thoroughly incompetent witness that he was—had revealed more than anyone might have expected; but—because of the closed nature of the session, designed not to embarrass the Democratic Party—the transcript would be confidential until the committee's eventual report. Kefauver's usual frank press summary of witness testimony would be suspended in the captain's case. The public would not be privy to Tubbo's testimony until weeks, perhaps months, after election day.

I'm sure Kefauver did this reluctantly; but the politics of it were unavoidable. Whether some deal with Tubbo had been cut in advance—and his "surprise" appearance was expected—or the senator instinctively toed the party line by temporarily covering up Tubbo's testimony, I couldn't tell you.

What neither Tubbo nor Kefauver had contemplated, however, was a certain sleazy private detective among the insiders in the gallery, a surveillance-savvy divorce dick whose briefcase contained a battery-operated miniature wire recorder about the size of a fat paperback book, with a spool handling two and a half hours without a reload. In other words, Drury's tapes may have been missing, but Heller's weren't. I sold them to Ray Brennan of the *Chicago Sun-Times* for a grand—a fact never revealed until now—and Captain Dan Gilbert's full committee testimony appeared in that paper on November 2nd . . . just in time to louse up the election for Tubbo.

I would rather have put a bullet in the fat fuck's brain; but had to settle for just ruining him. The man who plotted with Charley Fischetti to have Bill Drury and Marvin Bas murdered lost the sheriff's race by nearly four hundred thousand votes—and, even in Chicago, the Democratic machine was soundly trounced by protest voting from its own party, from key county offices to Senate majority leader Lucas losing to Everett Dirksen.

The day following the election, Captain Dan "Tubbo" Gilbert resigned in disgrace as chief investigator of the State's Attorney's office and from the police department itself. He had plenty of money for his old age, but the commodity he valued most of all—power—was lost to him forever.

17

Tim O'Conner lived on the far Northwest Side, on Forest View Lane off Milwaukee Avenue. I'd called Tim and told him I had something for him—Bill Drury's widow, Annabel, had asked me to deliver a personal item—and he said tonight would be fine.

A few weeks had passed since Tubbo appeared before the Crime Committee—the papers were still having a field day with the story, including speculation over who might have leaked the testimony (Kefauver blamed the reporting company who transcribed the court recorder's work). This was a Tuesday evening in early November and drizzly and cold, enough so that I'd zipped the lining into my London Fog.

I pulled the Olds into the Forest Preserve and walked across the woods, leaves crunching damply under my Florsheims, and angled through the trees until I came out at the dead-end street that was Forest View Lane. Tim's house was the last one on the end of the block, with no one directly across the street, and a vacant lot of knee-high weeds next door. A standard Chicago brown-brick bungalow, the squat, pitch-roofed one-story had an attic with an overhang and a big bay window in front of the living room, drapes closed, though lights burned behind them.

Carrying a paper bag about big enough for a sandwich, I walked up on the cement stoop and knocked and had just knocked a second time when Tim opened the door.

"Jesus, get out of the rain," he said.

I did, removing my fedora, shaking the beads of moisture off. My lanky host closed the door behind me and took my raincoat, tossing it over a straightback chair by the door. I pitched my hat on the same chair.

In a gym-style T-shirt and rumpled gray moleskin slacks, in his stocking feet, O'Conner looked lousy—his sandy blond hair uncut and unkempt, his blue eyes bloodshot, and his pockmarked complexion had taken on a grayish cast; already thin, he seemed to have lost some weight, which made the sharp features of his face seem less handsome, more exaggerated . . . and his nose was as red as if he were working on a huge pimple. But it was just the beer, which was on his breath, by the way.

"I guess you haven't been here since the divorce," he said, with an embarrassed chuckle, gesturing to the all but empty living room. To call the room, with its bare wood floor, sparsely furnished was a ridiculous understatement: facing a television console against the far wall was an easy chair with one of those lamp/end table combinations, several empty Pabst bottles on the table part, and that was all. No sofa or other chairs—a few newspapers tossed on the floor, some magazines, a couple more beer bottles. On the wall opposite his TV area was a formal fireplace, its mantel bare, though a mirror over it served to make the big empty room seem even bigger and emptier.

"I got the house," Tim said, "but Janet got the furniture."

And the kids. And any life inside these walls that might have been worth living.

"Hey, don't worry," he said, with a grin, putting a hand on my shoulder, "she didn't get the poker table. . . . Come on."

In the dining room—always an object of discussion between Tim and Janet—was a large octagonal poker table with a felt top and built-in chip holders. Tim had fashioned a piece of dark wood that could fit over it, so Janet could serve dinner to company (not in use at present); and the wall you saw entering from the living room still had the built-in china hutch—piled with a few paperbacks and pulp magazines now—reflecting the room's onetime schizophrenic functions.

"Why don't we sit in here," he said. "Beer all right?"

Indeed, chairs were all around the poker table, just as when Bill Drury, Tim, Lou Sapperstein, and a few other cops and reporters had regularly played poker here—what was it, once a month? Up until maybe three years ago.

"Beer is fine," I called to him. He had gone into the kitchen, off the dining room.

The skinny pockmarked man in the T-shirt came back with two sweating bottles of Pabst, no glasses, and he sat with his back to the kitchen doorway, and I took the chair right next to him, placed the brown paper bag on the table before me, making a little clunk.

"Lots of memories at this table," O'Conner said between gulps of beer.

"Yeah—huge fortunes passed hands. Sometimes as much as twenty-five bucks."

His laugh echoed sharply in the plaster-walled, carpetless room. "Yeah, you and your Black Mariah. Fucking wild cards."

"Threes and nines," I said.

"That's not real poker."

I grinned and swigged. "It wasn't real money."

"Except once a year."

"Yeah, that's right." Every December, sometime between Christmas and New Year's, we'd play one higher stakes game, bumping our quarter/fifty cents/a buck chips to a buck/five bucks/ten. On those occasions, hundreds of dollars had crossed this felt-covered table.

"Funny," Tim said, with a faint smile, holding the beer bottle in his palm as if he were going to toss it, "how conservative Bill always played."

I nodded, sipped the Pabst. "Even small stakes, he played like it was his life savings."

Tim shook his head, laughed a single hollow laugh. "I mean, a guy that took the kind of risks he did, in real life—and on a night out with the boys, he was a little old lady."

"You, on the other hand, were always a reckless fucker."

He laughed. "Yeah, I know. Sometimes I bluffed my way into some pretty good pots."

"Yeah, Tim, but you got greedy. Too much bluffing."

"Oh yeah? Your problem was, you never did bluff."

"I still don't."

He took another swallow, then nodded at the paper bag. "So what's that, your supper?"

"That's what I came to bring you. What Annabel Drury wanted you to have."

"Yeah?"

I pushed the bag toward him, like it was a pot he'd won. "Take it. She said he would have wanted you to have it—Bill's old partner, after all."

Tim put the beer down in a built-in coaster, and emptied the paper bag onto the table; this time it made a bigger clunk, as Bill Drury's nickel-plated, well-worn ivory-handled .38 police revolver dropped onto the felt tabletop.

"Oh Christ," he said softly.

"He carried that same piece from the day he made detective till the day he died," I said.

O'Conner was nodding, eyes glazed. "His late brother gave it to him. The reporter? Lots of . . . sentimental value."

"It was in his glove compartment, with a box of shells, when those sons of bitches shot him. . . . Like I say, Annabel wanted you to have it."

O'Conner hadn't picked it up; he was just staring at it, leaning an elbow against the table, fingertips pressed to his head.

Then he finished his Pabst off in a big gulp, and said, "I can use another. How about you?"

"No, I'm fine."

While he was in the kitchen, I took the nine millimeter Browning from my shoulder holster and held it beneath the table, where he wouldn't notice. I'd carried this weapon a long time, too. Different sentimental reasons, though.

A few moments later, he stumbled back in, sliding on the floor in stocking feet, with a fresh sweaty Pabst in hand, and sat down, rather heavily. He sighed and took several swigs of the beer.

"I miss him, that bald-headed bastard," O'Conner said. He had tears in his eyes. "I feel like I let him down."

"Well, sure you did—setting him up like that."

O'Conner looked up, sharply. "Is that what you think?"

I bestowed him a bland smile. "I don't just think it, Tim. I know it."

His forehead clenched, his eyes moving back and forth, as if trying to escape his head. "I loved Bill Drury. We were like brothers."

"Ever hear of Cain and Abel, shitheel?"

He backed away in the chair. "I think maybe you oughta get the hell outa here, Heller."

"No. Finish your beer. Let's talk."

He sneered at me—kind of a pathetic sneer, though—and picked up the .38 and pointed it at me. "Is this loaded?"

"Yeah. Just one bullet, though. Mine has a full clip."

Not quite smiling, O'Conner looked at me carefully. "You want me to believe you're pointing a gun at me right now, I suppose."

"That's right. . . . Of course, I could be bluffing."

He said nothing. Then he put the .38 down in front of him, again, and swigged his beer. "What do you want from me?"

"A few answers. A few holes I haven't been able to fill. This starts with Bill assuming you were a straight-arrow copper, like he was—that when you got tossed off Town Hall Station together, for covering up gambling, the both of you were being railroaded. What occurred to me was, you could be the reason Bill didn't know about the gambling in the district—you'd been there longer, you could've been, well, assigned to him, to steer him away from those joints."

He gestured with the hand that had the Pabst in it, and a little spilled. "Does this look like the home of a bent cop, enjoying the fruits of graft?"

"Actually, it does. This was a family home, right? Your

parents lived here before you? You grew up in this house, only child, if I recall."

The bloodshot blue eyes were fixed unblinkingly on me. "So what?"

"Speaking of sentimental attachment . . . don't shit a shitter, Tim. I'm a divorce dick—the husband doesn't end up with the house . . . not unless the wife ended up with more than just the kids and the furniture. Like, for instance, a hefty bank account. You must've made a hell of a settlement with Janet . . . all 'cause you couldn't keep your prick in your pants. What happened to that little dame you were dating?"

His mouth twitched; he swigged the beer. He belched and it echoed. "She dumped me. For a guy who had real dough. He owns supermarkets or something."

"Pity. And for this you got excommunicated? Couldn't you sweettalk Janet back? She was a hell of a fine girl."

"She was a bitch. You don't know anything about my life."

I shrugged; the nine millimeter felt remarkably light in my hand. "I know you've been in bed with Northside Outfit guys for a long, long time, Tim . . . which would include the late, very unlamented Charley Fischetti. I think you were . . . like I said, assigned to Bill Drury, to keep an eye on him. My guess is it's you who fucked around with the witnesses to the Ragen shooting, and muddied those waters, and got Drury suspended."

"I was suspended, too."

"Hey, that goes with the territory. It's sort of like . . . undercover work, but from the other end of the telescope . . . or gun barrel." I grinned at him. "You misdirected me, Tim—a very simple piece of misdirection, but a good one—by indicating your lawyer pal, Kurnitz, was working for the Kefauver Committee. Of course, he wasn't working for 'em, but with them . . . as he admitted to me, himself, the other day."

"So what?"

"So Kurnitz was Bill Drury's lawyer. I guess I figured Bas was Bill's lawyer, but they were just working on a matter of mutual interest—the downfall of Tubbo Gilbert.

Of course, Tubbo was an old pal of yours—he instigated the Ragen cover-up, in which you assisted."

He grunted a nonlaugh. "You don't have anything solid. Nothing but air."

"Maybe so, but it's foul-smelling air—like the worst gas Tubbo Gilbert ever passed . . . and that would have to be rank shit, wouldn't it? Kurnitz offered himself to the committee, as a conduit of friendly witnesses, when his real employer was the Outfit . . . or perhaps just Charley Fischetti. I'm a little unsure on that point—care to clear that up?"

"Fuck you."

"Well, I'm gonna say Kurnitz was leaking to the Outfit, in general, 'cause Giancana had access to the info. Halley wasn't the leak, nobody really on Kefauver's staff was the leak—it was Kurnitz, and his investigator . . . you . . . who were keeping the Outfit updated as to the committee's plans, evidence, and witnesses."

"It's just a theory. Nothing but a theory."

"Here's something that's not a theory: you and Kurnitz—Bill's trusted partner, and his trusted attorney—set up the meeting in Little Hell with the nonexistent 'new' witness in the Ragen case. Drury and Bas, the afternoon of the night they died, told me the witness was somebody Kurnitz lined up for them, an inmate at Joliet he represented."

He was shaking his head. "That's Kurnitz. Not me. I just worked for him, some. You want to sit and threaten somebody with a gun, go look him up."

"I'm not going to have to. You see, earlier today I had a meeting with Sam Giancana. In a sleazy joint called the Silver Palm. Ever been there? Anyway, I gave him the lowdown."

His eyes flared. "What?"

"I told Sam the whole sorry story. You see, by helping Fischetti and Gilbert hit Drury and Bas, you and Kurnitz betrayed the Outfit. Was it you, or Tubbo, who brought in those bent cops from Calumet City? Oh well, what does it matter? You see, the top Outfit boys, all but Charley, decided killing Drury in particular would bring unwanted heat down on them . . . which it did. So I figure Kurnitz will show up in the trunk of a car, some evening—and he won't be trying to sneak into a drive-in movie."

Shaking his head, his eyes huge, one hand a fist, the other clutching the Pabst bottle as if it were his lifeline, he all but yelled, "You fucking asshole . . . you crazy fucking bastard. . . . They'll come after me!"

"No. Not right away. I asked Mooney to give you a little time."

"Time?"

"Tomorrow . . . that's the earliest."

"What are you saying?"

"That the earliest Giancana would send somebody around, to deal with you, would be tomorrow morning. Of course, they may wait a while. Maybe it'll be a Christmas present."

He was breathing hard. "You're crazy. You're a fucking lunatic."

"That's a medical fact—it's on my service record. Some day it may come in handy, for an insanity plea."

He seemed on the verge of tears. "How could you go to Giancana with such tissue-thin evidence? This is a bunch of circumstantial bullshit! You suspect these things, Nate, but, Christ, you don't know them."

"I know them."

He slammed a fist on the table and the .38 jumped. "How? How can you be so goddamn sure?"

"It goes back to when you tied up that loose end at Riverview."

"Huh?"

"You know—when you plugged that moon-faced motherfucker in the back and in the head, getting even for Bill Drury. When you went all crazy with revenge. 'This is for Bill!' "

"I . . . I loved Bill Drury. He was—"

"Like a brother, yeah. But how did you know that guy from Calumet City was one of Bill's killers? I was the only one who saw them that night in Little Hell—and I didn't tell you."

His face went blank.

He swallowed. "You . . . you figured it, then? At that moment?"

I sighed. "No—too much was going on. I was busy grieving for a poor girl with bad taste in men. You arranged that abduction, didn't you? . . . Had those clowns grab Jackie and lure me to Aladdin's Castle. How you must have laughed when I called you to be my backup!"

He leaned forward, the pockmarked face long with attempted earnestness. "I didn't laugh, Nate. And . . . I could have shot you, that night. You know that's true."

"No, I don't think so—you weren't sure I hadn't told Lou or somebody else about meeting you, there. Better odds to let me live, and keep me thinking you were on my side, Bill's vengeance-happy partner cutting down the scum who killed him. Scum you hired, right?"

". . . That was Tubbo."

"Was it? Piece of work, old Tub. Like coming to me with that outrageous offer of fifty grand should I find the Bill Drury papers—the notebooks and tapes . . . when Tubbo knew all along *you* had them. Or was it Kurnitz? Bill would have entrusted them to one of you, his lawyer, or his partner. Either way, they've been destroyed."

"He gave them to me." O'Conner sounded almost proud of that.

My laugh resonated harshly in the hollow room. "Too bad—you could have sold them for big bucks to the Outfit . . . only that might have tipped 'em to your role in the murders of Drury and Bas. You even misled those Calumet City boys about the files—when their only real job was to dispose of Mrs. Rocco Fischetti . . . and me. Pity, to have something so valuable . . . that you had to get rid of. Did you burn them, Tim? Out in your fireplace?"

He didn't say anything.

So, for a while, I didn't say anything.

Then, quietly, Tim said, "So now you've told me."

"Now I've told you."

Eyes tensed, shaking his head, he asked, "Why? Why come here and confront me? Why not just let Giancana take me for a ride?" He searched my face, in desperation.

"Or is this . . . is this one last expression of a friendship we shared—to give me a few hours to get the hell out?"

I shrugged. "Well, it is out of friendship, in a way. More with Bill, than you. I don't think I want Annabel to have to suffer further, finding out that her husband's partner was a greedy psychopath who betrayed him. I thought I'd do you the favor of offering you a graceful way out."

He reared back. "And what would that be?"

I nodded toward the .38. "Bill Drury's gun. Your partner's weapon. Cops kill themselves all the time—ex-cops, too."

A hollow laugh, an unbelieving grin. "You expect me to pick this gun up, and shoot myself?"

"Yeah."

"One bullet in it, right?"

"Right."

"Why wouldn't I just turn it on you?"

"That's an option. But you even hint at pointing that gun at me, the gun I'm pointing at you will fire first."

"I might get lucky."

"At this table? Anyway, if by some fluke you shot me before I could stop you, Sam Giancana would still finish the job. You're a dead man, Tim. The question is, how do you want to go out?"

His head almost twisted off, from shaking side to side. "Suicide? Why the hell would I—"

"We can shoot it out right here, and I'll plead self-defense, and reveal your whole sorry history. Or you can die a tragic police hero, depressed over the death of his murdered partner."

"I'm a Catholic, Heller. I'm not—"

"You're an excommunicated Catholic, Tim. And do you really think you're going anywhere but hell? Jesus is going to forgive *your* sins?"

". . . He might."

"Then go out with a little class. Don't be just another gangland slaying. Don't be the Judas that made Annabel Drury's life even more miserable."

"What about my kids? You're a father."

"You sold them out a long time ago, Tim. Anyway, you

want them to remember you as a tortured soul, or a crooked cop? Up to you."

He swallowed again. "Cold. So cold. . . ."

Was he talking about me, or the temperature?

His eyes seemed woozy, suddenly. "You think I'm a piece of shit, don't you?"

"What does that matter?"

"You're worse than I am."

"Maybe."

He looked at me, then he looked at the pearl-handled gun. Me, gun, me, gun, me, gun, me, gun. . . .

He picked it up, careful not to aim it my way. He held it in his palm and looked down at it.

"Father forgive me," he said. "Forgive my sins."

And he lifted the revolver to his temple and squeezed the trigger. The echo was like a thunder crack in the room; blood and brains and bone matter splattered the empty china hutch, and he tumbled off the chair, sideways, onto the floor, somewhat on his back, his empty eyes staring up at me.

"Good choice," I said.

And I went out and got my coat and hat, walked unseen into the chill night—the drizzle had let up—and strolled across the woods to my Olds.

From May 1, 1950, to September 1, 1951, the Kefauver Committee heard over six hundred witnesses, racking up close to twelve thousand pages of testimony from minor hoods to major mob figures as well as government officials on every level. The senator's circus traveled to fourteen cities and put on public display, for the first time in any significant manner, the ongoing connection between crime, politics, and business.

The last stop on the Kefauver tour was the big one: New York, with the entire hearing televised. Notorious mob courier Virginia Hill—who, once upon a time, Charley Fischetti had introduced to Ben "Bugsy" Siegel—brought some sex into the midst of the violence; and former NYC mayor William O'Dwyer generated some genuine pathos, a crime-busting former D.A. brought down by corruption. The real star, however, was Frank Costello, the east coast's elder statesman among racketeers.

Or anyway, his hands became stars. Costello refused to be photographed, and the TV cameras focused on his nervous hands—tapping, rapping, clenching, unclenching, fingering cigarettes—accompanied by his whispery, raspy off-camera voice. He fudged, he fidgeted, he hedged, he refused to produce material, he stormed out, and of course refused to answer many of the questions on grounds of self-incrimination. Cited for contempt, sentenced to eighteen months, indicted and convicted for income tax evasion, Costello was a major mobster clearly brought down by the Crime Committee.

The Kefauver Committee turned out scores of recommendations, some commendable, others ridiculous. Of nineteen bills proposed by the committee, one—the Wagering Stamp Act—passed . . . and proved unenforceable. Of forty-five contempt citations to uncooperative witnesses, only three convictions resulted, the courts generally backing up the mobsters' fifth amendment rights.

On the other hand, the national race wire racket—Continental Press—was forced to shut down in 1952. And the hearings pressured the Immigration Service and IRS into prosecuting hundreds of mobsters during the next eight years. Even J. Edgar Hoover had to admit the existence of the Mafia. Convictions and deportations led to mob warfare, as various individuals and factions fought for control.

And in 1952, Estes Kefauver ran for president, his fame as a gangbuster helping him accumulate the largest number of committed delegates at the Democratic National Convention. But the party regulars—including Harry Truman, who'd been tainted by corruption the committee uncovered—controlled the uncommitted delegates, and Kefauver was denied the nomination.

Kefauver did become Adlai Stevenson's vice presidential running mate; the Demo duo lost to Eisenhower and Nixon, tried again in '56, and lost again to Ike and Dick. The senator played out the remainder of his congressional career as a strong, independent, progressive voice in national government. He died of a heart attack in 1963.

Kefauver's pit bull, Rudy Halley, used his fame on the Crime Committee to run as an independent and win a seat on—and eventually the presidency of—the New York City Council. He tried to be a reformer, without much success, and ran for mayor in 1953, losing as badly as Tubbo Gilbert had that sheriff's race. Oddly, Halley was associated with (legal) gambling interests toward the end of his short life; he died of pancreatitis in 1956. He was only forty-three.

The other counsel, George Robinson, who was from Maine, I lost track of.

The impact of Kefauver's televised hearings was perhaps the first real demonstration of the power of television. This was not lost on Joe McCarthy, in his efforts to capitalize on the public's paranoia fueled by the protracted war in Korea, and he convinced many Americans that Commies might be living next door or lurking under the bed. Ultimately the unforgiving tube brought McCarthy down, of course, revealing him in the Army hearings as a liar and a bully, and he died in disgrace, in 1957, in the same mental ward as his mentor, Jim Forrestal.

Columnist Drew Pearson's muckraking style paved the way for modern investigative reporting, but his real heyday was the 1950s. He died of a heart attack in 1969. Even more than Pearson, Lee Mortimer's successes were tied to the '50s. Married five times—calling into question Sinatra's insistence that Mortimer was homosexual—the *New York Mirror* columnist wrote several more *Confidential* books with Jack Lait, hosted a radio show, and died in bed of a heart attack in March 1963.

A heart attack took Rocco Fischetti, as well. He made peace with the Outfit, though his role was diminished; he maintained residences in Florida and in Skokie, Illinois. He told me once—we became, oddly enough, friendly again— that his sole ambition was not to die violently; he feared winding up shot to death in an alley, flung against garbage cans. He got his wish, dying a low-key death on a visit to relatives in Long Island, New York, in July 1964. He was sixty.

I never told him, by the way, that I was the one who busted up his trains.

Frank Sinatra made his comeback, as you may have heard, and he continued to be friends with Joey Fischetti, who received at least an occasional fee as a "talent agent," particularly for Sinatra's dates in Miami Beach, including at the Fountainbleau Hotel, with which Joey was affiliated.

In early 1951, Sinatra was asked to provide the Kefauver Committee with an interview, and he complied—a top secret one, at four in the morning in a law office at Rockefeller Center. He told them nothing—a list of gangsters was read off to him, and he informed committee lawyer Joseph Nellis he knew them "to say 'hello' and 'goodbye' to. . . . Well, hell, you go into show business, you meet a lot of people."

Perhaps because of my request to Pearson to apply gentle pressure, Kefauver accepted this private testimony and chose not to embarrass Frank by calling him as a hearing witness.

But Frank's mob connections would dog his heels his entire life—five grand jury subpoenas, two IRS investigations, a congressional summons, and a subpoena from the New Jersey State Crime Commission would follow over the years. So would a Congressional Gold Medal, presented to him by President Clinton in 1997, the year before Sinatra's death.

Joey Fischetti passed away some time in the '70s, if I recall, but Frank had long since grown tighter with one other mobster—Sam Giancana. Throughout the early '50s, following the Kefauver hearings, the leadership of the Chicago Outfit passed between Ricca, Accardo, and Giancana. During this period numerous gangland murders—all unsolved—were committed; one of the first was an attorney named Kurnitz, who turned up along that same Calumet City roadside as those two heroic police detectives. His throat had been slit and his tongue had been cut out and stuck in the new aperture.

In the early '50s, Giancana engineered a violent takeover of the numbers rackets from black policy kings. His interests eventually included Las Vegas, Mexico, and Cuba, and he ran in show business circles that included Sinatra, Joe E. Lewis, Keely Smith, and his longtime paramour, Phyllis

McGuire of the singing McGuire Sisters. He shared a mistress with President Kennedy, and his involvement with the CIA is thought to have led to his murder in his Oak Park home—shot in the back of the head, frying up sausages.

Paul Mansfield was true to his word and drove his wife Jayne to California, after he got out of the service; she kissed the ground hello, shortly after they crossed the state line. Shortly after that, she kissed Paul goodbye. She made it in Hollywood, but via New York, playing a Marilyn Monroe-like character in a Broadway play by the author of *The Seven Year Itch*; this led to a 20th Century Fox contract, and major motion pictures, most notably *The Girl Can't Help It*.

Jayne—like Mamie Van Doren (a onetime Charley Fischetti sweetheart)—became a road company Marilyn. Her sexbomb persona seeming increasingly passé as the repressed '50s gave way to the swinging '60s, she made a nudie cutie movie, promoting it by posing nude for *Playboy*, which led to a famous pornography charge for the magazine. Before her auto accident death in 1967, she had been reduced to TV guest shots, cameo appearances in movies, nightclub strip acts, and leads in low-budget foreign films. For all the highs and lows of her bizarre career, however, Jayne did achieve her goal of enduring stardom.

Jack Ruby made a name for himself, too.

The A-1 Detective Agency thrived in Chicago and Hollywood, and I maintained residences in both cities, though I would always be a Second City boy at heart. Sometimes I would stay in L.A. long enough to be jarred, on my return, by the changes in my town. Oh, the underlying casual corruption remained the same. But much of the character of the first half of the twentieth century in Chicago was getting chipped away at, as the second half got under way.

In 1960 the Chez Paree closed, for example, made irrelevant by the intimate likes of Mr. Kelly's, the Happy Medium, and Hefner's Playboy Club. Riverview amusement park shut down in 1967—all the famous rides sold off, the attractions demolished . . . including Aladdin's Castle.

The Federal Building was pulled down in 1965, and a new one with much less character took its place; but the

Monadnock Building still stands, and St. Andrew's Church is open for business.

As for Tim O'Conner, he got a hero's funeral—not as elaborate as those Calumet City coppers, but a nice send-off, though under the circumstances St. Andrew's was out of the question. No Bishop Sheil sermon and high mass for a suicide, after all. Everybody felt for Tim, caught up in despondency like that, over the death of his friend and colleague, Bill Drury.

A lot of people thought it was sad—tragic even—that poor Tim couldn't be buried in consecrated ground. That a nice Catholic boy like that had died while excommunicated, committing a mortal sin, and was condemned to burn in the flames of damnation for eternity.

Of course, I didn't buy any of that shit; but the thought sure as hell was comforting.

I Owe Them One

Despite its extensive basis in history, this is a work of fiction, and liberties have been taken with the facts, though as few as possible—and any blame for historical inaccuracies is my own, reflecting, I hope, the limitations of conflicting source material. Some minor liberties have been taken with time, primarily for reasons of pace—for example, moving the death of Charley Fischetti up slightly, so that the narrative would span weeks and not months.

This novel is a departure of sorts from the Nathan Heller "memoirs" of recent years. The first four Heller novels—beginning with *True Detective* (1983)—focused on Chicago and organized crime. With the fifth Heller, *Stolen Away* (1991), a new pattern for these novels was established, only tangentially involving Chicago and the mob: starting with his role in the Lindbergh kidnapping case, Heller has cracked famous unsolved historical crimes, most recently the Black Dahlia murder (*Angel in Black*, 2001).

In recent years, a number of avid readers of the series have suggested that Heller seemed overdue in returning to his Chicago roots. Commercial considerations—giving in to the obvious audience appeal of a world-famous crime (the Huey Long assassination, the Massie rape/murder case) or mystery (the Roswell Incident, the disappearance of Amelia Earhart)—have made it difficult to convince editors to allow Heller a return to his Chicago haunts. I thank my former editor, Joe Pittman, and present editor, Genny Ostertag, for their understanding and support of what might seem to be a departure from a successful format.

For Heller to develop as a character in his historical context, I considered it necessary for him to leave the '30s and '40s behind and move into the '50s and '60s. Since *The Million-Dollar Wound* (1985), in which real-life police hero William Drury was first introduced as a recurring figure in Nate Heller's life, I have known that the Kefauver inquiry—Drury's role in which led to his murder—was a necessary (and potentially powerful) subject for exploration in these memoirs.

This novel serves as an introduction to—and a bridge into—the 1950s and '60s, should my readers (and the publishing industry) be interested in following my detective and me into these fascinating, suitably crime-filled eras. Thus this novel centers not on a famous crime so much as a famous time in crime, when the TV-fueled shadow of congressional inquiries . . . not only Kefauver's beneficial one but McCarthy's injurious one . . . fell across the American landscape. The unsolved murder of William Drury—the theory behind the solution of which I, as usual, stand behind—may not have the household-name familiarity of some of Heller's previous cases; but it remains an historically significant, important, even pivotal crime.

My research assistant George Hagenauer and I began gathering material for this novel in 1985—and our first hurdle, sixteen years later, was locating the research materials we'd assembled for a book we had both back in '85 assumed would be happening soon; and our second one was refamiliarizing ourselves with that material, specifically, and with Chicago mob history, in general.

I had the additional chore of renewing my general Chicago chops (George, born and raised in Chicago, has this stuff in his blood). I always thank George for his help, but this time I really should shout that gratitude from a rooftop. (Also, though he hasn't taken an active role in the research in some time, Mike Gold was one of the original architects of the Heller Chicago/mob history; thanks, Mike.)

Much of what George gathered for *Chicago Confidential* was original newspaper material, and he also scoured the bound volumes of the Kefauver Crime Committee testimony, sending along to me reams of photocopied material from both sources. This book draws more than anything on the original coverage in the Chicago press and those bound volumes of testimony. The scene involving Dan "Tubbo" Gilbert's appearance before the Kefauver Committee incorporates material from a Gilbert appearance before the Chicago Crime Commission as well as newspaper interviews.

As indicated in the text, the lively journalism of Jack Lait and Lee Mortimer was key to this work; if my portrait of Mortimer was in any way unflattering, chalk that up to his karma . . . but know that I love reading the Lait/Mortimer *Confidential* books, which have had a huge influence on the Heller memoirs, never more so than this time around. *Chicago Confidential* (1950), *Washington Confidential* (1951), and *U.S.A. Confidential* (1952) all extensively cover the Chicago mob, the Drury story, and the Kefauver inquiry. I also consulted an imitation of their successful series, *Washington Lowdown* (1956), by Larston D. Farrar.

Most of the characters in this book are real-life figures and appear under their actual names. Jackie Payne is a fictional character, however, suggested by Rocco Fischetti's documented wenching and woman-beating, including throwing a former Miss Chicago out of the Barry Apartments penthouse, leaving her and her bags on the nearest street corner. Fred Rubinski is a fictionalized Barney Ruditsky, a real-life ex-cop turned private eye in Los Angeles. Tim O'Conner is a fictional character, as is lawyer Kurnitz; both have historical counterparts, though I do not mean to impart the sins of the fictional characters upon the real people. O'Conner is designed to suggest that traitors existed on the police force, while Kurnitz suggests the not too radical theory that criminal lawyers are sometimes as much criminal as lawyer.

My portrait of Estes Kefauver is drawn primarily from the following sources: *Estes Kefauver: A Biography* (1980), Charles L. Fontenay; *Kefauver* (1971), Joseph Bruce Gorman; *The Kefauver Story* (1956), Jack Anderson and Fred Blumenthal; and *Standing Up for the People: The Life and Work of Estes Kefauver* (1972), Harvey Swados.

Two books relating to Kefauver, however, must be singled out as particularly key to this novel: the first-rate scholarly work *The Kefauver Committee and the Politics of Crime, 1950–1952* (1974), William Howard Moore; and the senator's own *Crime in America* (1951), Estes Kefauver. Also, in addition to photocopies of actual testimony, I used the government document *The Third Interim Report of the Special Committee to Investigate Organized Crime in Interstate Commerce* (1951).

I am an enormous Frank Sinatra fan, with an extensive library of books on the singer, his life, and his art; the portrait in this novel—meant to be fair and even affectionate, without ducking certain realities—was primarily drawn from *Frank Sinatra: An American Legend* (1995, 1998), Nancy Sinatra; *Frank Sinatra: Is This Man Mafia?* (1979), George Carpozi, Jr.; *His Way: The Unauthorized Biography of Frank Sinatra* (1986), Kitty Kelley; *Sinatra: Behind the Legend* (1997), J. Randy Taraborrelli; and *The Sinatra Files: The Secret FBI Dossier* (2000), Tom Kuntz and Phil Kuntz, editors. Some Sinatra fans may object to my using the Kelley book as a source; I feel this is balanced out by the Nancy Sinatra biography, which has an excellent year by year (sometimes day by day!) breakdown of her father's remarkable life.

Jayne Mansfield and her first husband Paul are, obviously, real people; I remind my readers that these are, like all of the characterizations in this novel, fictionalizations. The story Vera tells in this novel about her rape is one reported in several books and something she apparently told from time to time; but I have reason to disbelieve it—and its suggestion about the paternity of her first child. Also, the events in her life described herein—including her studying at UCLA and her attempt to become Miss California, as well as Paul's objections to both—have been moved in time a few months, to accommodate the needs of this narrative. Consulted were *Jayne Mansfield's Wild, Wild World* (1963), Jayne Mansfield and Mickey Hargitay; *Jayne Mansfield* (1973), May Mann; *Sexbomb: The Life and Death of Jayne Mansfield* (1988), Guus Luijters and Gerard Timmer; *The Tragic Secret Life of Jayne Mansfield* (1974), Raymond Strait; and *Va Va Voom!* (1995), Steve Sullivan. Strait also published *Here They Are—Jayne Mansfield* (1992), with a new copyright and no mention of the earlier *Tragic Secret Life*, although they appear to be substantially the same book with different pictures.

Major sources for the Drew Pearson characterization were *Confessions of a Muckraker* (1979), Jack Anderson with James Boyd, and *Drew Pearson: An Unauthorized Biography* (1973), Oliver Pilat. Although I have gathered numerous books on Joseph McCarthy and the McCarthy Era, his characterization here primarily depended upon *The Life and Times of Joe McCarthy* (1982), Thomas C. Reeves, and *McCarthy—the Man, the Senator, the "Ism"* (1952), Jack Anderson and Ronald W. May. Jack Anderson wins the M.V.P. award for writing three of the books I used as sources on three different subjects touched upon (in addition to being a character—albeit an offstage one) in this novel.

Three books on Chicago crime were very helpful: *Barbarians in Our Midst* (1952), Virgil Peterson (with a Kefauver introduction); *Syndicate City* (1954), Alson J. Smith; and *To Serve and Collect* (1998), Richard C. Lindberg. The latter covers the Drury case in some depth, as does George Murray's *The Madhouse on Madison Street* (1965), a book on Chicago newspapermen in which Drury is viewed in the context of his journalistic endeavors.

Many other general Chicago books were consulted, including *Chicago's Famous Buildings* (1965, 1969), Arthur Siegel and J. Carson Webster; *Chicago Interiors* (1979), David Lowe; *Chicago on Foot* (1973, 1977), Ira J. Bach; *Kup's Chicago* (1962), Irv Kupcinet; *Lost Chicago* (1978), David Lowe; and a restaurant guide, *Vittles and Vice* (1952), Patricia Bronte, which provided Chez Paree background. My research associate George Hagenauer's *True*

Crime Series Three: G-Men & Gangsters (1992)—a card set, the first series of which we (notoriously) did together—was a handy useful resource.

The Riverview sequence draws upon my own memories of the park and George Hagenauer's as well as Chuck Wlodarczyk's valentine to the park, *Riverview: Gone but Not Forgotten* (1977). Some minor liberties, primarily geographic, have been taken.

Dozens of books about organized crime served as reference, most significantly: *Accardo: The Genuine Godfather* (1995), William F. Roemer, Jr.; *All-American Mafioso* (1991), Charles Rappleye and Ed Becker; *Blood and Power* (1989), Stephen Fox; *Captive City* (1969), Ovid DeMaris; *Capone* (1971), John Kobler; *The Don* (1977), William Brashler; *Double Cross* (1992), Sam and Chuck Giancana; *The Hollywood Connection* (1993), Michael Nunn; *The Legacy of Al Capone* (1975), George Murray; *The Mafia Encyclopedia* (1987), Carl Sifakis; *Mafia Princess* (1984), Antoinette Giancana and Thomas C. Renner; *Mr. Capone* (1992), Robert J. Schoenberg; *Mob Lawyer* (1994), Frank Ragano and Selwyn Raab; and *Playboy's History of Organized Crime* (1975), Richard Hammer.

Other helpful books included: *Jack Ruby's Girls* (1970), Diana Hunter and Alice Anderson; *Mid-Century Modern* (1984), Cara Greenberg; *Playing the Field: My Story* (1987), Mamie Van Doren with Art Aveilhe; *The Plot to Kill the President* (1981), G. Robert Blakey and Richard N. Billings; *Twentieth-Century Pop Culture* (1999), Dan Epstein; and *This Was Burlesque* (1969), Ann Corio with Joseph Di-Mona. Another Jack Ruby reference was "The Lost Boy," a 1999 *Gambling Magazine* article by John William Tuohy.

The Acapulco sequence drew upon the beautifully written *Now in Mexico* (1947), Hudson Strode, as well as *Around the World in 1,000 Pictures* (1954), A. Milton Runyon and Vilma F. Bergane; *Pacific Mexico Handbook* (1999), Bruce Whipperman; and *The Wilhelms' Guide to All Mexico* (1959), John, Lawrence, and Charles Wilhelm.

A number of books on L.A. and Hollywood were also sources, including *Death in Paradise* (1998), Tony Blanche and Brad Schreiber; *Great American Hotels* (1991), James

Tackach; and *Sins of the City: The Real Los Angeles Noir* (1999), Jim Heimann. Also, the WPA Guides for California, Los Angeles, Illinois, and Washington, D.C., were vital references.

Thanks to editor Genny Ostertag, for her strong support, and to my friend and agent, the indefatigable Dominick Abel.

As always, I am grateful for the love, support, and patience of my wife, Barbara Collins—the rare writer who can listen with interest and offer helpful suggestions to another writer when interrupted in the midst of her own work.

About the Author

MAX ALLAN COLLINS has earned an unprecedented nine Private Eye Writers of America "Shamus" nominations for his "Nathan Heller" historical thrillers, winning twice (*True Detective*, 1983, and *Stolen Away*, 1991).

A Mystery Writers of America "Edgar" nominee in both fiction and nonfiction categories, Collins has been hailed as "the Renaissance man of mystery fiction." His credits include five suspense-novel series, film criticism, short fiction, songwriting, trading-card sets, and movie TV tie-in novels, including *In the Line of Fire*, *Air Force One*, and the *New York Times* bestselling *Saving Private Ryan*.

He scripted the internationally syndicated comic strip *Dick Tracy* from 1977 to 1993, is cocreator of the comic-book features *Ms. Tree*, *Wild Dog*, and *Mike Danger*, has written the *Batman* comic book and newspaper strip, and the miniseries *Johnny Dynamite: Underworld*. His graphic novel, *Road To Perdition*, has been made into a DreamWorks feature film starring Tom Hanks and Paul Newman, directed by Sam Mendes.

As an independent filmmaker in his native Iowa, he wrote and directed the suspense film *Mommy*, starring Patty McCormack, premiering on Lifetime in 1996, and a 1997 sequel, *Mommy's Day*. The recipient of a record five Iowa Motion Picture Awards for screenplays, he wrote *The Expert*, a 1995 HBO World Premiere; and wrote and directed the award-winning documentary *Mike Hammer's Mickey Spillane* (1999) and the innovative *Real Time: Siege at Lucas Street Market* (2000).

Collins lives in Muscatine, Iowa, with his wife, writer Barbara Collins, and their teenage son, Nathan.